MARY McCARTHY, a Phi Beta Kappa graduate of Vassar College, began her distinguished career as editor and theater critic. In 1942 she published *The Company She Keeps,* her first work of fiction. Early stories were published in *The New Yorker* and *The Atlantic.* In 1949 she won the Horizon Award for her short novel *The Oasis,* and was given the first of two Guggenheim fellowships.

Her full-length novel *The Groves of Academe* came three years later, followed in dazzling succession by *A Charmed Life, The Group, Birds of America,* and, most recently, *Cannibals and Missionaries.*

Mary McCarthy has also taught literature, published collections of theater criticism, short stories, travel and literary essays, and a number of books on the politics of our time. In 1957 her autobiographical *Memories of a Catholic Girlhood* appeared.

A member of the National Institute of Arts and Letters, Mary McCarthy lives in Paris and Maine with her husband, James West.

THE HOUNDS OF SUMMER AND OTHER STORIES

MARY McCARTHY'S SHORT FICTION

A BARD BOOK/PUBLISHED BY AVON BOOKS

This volume contains all of the stories previously published under the title CAST A COLD EYE.

"The Hounds of Summer" and "The Appalachian Revolution" are published by special arrangement with Mary McCarthy.

AVON BOOKS
A division of
The Hearst Corporation
959 Eighth Avenue
New York, New York 10019

Copyright © 1944, 1946, 1947, 1948, 1950, 1954, 1963 by Mary McCarthy
Published by arrangement with Harcourt Brace Jovanovich, Inc.
Library of Congress Catalog Card Number: 80-69929
ISBN: 0-380-78196-4

First Bard Printing, August, 1981

BARD TRADEMARK REG. U. S. PAT. OFF. AND IN OTHER COUNTRIES, MARCA REGISTRADA, HECHO EN U. S. A.

Printed in the U. S. A.

10 9 8 7 6 5 4 3 2 1

TO BERNICE

ACKNOWLEDGMENT is made to the following periodicals in which these stories first appeared: *The New Yorker, Town and Country, Partisan Review, Mademoiselle*.

Contents

Contents

I

The Weeds

SHE WOULD leave him, she thought, as soon as the petunias had bloomed. With a decisive feeling of happiness, she set down her trowel and sank back on her heels to rest. Around her lay the brown earth of the converted vegetable garden, a slightly lopsided rectangle, across which careened the flower seedlings in rows that were both neat and unsteady, so that the whole planting, seen from a distance, looked like a letter written by a child who has lost his ruler. If only, she reflected, she had done it the way the book said and marked out the rows with stakes and string. Next year . . . Her heart turned over with horror as she perceived the destination of her thought. She had done it again. Next year, *of course,* she would not be here. She had been telling herself this for five weeks, yet she could not seem to remember it. Left to itself, her idle mind reached out lazily, unthinkingly, for a plan, as doubtless Persephone's hand had strayed toward a pomegranate seed.

She remembered all the times she had thought of leaving him before. But there had always been something—the party Saturday night that she did not want to miss, the grapes blue on the vines waiting to be made into jelly, the new sofa for the living room that Macy's would deliver next week, the man to see about the hot-water heater. And by the time the sofa had come, the man had gone, the jelly had been made, she would no longer be angry with him, or at any rate her anger would have lost its cutting edge and she would have only the dull stone of discontent to turn over and over in her palm.

Now, however, it was settled, this problem that had been agitating her since April, since the morning she had planted the sweet peas instead of packing her suitcase, as she ought of course to have done when he had uttered the unspeakable sentence. Now she had actually set a date for her departure, a date on a real calendar, and not simply on the calendar of her heart, where the years were written as days and it seemed always a matter of a few weeks at most before she would be back with her friends, a returned traveler with a fresh slice of life in her hands and many stories to tell. She had been trying since April to do it, all the while that she went on with her digging and watering and weeding, trying to imagine the flowers in their places in August and herself not there to see them, herself in New York in a hot furnished room. It was a little like imagining her own death, but there had been mornings when she had been almost able to do it, and then she would set down her tools and say to herself in surprise, Why, I can leave tomorrow. There is nothing to keep me here. Always, however, she would have forgotten the petunias, which were growing in flats inside the house and had therefore not fallen under her eye. Suddenly they would flash into her mind, white, ruffled, with yellow throats, blocked out in squares, alternating with squares of blackish red zinnias, with the heavenly blue of the scabiosa making a backdrop of false sky behind them; her heart would contract with love and despair as she saw that she could not leave them—she was in bondage unless they should die.

But to acknowledge this was to feel panic. Speaking to her of time and the seasons, the garden urged her to hurry, to go now, before it was too late, before the wheel, turning, should carry her once again on its slow journey through birth, reproduction, and death. Now for the first time she began to count the weeks. Her sensibility quivered in a continual anticipation of change; she took offense readily, pushed everything to extremes, and, in her mind, renounced her friends, her house, her china, a dozen times a day. Desperate measures occurred to her: if she were to kill the petunias . . . ? *Petunias are peculiarly subject to the damping-off sickness. Water cautiously,* warned the gardening book. She would stare at the pitcher of ice water on the luncheon table as the heir stares at the bottle of sleeping medicine by the bedside of his aging relative. But always her resolution softened; the grotesque temptation passed, and, trembling, she would slip out of the house, quietly, lest her husband hear her and detain her on some pretext (for he considered that she was working too hard, complained that he never saw her, that her temper was being ruined); she would collect the trowel, the spading fork, the hand cultivator, and let herself into her enclosure, fenced off against rabbits and woodchucks, and there begin once again her penitential exercise, her agony in the garden.

"Why do you do it if it gives you no pleasure?" her husband would ask. "Don't pretend you are doing it for me." She knew no answer to this; only once she had turned on him, saying, "Ah, you hate it because it is mine. You would like to see it all go to ruin." And truly she did not understand why she was doing it, unless it was somehow *against* him. It was as though she owed these plants some extra and conspicuous loyalty to make up to them for his jealous hostility, which was always waiting its chance, alleging urgent business, sexual desire, anything, to keep her within doors. Sometimes it seemed to her that she stayed on simply as the guardian and defender of these plants, to which she stood in a maternal relation, having brought them into existence. At other times it was cruder. She would not, she would tell herself grimly, give him the satisfaction of seeing her lose the investment of work and love she had made in this rich but difficult soil. She had made a mistake, she knew it; the nurseryman had warned her, "You're biting off more than you can chew." Now she would pause occasionally to look out at the weeds swaying in the light spring wind, pressing up against the fence of her enclosure, where they grew taller, fiercer, more luxuriant than they did in the field itself. It was as if the field were a hostile sea which billowed and swelled in the distance with a sort of menacing calm, and spent itself vindictively in that last breast-high green wave which it launched upon her rectangular island. At such moments, dread would seize her; she would shudder and turn back to her task, knowing that every minute must be made to count, lest she be inundated, her work and tools be lost in this watery jungle of nature. And always it was as if *he* were the ally of the weeds—he was fond of telling her, pedantically, that there was no botanical distinction between a weed and a flower. On mornings when she would hurry out after a rainy spell to find her brown space green with a two-day crop of wild mustard, she would feel him to be nearly victorious; tears of injury and defiance would stand in her eyes as she scratched the ground with the claw.

She could remember a time when it had not been so, when her borders had been gay with simple clear colors, pink and scarlet, lemon yellow and cornflower blue, when her husband had stood by in admiration, saying, "You have green thumbs, my dear." Then she had been ready enough to lay down her tools, to greet a friend, to go on a picnic, to give an order to her maid; then there had been summer afternoons when he sat on a bench with a drink while she let the hose play gently over the flower beds and stopped from time to time to take the glass from him and sip.

Later, kneeling out in the garden, she would try to decide at what moment the change had come. When

she had declined to go with him to the city because
there was no one to water the flowers? When he had
bought the dog that rooted up the tulips? Ah no, she
thought. It had been inevitable from the beginning that
the garden should have become suffused with suffering,
like a flower that is reverting to its original lenten
magenta, for everything returns to itself and a marriage made out of loneliness and despair will be lonely
and desperate. And if I have a garden to console me,
you will have a dog, and your dog will destroy my garden, and so it will go, until all good has turned to evil,
and there is not a corner of life that has not been
flooded with hatred. It had become meaningless to
draw up lists of grievances (her picture torn across the
middle and thrown in the kitchen wastebasket), for
to have a grievance is to assert that some human
treaty has been violated, and they were past treaties,
past reparations, past forgiveness; to invoke love, mo-
rality, public opinion was pure simony—in every bel-
ligerent country the priests are praying for victory.

How far it had gone she had never perceived until
yesterday. She was repeating the flower names to herself: black boy, black ruby, honesty, mourning bride
(ah yes, she murmured, that is I, that is I), snow-
storm, purity, and last of all the free package thrown
in by the seedsman which was designated Peace. Dear
God, she had exclaimed, it's as if I were growing flowers for a funeral blanket. Is it possible that I wish him
dead? And at once the vision of herself as a young
widow slipped into her fancy, like a view into an old
stereopticon. She saw herself pale and beautiful in
black, murmuring repentant phrases to some intimate
woman friend. (It's true that we didn't get along, but
I couldn't have wished this to happen. I am sorry now
for everything, and I would like to be able to tell him
so. If only he could have known that I loved him
after all.) Yes, she thought, if he were dead, I could
love him sincerely. And how practical it would be! She
would not have to give up anything—the Spode salad

plates, the garden, the candy-striped wallpaper in the living room. And she would not have to decide whether to take the roasting pan or leave it (it had belonged to her in the first place). All the objects she had nearly determined to relinquish if she were to leave him, all these things she considered already lost, would be restored to her. And she could move about among them alone; she could have everything the way she wanted it, there would be no one to stop her, no one to say, "Why do we have to have a soup *and* a salad course? You are spending too much money."

That was the queer thing, she thought; it was not a question of money. If he died, he would leave her nothing; the commissions would stop automatically, there would not even be any insurance. What he would do for her by dying would be to relieve her of the necessity of decision. How many women, she wondered, had poisoned their husbands, not for gain or for another man, but out of sheer inability to leave them. The extreme solution is always the simplest. The weed-killer is in the soup; the man is in his coffin. One regrets, but now it is too late; the matter is out of one's hands. Murder is more civilized than divorce; the Victorians, as usual, were wiser.

Really, she said to herself, I will have to get away if I am going to have such thoughts. And a dreadful presentiment flicked her heart, lightly at first, like the stroke of a lady's riding whip. What if I were to go in now and find him dead by his work table with the blueprints spread out before him? She saw, as if by second sight, what her remorse would be and knew that she could not bear it. In a moment she was stiff with fright. Clearly, she would have to go and look for him, but she could not move. Look, she said to herself, if he is dead the maid will come to tell me sooner or later. I do not have to find him. I can just stay here. But it was useless. By now she was certain that he was dead; one last hope, however, remained. If she were to get there quickly enough . . . She found herself running down the driveway. Outside his window she stopped. It was too high for her to see in. See, she said to herself, almost happily, perceiving the difficulty, there is nothing you can do. But a stratagem occurred to her. By a supreme effort of will she made herself pull up an orange crate and climb onto it. She looked in. There he was at his table, motionless; she could not make out whether he was breathing. For the first time, she saw him with detachment, a man in a brown suit slumped over some papers, like a figure drawn by a painter and left there, a figure unknown, without history, and yet intensely itself. He moved, and was human again; she knew him, she disliked him; it was all right, he was alive. She drew a deep breath and slipped quickly down from the orange crate, before he should turn his head and see her. All afternoon in the garden she kept congratulating herself, fondly, hysterically, as people do when they have had, or believe they have had, a narrow escape. Yet when he came out at five to call her and startled her by approaching quietly, she gave a long, piercing, terrible scream, a scream that seemed to linger in the air long after she had left the garden. In some way, he had caught her red-handed.

This morning, in the garden, the scream was still there. Overnight, delay had become dangerous. A break must be made. The part of her that put up preserves, built terraces, laid in oil for the winter, would have to come to terms at last with the part that knew the train schedules by heart and kept a ten-dollar bill hidden in its jewelry box. A path would have to be cleared through the thicket of obligations with which she had surrounded herself, and it was not, after all, essential that she should choose the thorniest way. If she could not renounce the petunias, she would have them and then go. The important thing was that she should not make a single plan that would carry her beyond the first of August. Resolutely, she picked up her trowel and stabbed it into the ground, next to a clump of nut grass with its bright, spearlike leaves. Probing carefully, she lifted the plant and saw with satisfaction that the nut was there, dangling from the long root. The point about nut grass was that you must be sure to get the nut; otherwise your pains were wasted—within a week the plant would be up again. Hoeing was out of the question; you had to dig, with a spading fork or a trowel. "Why don't you give it up?" her husband had asked, indifferently, when she had showed him the thousands of green spears of the grass pricking the ground she had just cultivated. "Oh, go away," she had answered, and yet, often, this was what she most wanted to do, to give up and lie down on her bed and never make another effort, to sleep and have her meals brought up and live like a weed herself, silent and parasitic. But always the flowers pressed their claims; she would picture a few starved cosmos plants waving their thin heads among the tall grasses, and she would feel her heart wrung, as if squeezed out by those strong inimical brown roots. Ah well, she said to herself now, next year will be another matter. Next year nature can have her way. Thank God, at any rate, I did not put in any perennials.

All the rest of the morning she worked along cheerfully. When her maid's voice called her in to lunch, she got up with docility. Walking along the lane, she noticed that the wild lilies of the valley were nearly in bloom. There was a shady space along the veranda that could easily accommodate them. With fertilizer and cultivation, the blossoms should, by next year, double in size. . . . Some plants with a good chunk of earth were already in her hands when she perceived what she was doing. "My God," she murmured, "my God," and dropped the plants back into the hole her trowel had cut. She pressed the earth down around them and trod on it with her foot. It had been a close shave, and the beating of her heart informed her, bluntly, that she must run no more risks. The whole property was pitted with traps for her; she walked in danger and there was no time to lose.

In the hotel, the door had not closed behind the bellboy when she picked up the telephone. She had no plans. Her imagination, working (how long?) in secret, had carried her only this far; she had conceived of the future, simply, as a hand, still wearing its glove, reaching out for a hotel phone. To her first five calls there was no answer. This was a possibility she had not counted on. In all her calculations, it was she who had been the doubtful element, she the expected, the long-overdue relation whose homecoming was hourly anticipated, she the beloved sister whose room had been kept just as she left it; and throughout the term of her marriage, the thought of her friends had jabbed at her conscience: they were waiting and could not understand what could be keeping her so long. Now, at the fifth attempt, she put down the receiver peremptorily, to cut off the drilling, importunate sound that her call, unanswered, was making. For a diversion, she drew a bath, saying to herself that it was still too early, that people were out of town for the summer, that one could not expect, et cetera. Yet, after the bath was over, she did not know what to put on, for she both counted and did not count on an invitation to dinner. To her sixth call she got an answer. How nice, said her friend, that she was in town; could she come Thursday for dinner? Thursday was four days off, and she fumbled a little in accepting. Her great news had become suddenly undeliverable. The context was wrong, yet the news remained, almost sensibly, in her mouth, thickening her tongue. She hung up in haste, lest her disappointment be audible on the other end of the wire. On her seventh call, she was informed that the party had moved to Connecticut; on her eighth, she made a date for lunch on the following day. She was conscious of her own folly in withholding her announcement; she needed help, a job, money, reassurance, but she could not break through the fence of social forms she found erected against intimacy. In these five years, she perceived, she had become a visitor, the old friend from out of town who is at the Biltmore for a few days; in her absence, the circle had closed; the hands she had once clasped now clasped each other and would not part to readmit her to the dance. They had forgotten her, forgotten, that is, her former self, which remained green only in her own memory; for her alone, time had stood still.

She left the telephone and began, reluctantly, to dress. Half an hour later, in the hotel dining room, a man eyed her, and though she bent her head strictly over her dinner, her mind vacillated, wondering whether a stranger might not ... Discretion, however, warned her that she could pay too high a price for a listener. I must be strong, she said to herself, and, slightly reassured by this small victory, yet shaken by the need she saw in herself that had exposed her to so commonplace a temptation, she paid her check. Back in her room, her magazines exhausted, she picked up the Gideon Bible and read doggedly through Kings and Chronicles, and at last fell asleep.

When she woke, it was too early to telephone anyone at an office. She had breakfast and read the help-wanted columns. There was nothing there for her. By ten o'clock her sense of flatness and embarrassment had grown so large that she could not bring herself to telephone anyone who might be able to get her a job. The inevitable question, the Why, stood ahead of her, bristling with condolence and curiosity; she was not ready for it. Better, she said to herself suddenly, to go to an agency, where no personal explanations were required. In ten minutes she was at Rockefeller Plaza, with the list of her qualifications ready on her tongue. But the sight of the Victory garden, the rows of young radishes, made her own garden take shape before her, like a sin she had forgotten to confess. Oh God, oh God, she said to herself, I am unfit—who will hire me?

And it seemed to her that she had not gone far enough; she must discard her whole identity. An inspiration seized her: she might hire herself out as a cook. She saw herself, anonymous, in a maid's room in the third story of a house in Pelham, saw the bed with the thin blankets and the lumpy mattress, the bath shared with the baby, or the lavatory in the basement. All the wretched paraphernalia of domestic service became invested with glamour for her—she might lose herself and be saved. If she were to go down to Fourteenth Street now and buy herself a cheap dress and some shoes, by tonight she might have a situation. She could leave her own clothes in the hotel room, and when he came to find her, he would find merely Bonwit Teller, Mark Cross, hat by John-Frederics, fragrance by Schiaparelli. She was already, in her mind, selecting the shoes for her new life (patent leather with bows which would do for her day out, or sensible, flat-heeled black?), when some part of her, her conscience or her good sense, warned her that it would not do. It was a child's dream of revenge (see to what lengths you have driven me). Regretfully, she relinquished the adventure.

Yet, she said to herself, I must do *something;* by tomorrow I shall be out of money. In her handbag were the few pieces of jewelry she had inherited from her mother. It occurred to her that this was perhaps the moment to sell them; after lunch, with cash in her pocket, she could approach the agencies with more assurance. She walked briskly up toward Fifty-ninth Street, feeling herself lifted once again by that wave of exultation that had brought her down from the country. She was free again, if only for a few hours; all decisions, commitments, were postponed. It was as though the old-gold and diamond shop which she entered presently were the last station in her flight; passing the jewelry over the counter, she divested herself of her last possession; the appraiser counted her out a hundred dollars, and she no longer had anything to lose. She stuffed the money into her pocketbook and hurried back to the hotel.

At the desk, however, she found a message, breaking her lunch date and asking her to call back. At once, her elation vanished. The day stretched empty ahead of her. She turned quickly back to the street and found a Hamburger Heaven, where she ate lunch. Afterward, she went to the movies, and when she returned to her room she did not telephone anyone, but lay on her bed reading the Gospel according to St. Matthew until she felt it to be late enough to go to sleep. She had eaten no dinner. The third day passed off in much the same way: again the movies, and at night the Bible.

On the morning of the fourth the telephone waked her, and she knew at once that it would be he. "Well," he said, "I found you." "Yes," she said. "It wasn't so hard." "No," he replied shortly. "Will you come down and have breakfast with me?" "No." "Oh, go to hell," he retorted, and hung up. When he called up that night, he was not sober, and it was she who hung up. She had seen nobody since her arrival. Since the first night she had eaten nothing but hamburgers, and sandwiches at drugstore counters. Notice of any sort had become painful to her: she was unequal to a headwaiter or a desk clerk; she passed in and out without leaving her key; she felt both conspicuous and obscure. She had gone to a single employment agency and filled out an application. Outside the door, she realized that she had forgotten to note down her previous experience, but she could not go back. She was hiding and waiting, both for him and for someone else, some friend or stranger who would come to help her in response to an appeal she had never made. She was living in a state of peculiar expectation, as though she had put an ad in the newspaper, an ad of the most total purport, which God perhaps might answer, and the message she daily expected to find, written out in the hotel's violet ink and shoved under her door, was not of an ordinary social nature.

Yet this sense of expectancy, of extravagant, unreasonable hope, had for its corollary during these days a strange will-lessness, an attitude of resignation and despair. She knew that it was absolutely necessary that she should bestir herself; her money would soon run out and she would be locked out of her hotel room. Yet she found that she actually looked forward to this catastrophe as a means of release; the credit manager might yet be the Saviour, who, as holy legend tells us, appears in strange disguises. She was, it seemed to her now, utterly at the mercy of chance: a notice of eviction might precipitate her future out of the solution in which it was suspended—she herself was powerless. In her present state, even her flight appeared to her to have been an act of supreme daring; she could not imagine how she could have summoned up the firmness of character to do it. In fact, she said to herself, if she could have foreseen the outcome, she would never have taken the last drastic step, but held it forever in reserve, a threat and a promise—and died, after thirty years of marriage, thinking how different her life might have been had she left him. What folly, she cried, what madness! She had exchanged the prison of the oppressor for the prison of the self, and from this prison there was not even the hope of escape. At six o'clock Thursday evening, she had not decided what to wear for dinner, a long dress or a short. She put two dresses on the bed, but the arguments for each were unanswerable, and at six-thirty she went out and walked until she found a Western Union office, where she sent a telegram of excuse to her hostess, knowing, as she did so, that she was cutting her last line of communication to the world, to the past, to the future.

Yet when he had not called her again by the morning of the sixth day, a faint hope began to ruffle her spirit, like a sea breeze on an August afternoon. If he had given up and returned to the country, something might still be salvaged. She had seen her resolve melt away in these long mornings in the hotel room, and she knew that she was no longer proof against him; if he were to summon, she would obey. With the dissolution of her belief in herself, her case against him had collapsed. Yet, if he were to abandon her, she knew that she would endure, simply because, physically, she was alive and possessed of a certain negative fortitude. Eventually she would go out, she would telephone, get a job, and gradually circumstances would knit a new web around her, as scar tissue will form over a wound, even if the surgeon has not been called to take the proper stitches.

On this sixth day, as the morning passed on and the telephone still did not ring, she felt her spirits rise and an almost forgotten gaiety take possession of her. Surely he must be gone, she said to herself, and now I am really up against it and perhaps it will be fun after all. The sense of being under surveillance was passing off, and she dressed quickly, in her best white dress, black shoes, and large black cartwheel hat. Nothing, she told herself confidently, is more urban than black and white in summer. It was three o'clock and she had had nothing to eat, but the emptiness of her stomach only added to her fine sense of lightness and bravery. The sound of her heels on the stone floor near the elevator was brisk and pleasing, she let her handbag swing gallantly on her bare, tanned arm. For the first time, on pressing the button, she knew precisely where she was going—to call on an old friend who had an important job in an advertising office—and she knew, furthermore, that it was going to be all right, that he would compliment her and take her out to cocktails at a nice place, and that there, over the second drink, an opening would come which would allow her to tell him, quite naturally, quite easily, that she had left her husband. When he would press her—gently—for a reason, it would be merely a question of finding the

right formula, of avoiding vindictiveness on the one hand and piety on the other, of packing the truth into some assimilable capsule which her companion could swallow without any noticeable discomfort. As the elevator descended, a sentence spoke itself for her (I would have left him long ago if it hadn't been for those damned petunias). This was the right note, she recognized at once, seeing in advance the effect it would make in her friend's face, where the struggle between incredulity and belief would resolve itself in laughter. She foresaw a whole train, a lifetime, of these sentences. (But you say you left him five days ago; what have you been doing ever since? I've been lying in my hotel room reading the Gideon Bible.) She smiled, feeling herself on home territory. She was back at her port of embarkation, which she had set forth from five years before, back to her native patois, where jest masks truth but does not deny it.

The elevator doors opened and she saw her husband sitting in the lobby.

Two days later, he unlocked the door of the house and gave her a slight shove forward, as though she were a dog or a truant child. Her first impression was that the house had in a week grown older and shabbier. She stood in the doorway of the living room, looking about her with the eyes of an observant stranger. She noted the paint peeling on the window frames, the place where the wallpaper had been patched and the stripes did not quite meet, the blue chair that had never belonged there in the first place, the stain where her own head had rested on the back of the sofa. Two rather tacky-looking bouquets of bridal wreath stood on the marble-topped coffee table which she had cut down from an old piece; very plainly, they said Welcome Home in the floral language of her maid. Generally, when this kind of thing happened to her, when a room or the face of a lover did not measure up to memory, she would narrow her eyes, as she did to look at herself in the mirror, till the focus had changed and the image become a little blurred; then, with the quick hand of fancy, she would bestow a few decorations on the object—a bowl of flowers, a glass cigarette box—a look of irony, or a smile; and in a few moments all would be well, the face or the room would have subsided, and her eyes, now wide open, could run over it with love. This time, however, though she narrowed her eyes out of force of habit, nothing of the sort happened; the room became dimmer but it did not reassemble itself. "Well," said her husband, rather heartily, in his business-as-usual tone, "everything looks the same." This statement came in so patly that she made the mistake, fatal in marriage, of speaking to him as an intimate. "Does it?" she asked. "Really? It looks queer to me. The colors look as if somebody had mixed black in them. Do you suppose she has changed the light bulbs?" "Don't be silly," he said, sweeping her ahead of him toward the staircase. "Why should she do that?" "Let's have dinner right away," he added, pushing her slightly again, as though he had expected her to express some morbid and contradictory wish. She obeyed him, mechanically, as she had done ever since she had seen him sitting in the hotel lobby. Her defeat seemed to her shameful and absolute. Fortunately, however, her feelings had died in her; there was no rebelliousness, no resentment—in the conquered country, the officials conferred quietly with the captors and the underground movement slept.

What troubled her all evening was merely the notion that something had happened to the lighting. Across the table in the dining room, she could barely see her husband's face, though the customary twelve candles were burning. In the middle of the meal, she excused herself and got up to turn on the electricity. This was not an improvement; now her husband's face appeared to be unnaturally white. The food also seemed to her to have been tampered with. Her husband was eating with apparent relish; still, she could not disabuse herself of the idea that there was something wrong—perhaps the maid had forgotten to put the sherry in the stew? "You are tired," said her husband warningly, and she accepted this explanation with gratitude. After dinner, nevertheless, she could not restrain herself from going around to each of the lamps to see if there might be dust on the bulbs. But her finger came off clean.

In the morning, the visual derangement persisted. Her eye was caught, on waking, by a window shade which had been white when she had gone to New York; this morning it was certainly ivory. Slightly frightened, she closed her eyes and took refuge in sleep. When she woke, it was to the light sound of the glass bell calling her to lunch, and to an instant conviction of disaster. There was something wrong, something she had forgotten, something more than the persistent queerness of the light or the fact of her being back once again in her husband's bed. But her memory would not yield it up until, during a pause in the lunchtime conversation, she happened to glance out the window and saw on the sill the boxes containing the dead petunias. Her husband heard her gasp and his eyes followed hers. "What's the matter?" he said. "Nothing," she replied. "Something I remembered." He did not pursue the topic, and later, when he asked the question ("Have you been out yet to look at your garden?"), she perceived, with relief, that he was unaware of its significance. For him the question was a mere token of politeness, a bone tossed to the idiosyncrasies of her taste. He was still going through the motions of treating her, rather nervously, as a guest, but his heart was plainly not in it, for he did not trouble to wait for her answer.

For her, however, the question had a more fateful sound. She knew at once that she ought at least to go out and look, yet she put it off, for a day, for two days, while she did nothing but lie on her bed, declining to go to the market, plan the meals, make the

French dressing, sleeping from time to time, as she had done in the hotel, and waking always with that terrible start of knowledge that tells us, as we come out of ether or alcohol, that something has changed in our lives, though we are not yet sure what it is. If her husband's question had not been repeated a second and a third time, she might never, she told herself, have made the nearly unbearable effort that took her into the toolshed for her trowel and cultivator and sent her slowly down the garden path to the enclosure in the fields. But the third time his question had had an anxious perplexity in it. Her avoidance of the garden had begun to seem to him abnormal; his mind must be set at rest. For (it had become more and more apparent) he had no comprehension at all of the events of the past week. He imagined that the whole affair was a sort of triumph, that he, the conquerer, guardian of the hearth, had pursued the fugitive nymph and wooed and bullied her home by the sheer force of his will. It had not occurred to him for an instant that the collapse was interior, that, like France, she had fallen, limp, corrupt, disgraced, into the arms of the victor, and so long as he did not perceive this, she had a little bargaining power left. But for the preservation of the illusion, it was necessary that he should believe her unchanged, should have no suspicion of the docility that placed her, not only at his mercy, but at the mercy of every event. Her long hours in her room she had excused on the grounds of emotional exhaustion, but this could hardly be expected to last forever. Already he had begun to look a little critically at the meals, to run a finger over a table that had not been dusted—the holiday, his voice indicated, was over. And now, as she passed his window, she knew that the sound of her footsteps were reassuring to him; it signified the return to normalcy, the resumption of hostilities.

The garden had waited too long, she warned herself; she was too late. Common sense alone could tell you what you might expect to find if you left a garden alone for ten moist days in June. She was prepared for the worst. Yet halfway down the path apprehension gave place to hope, and she began to run, as though this final burst of speed could make up for a long tardiness, as though she might catch the garden in the moment of transformation, effect a last-minute rescue in the very teeth of probability. The garden, however, was gone. Her first impression was that it had disappeared without a trace. In ten days the weeds had swallowed it. The brown enclosure had turned green; the very markers that indicated the rows had vanished, and of the whole enterprise only the fence remained, an absurd testimonial to the fact that this rectangle had been, at one time, the scene of human endeavor. With the first shock, she closed her eyes: this was the nightmare vision she had wrestled with all spring, a ferocious tableau vivant entitled The Triumph of the Weeds, which had appeared again and again to halt her on the road to freedom, to harrow her susceptibilities and appeal to her pity and love. She had turned back before it a hundred times, and when at length she had hardened her heart, she had told herself, I will not be there to see it. Now, however, it was all as she had imagined it, except that the season was not so far advanced and she was here in the midst of it, while the hot furnished room was distant beyond desire. When she opened her eyes again, it was not with the hope of finding some mitigating circumstance, but rather with a kind of morbid appetite to embrace the full details of her disaster. Now she made out the individual weeds, and she saw that while in the field outside there were buttercups and a few daisies already open, here, in her enclosure, flourished only the most virile, the most virid, the most weedlike weeds, the coarse growers—burdock, thistle, milkweed, Queen Anne's lace; the crawlers—carrotweed, Jill-run-over-the-ground, and especially the choking nut grass, which crawled beneath the earth's surface and sprouted fiercely above it. No doubt, she said to herself, there was some natural explanation for this—the rankest weeds were perhaps the strongest and their seeds had a longer viability— yet common sense would not prevail; her heart accepted the phenomenon as a judgment and a curse.

It is hopeless, she murmured to herself, leaning against the fence, hopeless; and for the first time her spirit made an acknowledgment of defeat that was not provisional in character. Up to this moment there had been in her mind small recesses of hope to which her thoughts had fled secretly, unavowedly; in her contract with reality, an escape clause which permitted her to believe that what had been done was not irretrievable, that—in this case—dry weather might have retarded the weeds or some magic helper hoed for her (her maid, a thoughtful neighbor, a small boy employed by her husband?); now solidly before her lay the brutal *fait accompli,* the lost garden, irrecoverable, for though something might still be salvaged (a few gray cornflower plants could be made out in the mat of vegetation at her feet), the original design, the mirror of absolute beauty in which she had glimpsed her own image, was shattered. She sank listlessly to the ground and sat looking about her. Quite simply a sentence came to her and she spoke it aloud: "Now," she said, "I have nothing to live for."

The patent absurdity of these words acted as an astringent. The voice of common sense spoke again, saying, After all, you have a life expectation of at least forty years and you have got to do something with your time, you cannot just go to pieces, and in any case people do not live for gardens, but for ideals, principles, persons. This particular garden is ruined, but it is still possible to transplant. A second-best garden can be made out of the cornflowers, the zinnias, the cosmos, perhaps even the scabiosa. You can move the stronger plants and in August you will have flowers on the table. She presented this idea to her emotions and waited for the familiar bustle of activity, the rolling back of the sleeves, which turned her heart on such occasions into a large and hospitable house that is being made ready for an evening party. But the motors of anticipation remained cold. The second-best garden could not, even momentarily, command her belief. Like an adopted child, or a second husband, it could never make up to her. The weeds had finished all that. The weeds were, in fact, her garden, the end product of her activities, and the white foam that children call spit, which she saw clinging to the young grasses, was the outward mark of her disease. She remained sitting on the warm ground, idle, without thought or feeling, but ashamed to go back to the house.

This time she heard her husband's footsteps approaching, but out of pride she would not look up, even when she felt him stop just behind her at the entrance to the garden. "Gosh!" he said. "What an awful situation!" "Yes," she answered defiantly. "It's ruined." There was a silence during which she imagined him to be shrugging his shoulders. Anger began to boil up in her again, and she spun around to face him. The language of their old quarrels rose to her lips, the classical formulae of accusation and outrage. (See what you have made me do, you wanted this to happen, you are glad), but she was arrested by the expression of his face, which was neither jubilant nor indifferent, but full of simple curiosity and wonder. The weeds had finally made their impression on him; never before had he really believed in them; he had considered them to be a chimera of her dark imagination. Now he stood awestruck by this fearful demonstration of their authenticity, and for the first time the two of them shared in silence a single emotion. "What is that awful stuff?" he asked at length, bending down to pull up a spear of nut grass. The root broke off in his inexperienced hands. "Not that way," she said. "Look." Her trowel came up with the nut secure.

"This is the weed I've been talking about all spring."
He examined it, turning it over between his fingers
in his methodical way. "Why, it's a little bulb," he
said. It was not worthwhile to correct this statement;
to make the botanical distinction between a bulb and
a tuber might simply provide a distraction from the
mood of repugnance and terror that had brought them
close for a moment. She longed to rush him ahead
with her into the particulars of her loss, to say, See
what I have been up against, see the sorrel, the field
grass, the carrotweed, see where the sweet peas would
have been, see where I dug the trench and strewed it
with manure, think of the liming and the watering and
weeding; she was filled with a kind of wild excitement
and joy that he, who had never acknowledged the
garden in life, should meet it, as it were, post-
humously, and pay his respects. Yet prudence or tact
restrained her. The work of initiation could not be
hurried. He stood on the brink of her agony in the
garden; his wide feet in their brown shoes were
planted on one of the surviving cornflowers, as though
to illustrate the text of his inculpation—but he must
not be pushed. It was enough that he should share,
however vaguely, her burden of loss, that her be-
reavement should to some measure be accepted as
his. She waited, half-frightened, half-exalted, for what
he would say next.

"Gosh!" he repeated, with intensified feeling, and
now she was sure it was coming, the miracle she expected, which might take the form of an embrace, a
cry, an apology, but which would be in essence a la-
ment, not so much for the garden as for her, for the
dead young lady he had brought back from New
York, whom he kept propped up in bed, at the breakfast table, on the sofa, in the odor of corruption.

"You have your work cut out for you," he said. For
an instant she believed that she had not heard him
properly.

"Maybe we can get a boy to help you," he continued in a matter-of-fact tone.

It was over, she knew it at once, yet she made a last appeal. "The garden is ruined," she said in a stubborn, hostile voice, but speaking slowly and emphatically as though to direct his attention to the importance of this statement.

"Nonsense," he replied briskly. "You are always so extreme. I'll call up Mr. Jenkins tomorrow and see if he can send . . ."

At the mention of the neighboring farmer, her mouth opened and she began to scream. "I'll kill you if you do!" she shouted. Picking up the spading fork, she plunged it wildly into the ground, tossing sods and plants into the air in a frenzy of destruction. The loose earth fell on her hair, on her face, down which tears were running. She was aware that she cut a grotesque and even repulsive figure, that her husband was shocked by the sight and the sound of her, but the gasping sobs gave her pleasure, for she saw that this was the only punishment she had left for him, that the witchlike aspect of her form and the visible decay of her spirit would constitute, in the end, her revenge. She continued to lay about her with the spading fork, though the original fury had already passed off, until his solid, uneasy figure had disappeared from view, until his last words no longer sounded in her ears.

It was late in August when he came into the living room with a heterogeneous bouquet in which she recognized some of the stubborner flowers of her garden, cosmos and cornflowers and a few blackish red miniature zinnias. Mixed in with these were some weeds, pinkish sprays of bouncing Bet and the greenish-white clusters of Queen Anne's lace. There was no doubt of it, he had been visiting her garden, and this was not the first time. Toward the end of June she had heard him outside the window, swearing, as he tied up rambler roses; in July, he had brought in raspberries, saying, "Can't we have these for dinner?" The berries were soft and broken—he had been too late in the harvest. She lay now on the sofa, reading a detective story, watching him as he brought in a vase too tall for his bouquet and crammed the flowers into it. She felt no impulse to correct him; his clumsiness, in fact, pleased her, the ugliness of the bouquet pleased her, just as the stain on the coffee table had pleased her, the spot on her maid's uniform at lunch. She basked, as she had been doing all summer, in a sly private satisfaction. She was broken but she was also irreplaceable, and her continued physical existence must be, she thought, an unending reminder to him of everything he had lost. She was enjoying in real life the delight that is generally experienced only in daydreams, the sense of *when I am dead, how they will mourn for me, how valuable I shall become to them when I am no longer theirs*.

She could see her own case now with the detachment of a historian. Between them, he and she had killed off the part of her that had always excited his anxiety and irritation, the part of her which regarded nothing as final, which was continually planning, contriving, hoping, which lived in the future and slept, like a fireman, fully dressed for an emergency. It was this part of her which had dreamed of flight and deliverance, but it was also this part which had created for itself the small mirages of duty and pleasure which had held her to him for five years. These were not, as she had thought, antithetical selves, but the same thing, the creative, constructive principle which, in its restless anticipation of change, built structures of semi-permanency —a series of overnight cabins that in their extension formed, not precisely a city, but at least a road, a *via vitae*.

It was this part of her which had incurred his jealousy, for it was obliged to live slightly estranged, to make large investments of passion in private enterprises; yet it was this part of her he now wished back,

for he saw that this had been the nerve, and he now
longed for a recurrence of the very symptoms whose
presence, three months ago, he had detested. Now, by
a hundred spells, he was attempting to bring about a
resurrection. He appealed to her housekeeping instinct, to her esthetic sense, to her vanity, to her pity;
his very clumsiness was an appeal for help, and it was
not that she did not hear these appeals; she heard, but,
as in a dream, she was incapable of action. What it
was all leading up to she understood plainly: a moment ought to come when she would rise miraculously
from the sofa, sweep the absurd bouquet from his
hands, shake it lightly into form, call for a new bowl,
and enshrine the product on the mantelpiece, while he
stood by, awkward and grateful, as at a religious ceremony, a secular Easter mass. Yet now she could only
lie back and watch, with lowered eyelids, pretending
to take no notice, enjoying her poor-man's pie of irony
and contempt.

For the pleasure she took in her untended house, in
her careless and unsupervised maid, in her neglected
garden (which, however, she had never, since June,
seen) was purely negative in character, a compensa-
tion for disability. The discomfort inflicted on her husband by the loss of her imaginative faculty could never
atone to her for the joy she had once had in the exercise of it. Lying on the sofa, looking about at the dusty
bare room, she would feel excruciating stabs of remorse, like the pains in an amputated limb. She would
get up and start at some task, but before the candle-
sticks were half polished, her interest would have died
and she would leave them in the sink for her maid to
finish. It could not, it seemed to her, go on much
longer, and she prayed for him to abandon her. (Her
going, on her own initiative, had become utterly out of
the question.) On him her life now depended; where
renunciation, the withdrawal of love, had blackened
the loved objects as frost blackens the flowers in an
autumn garden, he alone had survived, evergreen,

sturdily perennial, in the season of death. Disliking him as she did, she had never bothered to renounce him, and now her eyes would come to rest on him with a kind of relief—the familiar detested object in surroundings grown strange and terrible. Her glance held in it also an element of calculation: how long, she asked herself, will he be able to stand me? Her own endurance had become infinite, for she no longer lived in time, but he, being real, being alive, might reach in measurable stages the threshold of domestic suffering.

He set the vase down on the table, took his hand-kerchief, and dusted the surface in a rather bustling way, like a woman who rattles dishes in the kitchen to awaken a sleeper whom she does not wish to be so rude as to call. He cleared his throat.

"You have some beautiful flowers out back."

She sat up at last to look at him directly, but made no reply.

"You ought to go out and see them."

She watched him hesitate and then think better of what was in his mind to say. He is afraid of me, she thought, with a touch of pity.

"We ought to have some more of them in the house," he continued, enthusiastically. "You have got all sorts of things back there. Even your weeds are wonderful," and he went rattling on nervously, de-scribing the scene in the fields, suggesting improve-ments—a professional tree surgeon to come for the old apple trees, a wattled fence along the lane, plans she had once proposed and he rejected. She was only half listening; the very idea of these improvements now seemed to her preposterous; one might as well paint a mural in a condemned house.

Seeing that she would not reply, he halted and tried a new tack. He came up to her and took her hand. "I miss the way this room used to look," he said in a voice that was quite new with him, wistful and child-like in its directness. "Those yellow things you used to have on the coffee table." For a moment now, she saw it all through his eyes, saw a vision which was less precise and accurate than hers, a rather smeary vision in which the pale, clear, lemon yellow he was thinking of (African marigold, carnation-flowered, yellow supreme) was likely to be confused with the orange of French marigold or of cosmos orange flare, a vision in which energy and whopping good intentions counted for more than anything else and the bigger a flower the better—but nevertheless a vision, an ideal of beauty, of love and the lavish hand; and the sense of his loss, his large, vague loss, overwhelmed and engulfed her own.

She pressed his hand lightly, murmuring, "Yes, I remember," and then let his fingers drop. He regained her hand, however, and squeezed it. She felt, as once before in the fields, that he was on the verge of some fine avowal. She herself, only now, had made the great leap from pity to sympathy; she grieved for his predicament, of which she herself was the determining factor; could he likewise grieve for hers, whose existence he had never acknowledged, weep with her at last because she could not leave him, because the courage, the more attractive alternative, whatever it was that might separate them, was lacking? "I've always loved your flowers," he said, his voice blurred and high with emotion. "You know that."

As her ears admitted this lie, this tearful, sentimental, brazen lie, her whole nature rose weakly in rebellion. How dare you, her heart muttered, how dare you say it? Nothing could have been—and at such a moment!—more dishonest; she could have cited him fifty instances which would have controverted him utterly. But the heartfelt insincerity of these words went beyond contradiction, beyond hypocrisy, into regions of spiritual obstinacy and opacity impenetrable to reason, where reason, in fact, and conscience had been cruelly blinded by the will, the will which demanded that everything should be always all right, which had, as it

were, legislated the bouquet on the mantelpiece by a
kind of brutal denial of color, of tonal values, of the
harmony of textures, and which was now enforcing its
myth of a harmonious marriage, of tastes and occupa-
tions shared, by dictatorial fiat.

And yet there had been the tears in the voice. . . .
What the tears meant, she perceived, was that he did
love the flowers, now that she had not got them, now
that they were no longer dangerous; they had passed,
for him and for her, out of experience into memory,
and here in this twilight world he could possess them
—and her—with a terrible blind rapacity. She saw
also that her pity had been wasted, that he had got her
where he wanted her; she had been translated, bodily,
into that realm of shadows where the will was all-
powerful, the city of the dead. She herself was no
more to him now than an oak leaf pressed in a
schoolbook, a tendril of blond hair, a garter kept in a
drawer. But this was, for him, everything: it was love
and idolatry. The lie was a necessity to him, a cardinal
article of faith. To protest was useless. He could not
be shaken in his conviction, but only be annoyed, confused, thrown off. And in a final thrust of rejection,
she yielded, conceding him everything—flowers, facts,
truth. Let him put them into his authorized version;
she had failed them, and would do so again and again.
With him, they would see service.

She tightened her clasp on his hand.

"Yes," she said mistily, "I know."

The lie came easier, after all, than she would have
thought.

The Friend
of the Family

HIS GREAT QUALIFICATION was that nobody liked him very much. That is, nobody liked him enough to make a point of him. Consequently, among the married couples he knew, he was universally popular. Since nobody cherished him, swore by him, quoted his jokes or his political prophecies, nobody else felt obliged to diminish him; on the contrary, the husbands or wives of his friends were always discovering in him virtues their partners had never noticed, and a husband who was notorious for detesting the whole imposing suite of his wife's acquaintance would make an enthusiasm of the obscure Francis Cleary, whom up to that time the wife had seldom thought about. In the long war of marriage, in the battle of the friends, Francis Cleary was an open city. Undefended, he remained immune, as though an inconspicuous white flag fluttered in his sharkskin lapel. The very mention of his name brought a certain kind of domestic argument to a dead stop. ("You don't like my friends." "I do too like your friends." "No, you don't, you hate them." "That's not true," and—triumphantly—"I like Francis Cleary.")

A symbol of tolerance, of the spirit of compromise, he came into his own whenever one of his friends married. A man who in his single state had lunched with Francis Cleary once or twice a year would discover to his astonishment, after two or three years of marriage, that Francis Cleary was now his closest friend: he was invited regularly for weekends, for dinner, for

38

cocktail parties; he made the invariable fourth at bridge or tennis. Though he might never have been asked to the wedding ceremony (and in fact it was more usual for the wife to have him introduced to her quite by chance a few months later, in a restaurant, and to experience a kind of Aristotelian recognition— "Why hasn't Jack ever spoken of you? You must come to dinner next Thursday"), his azalea plant or cyclamen would be the first to arrive at the hospital when the baby was born.

If it was the wife who had originally been Francis Cleary's friend, the graph of intimacy would follow the same curve. A mild admirer who had always figured in the background of her life, imperceptibly he would have slid to the very center of the composition: he came to stay for two weeks in the summer, played chess with her husband, and took her to dinner when she was alone in town. He had become "your friend Francis Cleary," a walking advertisement of her husband's good nature. "How can you say I am jealous?" he would ask. "You had lunch with Francis Cleary only last week." Left by herself with this old friend, she would—as she had always done—get bored, play the phonograph, make excuses to go to the kitchen to see how the maid was getting along with the hollandaise. Yet at her husband's suggestion she would invite him again and again, because his presence in the house reassured her, told her that marriage had not really changed her, that she was still free to see her own friends, that her husband was a generous, fairminded man who could not, naturally, be expected to share every one of her tastes. Moreover, it was so *easy* to have Francis Cleary. When her real friends came, something unpleasant usually happened—an argument, an ill-considered reference to the past—or if nothing actually happened, she suffered in the expectation of its happening, so that when they finally left she echoed her husband's "Thank God, that's over!" in the silence of her heart. A few awkward evenings, a

weekend would serve, in most cases, to convince her
that the love she felt for her friends was a positive
obstacle to her happiness; and she would renounce it,
though perhaps only provisionally (telling herself that
surely, later on, in precisely the right circumstances
Jim would come to see these people as she did—just
as she was sure that sometime, next week or next year,
Jim would come to like string beans, if she served
them to him in a moment of intimacy and with precisely the right sauce). Meanwhile, however, it was
certainly better to have Francis Cleary, who was after
all a close friend of her real friends (had she not met
him through them?), and as the years passed the distinction between her "real" friends and Francis Cleary
would blur in her mind and she would imagine that
he had always been one of her dearest associates.

His social mobility derived from the fact that he
was capable of being used by other people as a symbol, and a symbol not only of an idea (e.g., tolerance)
but of an actual person or persons. Thus a husband,
drawing up a guest list for an evening party, might remark to his wife, "How about having the Caldwells?"
(or the Muellers or the Kaplans). "Oh my God," his
wife would shriek, "do we have to have *them?*" "I
like them." "They're awful, and besides they won't
know anybody." "They're old friends of mine. I owe
them something." "Have them when I'm away then—
you know they can't stand me." "Don't be silly.
They'd be crazy about you if you'd give them half a
chance." In desperation, the wife would cast about
her. She saw her party, her charming, harmonious,
mildly diversified party, heading straight for shipwreck
on the rock of her husband's stubbornness. Then all at
once an inspiration would seize her. "Look," she
would say, in a more reasonable tone, "why don't you
ask Francis Cleary instead? He'd get along very well
with these other people. And he's your friend, just as
much as Hugh Caldwell is. You're wrong if you think
it's a matter of the Caldwells' being your friends. It's

just that they wouldn't fit in." And the husband, reading the storm warnings as clearly as she, telling himself that if he insisted on the Caldwells his wife might treat them with impossible rudeness, and that even if she did not, she would make her concession an excuse for filling the house for months to come with her intolerable friends, that he might win the battle but lose the war, would reluctantly, grudgingly, consent. After all, Francis Cleary belonged to the circle of the detested Caldwells. To have him would be to have their spirit if not their substance, and, to be perfectly honest—he would say to himself—wasn't it the principle of the Caldwells rather than their persons that was the issue at stake?

Another hostess, on slightly better terms with the prospective host, or perhaps merely a better tactician, would begin differently. "Darling," she would say, looking up from the memorandum pad on which already a few names had been neatly aligned. "I have an idea. Why don't we ask Francis Cleary?" The air of discovery with which she brought forth this proposal would accord oddly with the fact that they always did have Francis Cleary at their parties, but the husband, who had been fearing something much worse (some old school friend or a marvelous singer she had met at a benefit), would in his relief not notice the anomaly. "All right," he would say, grateful to her for her interest in this rather dull old business associate, and before he had time to change his mind, she would have telephoned Francis Cleary and secured his acceptance. Then, when the question of the Caldwells was raised, she would pout slightly. "Oh," she would say, "don't you think that makes too much of the same thing? After all, we're having Francis Cleary, and I do think it's a mistake to have a bloc at a party." "I don't know." "Oh, darling, you remember the time we had all those Italians and they sat in the corner and talked to each other. . . ."

In either case, the outcome was the same. Francis

Cleary would appear at the party, representing the absent, unassimilable Caldwells. He was their abstraction, their ghost. Unobtrusive, moderately well bred, he would come early and stay late. He made no particular social contribution, but the host, whenever he glanced in his direction, would feel a throb of solidarity with his own past, and at some point in the evening he and Francis Cleary would have a talk about the Caldwells and Francis would tell him all about Hugh Caldwell's latest adventure. Not ordinarily a brilliant talker, in this particular field Francis Cleary was unsurpassed. He was a master of the second-hand anecdote, the vicarious exploit. Hugh Caldwell, who suffered dreadfully from asthma and had a distressing habit of choking and gasping in the middle of his sentences, never could have done himself the justice Francis did. In fact, Hugh Caldwell, telling his own stories, interposed an obstacle, a distraction—himself, the living, asthmatic flesh—between the story and the audience. As the movies have supplanted the stage, and the radio the concert hall, so Francis Cleary in modern life tended to supplant his friend, Hugh Caldwell, and in supplanting him, he glorified him. He was the movie screen on which the aging actress, thanks to the magic of the camera and make-up man, appears young and radiant, purged of her wrinkles; he was the radio over which one hears a symphony without seeing the sweat of the first violinist.

And yet, like all canned entertainment, Francis Cleary produced, in the end, a melancholy effect. To listen to him too long was like going to the movies in the morning; it engendered a sense of alienation and distance. Eventually, the host would move away, his desire to see Caldwell killed, not quickened, by this ghostly reunion, as the appetite is killed by a snack before dinner, as the taste for van Gogh's paintings was killed by the reproductions of the "Sunflowers" and "L'Arlésienne" that used to symbolize cultural sympathies in the living rooms of Francis Cleary's friends. But as the lesson of "L'Arlésienne" prevented hardly anyone from making the same mistake with Picasso's "Lady in White," so the lesson of Hugh Caldwell never prevented the host from allowing Francis Cleary to substitute on some other occasion for another old friend who was distasteful to the hostess, and many parties would be composed exclusively of Francis Clearys, male and female, stand-ins, reasonable facsimiles, who could fraternize with each other under the Redon or the Rouault or the Renoir reproductions—ready with anecdote, quotation, and paraphrase, amiable and immune as seconds at a duel. Afterwards, the host and hostess, reviewing the situation, would be unable to decide why it was that though everybody stayed late, got drunk, and ate all the sandwiches, nobody had had a particularly good time. And the failure of the party, far from causing bitterness or recrimination, would actually draw them together. Murmuring criticisms of their guests, they would pull up the blankets and embrace, convinced that they preferred each other, or rather that they preferred themselves as a couple to anybody else they knew.

But what about Francis Cleary riding home in a taxi with his female equivalent? Sex was not for him; his given name disclosed this—it could be either masculine or feminine; nobody ever called him Frank. He might be a bachelor or a spinster; quite often, he was a couple, but a couple which functioned as an integer. If he had begun his Francis Cleary existence as a single man, it was unwise for him to marry, for a wife might define him too sharply, people might like her and then other people would dislike her; before he knew it, through her, he might become the issue rather than the solution of a dispute. To say that sex was not for him does not mean that he did not sometimes have girls, or, in his female aspect, men; he might even have been in love, but since nearly the whole area of his life was public and social, this one small reserved section which he kept for himself was private, intensely so. His romantic activities, if he had any, were extracurricular. They did not interfere with his social function, and it is impossible to tell which was cause and which effect: was it the fact that he had very early in life fallen in love with the married lady that placed his weekends and his evenings and his vacations at the disposal of his friends, or had he recognized from the very beginning that he was cast for the part of the professional friend and arranged his affairs accordingly, cultivating without real predilection sexual tastes so impossible that they must be forever gratified *sub rosa,* under assumed names, in Pullman cars, alleys, cheap hotel rooms, public parks? How was anybody to know? In some of his manifestations, it seemed quite plain that design was at the bottom of it, that love had been gladly foregone for the sound of the telephone bell. He would hint at a disastrous passion or a vice to each of his married friends when the intimacy reached a certain stage, like a stranger on a train who after a given amount of conversation produces a calling card, but these confessions had a faint air of fraudulence or at least of frivolity: how could anyone take very seriously a passion or a morbid inclination which left its victim free every day from five until midnight and all day Sundays and holidays? Nevertheless, his confessions were accepted, often with a kind of gratitude. They served to "explain" him to new acquaintances, who might have thought him peculiar if they had not been assured that he kept a truly horrible vice in his closet.

In other cases, there appeared to have been no calculation. He thought sporadically of marriage but kept looking for "the right person," who was assumed to exist somewhere just beyond the social horizon, like a soul waiting to be born. Yet whenever a living being materialized who wore the features of the right person, she was found to be already married or indifferent or tied to an aged mother or in some other way impossible. So the vigil continued, until time made it an absurdity, and at fifty Francis Cleary ceased to yearn, ascribed his fate to a geographical accident (everybody has his double and everybody has his complement, but not necessarily in New York or even in America), to an over-romantic temperament, or simply to the bad habit, contracted in adolescence and never overcome, of falling in love with married women, which made him regard every woman who lacked a husband as essentially incomplete. Putting love behind him, Francis Cleary would throw himself more actively than ever into the occupation of friendship, the life of visits, small gifts and favors exchanged, mild gossip, concern over illnesses, outings for the children, and would, quite often, experience a kind of late blooming which would inspire all his friends to hope that he was at last on the verge of marriage, while in reality it was the abandonment of the idea of marriage that had permitted his nature, finally, to express itself. In this aspect—the aspect of innocence—Francis Cleary was almost lovable. Certainly he commanded the affection if not the active preference of his friends, and those husbands and wives who had accepted him as the lesser evil grew to like him for himself. It is significant, nevertheless, that he was liked for goodness of heart, which does not provoke envy, rather than for talent, charm, or beauty, which do. And goodness of heart notwithstanding, it was still a chore to dine or take a walk with him alone, and if by chance in these *tête-à-têtes* a muted happiness was achieved, his companion could never quite get over it, referred to the occasion repeatedly in conversation ("You know, I had quite a good time with Francis Cleary the other day"), as though a miracle had been witnessed and virtue been its own reward.

Yet here perhaps there has been a confusion of identity. It is likely that the Francis Cleary we have just been speaking of, the good, bewildered, yearning Francis Cleary, was never the true Francis Cleary at

all, but an uncle for whom the real one, the modern
one, was named. Whenever they met the good Francis
Cleary, his friends were struck by a certain anachro-
nism in his character; they would say that he reminded them of their childhood, of a maiden aunt who
did the mending, or a bachelor great-uncle who gave
them a gold piece every Christmas morning and left
his watch to them in his will when he died. The true
Francis Cleary had no such overtones. He was as much
a product of the age as nylon or plywood, and he could
be distinguished from the others, those uncles and
aunts of his who lingered on in a later period, by the
fact that one did not pity him. One could not mourn
for Francis, because he did not mourn for himself. He
cast no shadow behind him of thwarted ambition, un-
consummated desire, lost ideals. Indeed, one had only
to set the word *frustration* beside him to see that the
very conception of frustration was outmoded, hopelessly provincial—perhaps in the Middle West, in
small towns, men still walked the streets restlessly at
night, questioning their fate, wondering how it might
have been otherwise, but in any advanced center of
civilization, people, like sheets, came pre-shrunk; life
held neither surprises nor disappointments for them.

And your true Francis Cleary was the perfect san-
forized man, the ideal which others only approxi-
mated. He appeared to have no demands whatsoever
—that was the beauty of him. Or rather, as in a correctly balanced equation, demands and possible satis-
factions canceled out, so that the man himself, i.e., the
problem, vanished. When an apartment door shut behind him, it was as if he had never been. Nobody discussed him in his absence, or if they did, it was only
as a concession to convention. Once or twice a year,
he had a small, official illness, and in his comfortable
hotel apartment received flowers, books, and wine-
flavored calf's-foot jelly from his friends. Like everything else about him, these illnesses had a symbolic
character: they permitted his friends to bestow on him

tokens of a concern they did not feel. Without these illnesses, his friends might have grown to think themselves monsters of insensibility—was it, after all, *natural* to have a close friend whom you never gave a thought to? Francis, farseeing, provident, took care that such questions should not arise. He could no more afford to be a thorn in the conscience, the subject of an inward argument, than to be the occasion of verbal debate. The true friend might languish in furnished rooms with pneumonia and only the girl across the hall to help, or fight delirium tremens in Bellevue, but Francis' sore throats were always well attended. In the same way, he would from time to time present his friends with some innocuous little problem (should he go to Maine or New Hampshire during his vacation?) with the air of a man who asks for help in the most serious crisis of his life. His friends would loyally come through with advice and travel booklets, reminiscences of childhood summers, letters of introduction, and feel, when Francis set off at last to the place where he had intended to go originally, that they had stood by him through thick and thin, that the demands of friendship had been handsomely satisfied.

Once in a great while, when a friendship showed unmistakable signs of limpness (when a husband and wife seemed to be falling in love with each other again, or had reached the point of estrangement where each saw his own friends, or began to cultivate the acquaintance of another Francis Cleary, a competitor), Francis would go so far as to borrow money from the husband. These loans were of course mere temporary accommodations, and the warm glow of generosity felt by the husband almost always served to restore the circulation of the friendship. Still, during the short time he had the money (he usually waited until the twenty-seventh to borrow and then paid it back promptly the first of the next month), Francis was always very nervous. Once or twice he thought he had seen fear in the husband's eyes, fear that financial

need would turn "that nice Francis Cleary," as the
wives often called him, into another "poor old Frank."
Was it possible, he believed the husband was asking
himself, that he could have been deceived? Had importunity, cleverly disguised, always lurked in this old,
old acquaintance, and had it waited this long to strike?
The classic phrase of male disillusionment, *"I thought
you were different,"* trembled visibly on his lips, and
Francis saw himself slipping. The moment, of course,
passed. Francis repaid the money, and the husband,
metaphorically wiping the sweat from his brow, wondered how he could have doubted him. Certainly
Francis was different, had always been so. The friends
who had been with him at school or at college, and
who could remember him at all, were absolutely at
one on this point.

Even there, at the very beginning, importunity had
been excluded from his nature. The desire to excel, to
shine, to be closest, best friend, most liked, best
dressed, funniest, had played no part with him. He
had been content simply to be there, to be along, the
unnoticed eye-witness. Wherever he had gone to
school, whether it was Exeter or P. S. 12, whether
Yale or Iowa or Carnegie Tech, the Chicago Art Institute or Harvard Business, he was the man that
nobody could think of a quotation for when the year-
book was being compiled; and if you opened the year-
book today you would find the editors' defeat
commemorated by a blank below his photograph. Yet
he had not been disliked, for there had been in him
none of the burning hunger, the watchfulness, the
covert shame (however carefully masked by studious-
ness, indifference to society, eccentricity, geological
field trips, bird walks) that brand the true outsider
for the vengeance of those inside. During the rushing
period he had been neither too anxious nor too self-
assured nor too indifferent, with the result that, in
many cases, he was pledged to a slightly better fraternity than he might have expected to make; and in the

cases where he was overlooked in the general excitement, the omission was always remedied—he was
quietly taken in later on, in the junior year instead of
the sophomore. And the welcome given him, whether
tardy or prompt, never failed to create a small commotion among the outsiders, who knew themselves,
correctly, to be more brilliant, better looking, richer,
better scholars, better athletes, better drinkers, or
whatever was considered valuable, than he. Inevitably, they construed the pledging of Francis Cleary as
a calculated affront to themselves. Then and thereaf-
ter, forever and ever, the choice of Francis Cleary was
not an affirmation of something, but a negation of
something else.

Thus, in the family we were talking about, if Francis Cleary was for the husband a substitute for Hugh
Caldwell, for the wife he was the flat denial of Hugh
Caldwell. Mr. Caldwell, sitting in his lumpy armchair
in the Village, might have been solacing himself for
the fact that he was not invited to the Leightons with
the idea that the wife was simply a bitch who would
not let her husband see his rowdy old friends. But
when Francis Cleary, another of John Leighton's
friends of the same vintage, dropped in to see him,
fresh from a cocktail party at the Leightons', Mr.
Caldwell could no longer mistake her meaning. It was
he personally who was being excluded, and if he
stared at Francis Cleary and asked himself, "What in
the name of God has this guy got that I haven't?" this
was precisely the question Mrs. Leighton intended to
leave with him.

At this point the reader may ask what possible motive Mrs. Leighton could have had. What drove her to
persecute a man whom she hardly knew, who could
not, even if he had wished it, have done her the slightest injury? The reply can best be put in the form of a
further question. Let anyone to whom Mrs. Leighton's
behavior seems inexplicable, or at any rate odd, ask
himself why he does not like his wife's friends. Is it

really—as he is always telling himself—that they are
unattractive or that they bring out the worst in her,
encourage her to spend too much money or to think
about love affairs, or that they talk continually of
things and people of whom he is ignorant, or that they
borrow from her or take up too much of her time? Is
it even, to be franker, that he is jealous of them? This
explanation too is insufficient, for we can look around
us and find husbands who will not allow their wives'
friends or relations in the house but who display an
amazing cordiality toward their wives' lovers, and we
can find husbands who positively reject their wives' affection, who treat it as a bore and a nuisance, who yet
will use every means to deprive their wives of what,
from any sensible point of view, ought to be an outlet,
a diversionary channel for that affection—the society
of friends. Is not *envious,* rather, the word? Will the
dubious reader acknowledge that his wife and her
friends possess in common some quality that is absent
from his own nature? It is this quality that attracted
him to her in the first place, though by now he has
probably succeeded in obliterating all traces of it from
her character, just as the wife who marries the young
poet because he is so different from all the other men
she knows will soon succeed in getting him to go into
the advertising business, or at the very least set up
such a neurosis in him that he can only write one
poem a year. What passes for love in our competitive
society is frequently envy: the phlegmatic husband
who marries a vivacious wife is in the same position
as the businessman who buys up the stock of a rival
corporation in order to kill it. The businessman may
at the beginning delude himself with the idea that the
rival company has certain patents which he very much
wants to exploit, but it will shortly appear that these
patents, once so heartily desired, are in competition
with his own processes—they will have to be
scrapped. We cannot, in the end, possess anything that
is not ourselves. That vivacity, money, respectability,

talent which we hoped to add to ourselves by marriage are, we discover to our surprise, unassimilable to our very natures. There is nothing we can do with them but destroy them, deaden the vivacity, spend the money, tarnish the respectability, maim the talent; and when we have finished this work of destruction we may even get angry—the wife of the poet may upbraid him because he no longer writes poems, or the dull husband of the gay girl may reproach her for her woodenness in company.

Yet now a distinction must be made. In some cases, it is our wife or our husband who is the direct object of our envy and our desire, and in these marriages the friends are mere accidental victims; we have nothing against them personally; if we hate them it is because we have seen them smiling with our wife. But there is another kind of marriage, where it is the partner who is the accidental victim: simply a hostage whom we have carried home from a raid on the enemy, that is, on the circle of the friends. We bear this person no actual ill-will; we may even pity him as we lop off an ear or a little finger in some nicety of reprisal. He himself is not the object of revenge, he is merely the symbol of our hostility, usually for some group, class, caste, sex, or race. Such cases are generally marked by a crude and striking disparity between the husband and the wife; observe the communist married to the banker's daughter, the anti-Semite who marries the beautiful Jewess, the businessman who marries an actress and makes her quit the stage. These marriages are exercises in metonymy: the part is taken for the whole, the symbol for the thing symbolized. One might think, in the case of the businessman and the actress, that he had taken leave of his senses—why marry an actress if not to sit in the front row at her first nights?—if one did not know that his college life had been poisoned by his failure to make the Thespian Society, and that his secret vendetta against the stage had already expressed itself in certain Times

Square real estate operations, in investments in radio and movie companies, and, once, in an anonymous note addressed to the Commissioner of Licenses pointing out an indelicate passage in a current Broadway hit. The communist who subjects the banker's daughter to the petty squalor of life on Thirteenth Street—the unmade studio couch, the tin of evaporated milk flanking the rank brass ash tray on the breakfast table, the piles of dusty pamphlets, the late meetings, the cheap whiskey without soda, the hair done over the washbasin with wave-set bought from a cut-rate druggist—this man may be actually repelled by the conditions in which he obliges her to live; but his home is a stage kept set for the call her horrified father will pay them. And the anti-Semite who marries a beautiful Jewess may imagine that he has been carried away by love, treat her with great kindness, and exempt her from the Jewish race by a kind of personal fiat, declaring over and over again to himself and possibly to her that he married her in spite of her relations, her mother, her sister, her hook-nosed uncles, while in reality he is bored with his wife (who actually does not seem very Jewish), and it is the yearly visit of his mother-in-law to which he looks forward with sadistic zest. Summer after summer, he may promise his wife that he will not use the word "kike" in the old lady's hearing again, but somehow it always slides out, the old lady goes upstairs in tears, and the marriage has once again been consummated.

This distinction must be noted for the sake of clarity, though to the friends and to the wives and the husbands it makes really very little difference whether they are disliked for themselves or for some more irrelevant reason. The child struck by a bomb is indifferent to the private motives of the bombardier. Thus, with the Leighton couple, to return to our original question, Mrs. Leighton may have detested Hugh Caldwell because he or someone like him had once run a crayon through her sketch at a night class at the

Art Students League or because she was a stylist at Macy's and he a practicing nudist, or for any other reason that sprang from a divergence of interests. Or she may have found only one thing to disparage in Mr. Caldwell—his feeling of friendship for her husband. In either case, the result would be the same; whether from inclination or merely to spite her husband, Mrs. Leighton would see to it that Mr. Caldwell was not at home in her nice new house.

There are people who, whatever their good intentions, cannot renounce love, and there are people, a larger number, who cannot renounce victory. Thus, to take the second category first, a woman like Mrs. Leighton is not playing the game when she pretends to have sacrificed something by having only Francis Clearys at her parties; the jealousy and anger of the excluded Hugh Caldwell more than repay her for any superficial boredom she may have experienced during the evening. A still worse cheat is the anti-Semite who asks a Jewish Frances Cleary, a second cousin of his wife's, time after time to his house so that he may later express the most cruel and hair-raising opinions without being accused of bias. Most monstrous of all was the businessman already alluded to who married the actress and whose hatred of theatrical people stopped short of a young Francis Cleary, a radio actor with whom the wife had once played a season of summer stock. This man, whose name was Al, enacted for several months a pseudo-friendship with Francis. He invited him to lunch downtown, introduced him to radio magnates, listened to his morning broadcasts; the wife, the former actress, was at first bewildered and touched by these attentions, which she conceived to be overtures of love, and she began to look forward to the time when the house would be filled with her real friends, the playwrights, directors, and legitimate actors whom she missed so much in the country. It was not until her husband began to talk continually of the superiority of the verse drama of the air to the box-like drama of the stage that she perceived the malignancy of his design. Her answer was direct and militant. She treated Francis exactly as if he had been a genuine enthusiasm of her husband's—one night, without the slightest provocation, she turned him out of the house.

This shocking experience was crucial for the young actor Francis Cleary. It confirmed in him the sense, not yet quite solidified, of the perils of his position. For nearly two hours, as he paced the station platform, waiting for the train that would take him away from Fairfield County, away from important men who professed to admire Norman Corwin and were going to take him to lunch with the president of the Red Network, for this long-short intolerable time, he felt himself identified with the lot of humanity, with the mothers-in-law, sisters, true friends, ex-lovers for whom life is a series of indignities, with all those who, having attached themselves, are in a position to be dislodged. His heart cried out against the false husband who had not raised a hand to save him; it cried out and at length he hardened it. From this time on, Francis took the most energetic measures lest the taint of affection poison one of his friendships, and his reluctance to be identified with either partner to a marriage passed as devotion to the family, especially in doubtful cases like the Leightons', where to avoid the slightest appearance of partisanship, he concentrated his attention on the children and was always playing games with them on the floor or taking them out to the zoo or to holiday marionette shows—to the point that many of his friends kept remarking to each other that it was such a pity that Francis had never married because he was obviously mad about children. And though many of the children did not at all care for Francis and would even prefer sitting at a bar while their father drank with some dubious confederate to the most delightful outing Francis could offer them, others, more successfully educated by their parents, would take the name for the thing and being told that Francis adored them would docilely adore him back, to the limit, at any rate, of their capacities. But in either case, the mother, watching her child set out hand in hand with Francis to some accepted childish objective, was spared the slightest misgiving lest the child positively enjoy himself with Francis. Her own feelings about Francis assured her that there was no danger whatever that the child would get anything better than what he was used to at home.

In most instances, these precautionary measures were sufficient to keep Francis his status as friend. He watched, with professional amusement, the struggles of his younger counterparts to extricate themselves from the depths of a closer relation. He himself could never again be fooled when a husband or a wife, out of sheer malignance, would pretend to like him, seek out his company, complain that he was not asked to dinner often enough, lunch with him frequently alone, strike up a correspondence with him, till the other member of the couple would go nearly mad with exasperation and feelings of injustice, asking himself (if it were the husband) a hundred times a day how Dorothea could tolerate that lumpish little bore when she had a tantrum in the bedroom every time one of his real friends, one of his interesting friends, set a foot in the apartment. Francis could foretell, almost to the hour, the date of the inevitable rupture, and if it had not been for professional competition he might have warned his young namesake not to go to the Leightons' on the night that John Leighton, *for absolutely no reason,* would break a highball glass over his head. He himself practiced such discretion in these matters that he occasionally resorted to flight when there was no real necessity for it. The smallest compliment paid him by a husband or a wife would make him suspect a danger, and he would scurry away to safety before the friendship had got half started, while the couple, who had been counting on him to replace the people they liked in their social life and had no morbid designs at all, would ask themselves what they could have done to offend that nice Mr. Cleary.

The night on the station platform had left him with its mark. Where formerly the desire to be loved, noticed, esteemed, had, if it ever feebly stirred in him, been repressed without a pang, now the *fear* of being loved became a positive obsession with him. He saw annihilation stare at him in any half-affectionate glance. Though his whole activity was given over to the manipulation of the symbols of devotion—presents, visits, solicitous inquiries, games, walks in the country—still the validation of a single one of these tokens would suffice to ruin him, just as, it is presumed, the introduction of a single five-dollar gold piece into the channels of our currency would upset our entire monetary system. The liking of a single human being would translate him into the realm of measures and values, the realm of comparisons. Someone had valued him, and the whole question of his value was opened. From being a zero, the dead point at which reckoning begins, he became a real number, if only the tiniest fraction, and thus entered the field of competition. Or to put it another way, he passed from being an x, an unknown and inestimable quantity which could be substituted for a known quantity (Hugh Caldwell) in any social equation, to being a known quantity himself, that is he passed from algebra into arithmetic. He no longer represented Hugh Caldwell, but existing now on the same plane was capable of being compared with him. However, his whole merit had consisted of the fact that nobody could possibly like him as much as Hugh Caldwell could be liked; and indeed if anybody liked him one-half, one-quarter, one-tenth as much, it was enough to finish him as the family friend.

A husband, hearing his wife's voice quicken as she answered Francis Cleary's telephone call, would be startled into asking himself the impermissible question: *Why do we see that fellow?* The light fervor of his wife's tone jarred on his sense of what was fitting; it breached some unspoken agreement—she was not playing fair. He felt as if he had been duped. From that moment on, he disliked Francis Cleary intensely, and his wife would have to fight to get him invited to a party, just as if he had been one of her own friends. If she were loyal in her attachments, she would soon find herself trying to see him when her husband was out of town or working late at the office; she would meet him between engagements in the bars of quiet hotels. But this illicit atmosphere was deeply uncongenial to Francis. Her affection, her fidelity, could not begin to make up to him for the fact that he was no longer asked to her house. Indeed he hated her for that affection, which, as he saw it, was responsible for all the trouble. Like the husband, he experienced a sense of outrage; he too had been betrayed by her. With her inordinate capacity for friendship, she had gulled them both. She, on her side, became aware that Francis was suffering from his exclusion. She imagined (this particular wife was rather stupid) that he missed his old friend, her husband; and to save Francis pain she began to lie. "Jerry misses you terribly," she would tell him, "but we see hardly anybody any more. Jerry hasn't been feeling well. We say home and read detective stories. . . ." Francis, of course, knew better, and eventually it would happen that he met them when they were dining out with a large party of friends, and the poor wife's duplicity would be exposed. All her nudges and desperate, appealing glances went unanswered—Jerry would not invite Francis to sit down at their table. After that, Francis was always too busy to see her when she called. If anybody mentioned her name, he spoke of her with a rancor that was for him unusual, so that people assumed either that she had come between Francis and his old friend, her husband, or that she had tried to have an affair with Francis and failed. Of the husband

he continued to speak in the highest terms, thus rein-
forcing both of these theories. And his admiration was
not simulated. He respected Jerry for the contempt in
which Jerry held him—it was an attitude they shared.
As for the unfortunate wife, she could never make out
what had gone wrong. In the end, she came to believe
her husband when he told her, as he frequently did,
that she had no talent for human relations.

Between the Scylla of an Al and the Charybdis of a
Jerry's wife, Francis steers his uneasy course. Perhaps
it is the vicissitudes of this life, the vigilance against
the true and imaginary dangers, that are responsible
for the change in Francis. Certainly it has been hard
for him to be obliged, every year or so, to re-examine
his premises. Francis had, it seemed to him, made a
good bargain with the world. Yet whenever a Jerry's
wife took a fancy to him, he questioned his own
shrewdness. If she likes me, he would ask himself,
why wouldn't others, and if likes, why not loves, and
does she really and how much? It would be weeks, after such an experience, before Francis could silence
these questions. Like a businessman, he feared that
he had closed his deal with life too soon; the buyer
might have paid much more. And as the businessman
can only set his mind at rest by assuring himself that
the property he disposed of was really good riddance
of a negligible asset, so Francis' one recourse was to
persuade himself once again that he had been perfectly correct in setting the zero, dejected yet triumphant, opposite his own name. But however successful
as auditing, these midnight reckonings must have been
painful, even to Francis; one night his anesthetized
spirit must have awakened in rage and spite.

Or perhaps nature does abhor a vacuum; perhaps
the wall of the sealed, sterile chamber that was Francis' nature collapsed from atmospheric pressure, and
in rushed all the unattached emotions—that is, hatred,
envy, fear, which, unlike love, do not cling to a definite
object—that float, gaseous, over man's sphere. At any

rate, Francis has been changing. Under our very eyes, he has been turning into everything that he, by definition, was not. If you have failed to notice the steps in this process, it is because you are so much in the habit of *not* thinking about Francis that he could transform himself into a snake on your parlor floor without attracting your attention. Your indifference has been a cloak of invisibility behind which he has been preparing for you some rather startling surprises. But now that your memory has been jogged on the point, you will recall that his manners, while never highly polished, were once more acceptable than they are today. There was a time, for example, when he left your cocktail parties promptly at seven-thirty, taking with him one of the more burdensome women guests for a *table-d'hôte* dinner in the Village. But in the course of years his leavetakings have been steadily retarded; soon your wife has been cooking scrambled eggs for him at nine o'clock; and now you are lucky if at midnight or two or three you do not have to make up a bed for him in the spare room or, at the very best, take him home in a taxi and open his door for him. Once it was the interesting guests who stayed, disputing, quoting poetry, playing the piano, singing; today the fascinating people have always somewhere else to go, and every party boils down to Francis Cleary; you do not question this, possibly, but accept it as an analogy to life.

Perhaps it is Francis' growing addiction to drink (he no longer waits for you to notice his empty glass but helps himself from the shaker or inquires boldly, "Did someone say something about another drink?") that keeps him late and is also responsible for the mounting truculence of his conversation. In the old days Francis was always prompt to shut off one of his anecdotes when his companion's interest slightly wavered away from him; indeed, much of his conversation seemed to be constructed around the interruption he awaited. Gradually, however, he has become more adhesive to his topics. He may be interrupted by the arrival of a

newcomer, the host may excuse himself to fetch somebody's coat, or the hostess may go in to look at the
baby—but Francis has put a bookmark in his story.
"As I was saying," he resumes, when the distraction
has passed. Furthermore, his opinions, which he used
to modulate to suit the conversation, never taking up
a position without preparing a retreat from it, have
now become rigid and obtrusive. This is particularly
true of him in his female aspect. Frances Cleary, once
the indistinct listener, now arrives at a party with a
single idea that haunts the conversation like a ghost.
This idea is almost always regressive in character, the
shade of a once-live controversy (abstract vs. repre-
sentational art, progressive vs. classical education),
but the female Frances treats it as though she personally were its relict; any change of subject she regards
as irreverence to the dead. "Others may forget but I
remember," her aggrieved expression declares. If the
hostess is successful in deflecting her to some more
personal topic, a single word overheard from across
the room will be enough to send her train of ideas puff-
ing out of the station once more. She has dedicated
herself, say, to the defense of Raphael against the menace of Mondrian; momentarily silenced, she will instantly revive should one of the other guests be so
careless as to remark, "She's as pretty as a picture."
"You can talk about pictures all you want," Frances
will begin. . . .

In the male Francis Cleary this belligerency is more
likely to take a physical form. More and more often
nowadays, Francis breaks glasses, ash trays, lamps.
His elbow catches the maid's arm as she is serving the
gravy, and the hostess's dress must go to the cleaners.
All during an evening, he may have been his old un-
demanding self, but suddenly, at midnight, a sullen-
ness will fall on him. "Oh, for Christ's sake," he will
ejaculate when the talk goes over his head. Or he may
grab someone else's hat and stumble savagely out,
knocking over a table on his way.

As a couple, he does not drink too much. On the contrary, he quietly but firmly refuses the third and even the second drink. He arrives early, the two of him, and ensconces himself on the sofa (the Clearys of all numbers and genders have an affinity for the sofa, which they occupy as a symbol of possession). From this point of vantage, he, or shall we say for convenience' sake, they, overlook the proceedings with a kind of regal lumpishness. Though their position as friends of the family may be new and still insecure, they treat the very oldest and dearest members of the wife's or the husband's circle (the college roommate, the former lover) as candidates for their approval. They do not consider it necessary to talk in the ordinary way, but put sharp, inquisitorial questions to the people that are brought up to them ("Would you mind telling me the significance of that yellow necktie?" "Why do the characters in your novels have such a depressing sex life?"), or else they merely sit, demanding to be entertained.

Like the drinking Francis Cleary, they stay until the last guest has gone, and present a report of their findings to the host and hostess. Nothing has escaped them; they have noticed your former roommate's stammer and your lover's squint; they have counted the highballs of the heavy drinker and recorded the tremor of his hand; the woman you thought beautiful is, it turns out, bowlegged, and the lively Russian should have washed his hair. And they present these findings with absolute objectivity; they do not judge but merely report. Though each human being is, so to speak, a work of art, the Clearys are scientists, and take pride in disobeying the artist's commands. If the artist places a highlight at what he considers a central point of his personality, a highlight that says, "Look here," the Clearys instantly look elsewhere: the expressiveness of a man's eyes will never blind them to the weakness of his chin. And you and your wife, who have hitherto obeyed the laws of art and humanity and looked where you were told to look, are now utterly confounded by this clear, bleak view. Your friends whom you regarded as wholes are now assemblages of slightly damaged parts. You are plunged into despair, but you do not question the Clearys' right to conduct this survey, for their observations are given a peculiar authority and force by the fact that they refer to the other guests—whom they have just met—by their first names. "John drinks terribly, doesn't he?" they say, and it is useless for you to pretend that this particular evening was exceptional for your friend—that "John" asserts a familiarity with his habits that is greater, if anything, than your own. By the time they have finished their last glass ("Just a little cool water from the tap, please") and you have seen them to the door you and your wife are utterly drained of energy and belief. There is not even a quarrel left between you, for they have exposed your friends and hers with perfect impartiality. Your world has been depopulated. You have only each other and the Clearys.

Your sole escape from this intolerable situation is for one of you to blame the Clearys on the other. You can divide them up between you. If the husband, say, can be held responsible for Mr. and Mrs. Cleary ("*You* were the one who insisted on having them"), the wife can take Francis as her charge. You can treat them, that is, as friends, and this will immediately result in the exclusion of both factions. But now a super Francis Cleary must be found, a zero raised to a higher power, a negation of a negation. The search may be long, you may wander down false trails, but finally one night at a cocktail party you will find him, the ineffable blank, and you and your wife will seize him and drag him home with you to eat sandwiches and talk excitedly like lovers, of why you have never met before. Your difficulties are over, your wife smiles at you again, and when the two of you stand in the doorway to see him off, your arm falls affectionately across her shoulder.

But alas the same process is about to begin again, and the stakes have been raised. Your new nonentity is larger and emptier than your original little friend; naturally, he commands a higher price. Dozens of other couples are competing with you for this superb creation; he does not hold himself cheap. You realize very quickly from the envious glances your colleagues and neighbors cast toward him whenever you display him at a public gathering that if you want to hold on to him you will have to pay through the nose. Gone are the potted plants, the Christmas cheeses, the toys for the children that were regularly issued by the old Francis Cleary. The super friend gives nothing; he does not even try to make himself agreeable; he will not talk to old ladies or help with the dishes or go to the store for a loaf of bread. His company is all you will ever get of him, and the demands he makes on you will grow steadily more extortionate. If you want him around, his demeanor will tell you, you will have to give up your former friends, your work, your interests, your principles—the whole complex of idiosyncrasies that make up your nature—and your only reward for this terrible sacrifice is that your wife will have to make it too. Soon he will be bringing his own friends to your house, and these friends will be the other couples with whom you share him (did you imagine that he could confine himself to *you*?). Already he borrows your money, your books, and your whiskey.

He will stop at nothing, for he has always hated you and now he knows that he has got you where he wants you—you cannot live without him. Watching this monster as he sits at his ease on your sofa, your wife may look back with feelings of actual affection on your queer old friend, Hugh Caldwell; but now it is too late. Hugh Caldwell spits at the mention of your wife's name, and, quite possibly, at the mention of your own; and, anyway, you ask yourself, are you really sure that you want to see Hugh Caldwell again, especially if it would mean that your wife, in return, could see one of her old friends? No, you say to yourself, we cannot have *that;* there must be some compromise, some middle way—it is not necessary to go so far. Your mind beats on the door of the dilemma. Surely somewhere, you exclaim silently, somewhere in this great city, living quietly, perhaps, in a furnished room, there is a friend whom neither of us would have to feel so strongly about. . . . Some plain man or woman, some dowdy little couple of regular habits and indefinite tastes, some person utterly unobjectionable, unobtrusive, undefined. . . . With loving strokes, you complete the portrait of this ideal, and all the while there he sits, grinning at you, the lesser evil, but you do not recognize him.

After all, you say to yourself, my requirements are modest; I will give up anything for a little peace and quiet. You forget that it was in the name of peace and quiet that this despot was welcomed—just as the Jewish banker in the concentration camp forgets the donation he made to the Nazi party fund, back in 1931, when his great fear was communism; just as Benedetto Croce, anti-fascist philosopher, forgot in Naples the days when he supported Mussolini in the Senate at Rome, because order was certainly preferable to anarchy and bolshevism was the real manace. You cannot believe, you will not ever believe, that your desire for peace and quiet, i.e., for the permanent stalemate, has logically resulted in the noisy oppressor on the sofa. On the contrary, his presence there seems to you a cruel and unaccountable accident.

You are not happy with your wife but you do not want change. In a more romantic period you might have dreamed of voluptuous blondes, fast women and low haunts; you might even have run off with the lady organist or the wife of the Methodist minister. But you are a man of peace and careful respectability. You do not ask adventure or the larger life. Though at one time, theoretically, you may have desired these things,

you have perceived that adventure for one can readily
be the excuse for adventure for all, and who knows
but what your wife's or your neighbor's capacity for
adventure might be greater than your own? If all men
were created equal, programs for achieving equality
would not exist. The industrialist would welcome the
people's army into the gates of the factory, if he could
be sure that nobody would be any better off than he.
We do not want *more* than anyone else, though we
may take more for fear of getting less. What we desire is absolute parity, and this can only be achieved
by calculating in a downward direction, with zero as
the ultimate, unattainable ideal. Our lives become a
series of disarmament conferences: I will reduce my
demands if you will reduce yours. With parity as our
aim, it is impossible to calculate in an upward direction, for a nation will be allowed a navy which it has
not the productive capacity to build, or a man may be
granted freedoms which he has not the faculties to exercise, and gross inequalities will immediately result.

So long as you and I cannot accept the doctrine
"From each according to his capacities, to each according to his needs," the totalitarian state will supply
the answer to the difficulties of democracy and Francis
Cleary will be the ideal friend. At this very moment,
you are planning to overthrow the incumbent Cleary,
who happens to be staying with you for the weekend.
In a loud voice he has demanded something to eat,
though he finished lunch only an hour ago. Your wife
has rushed out to the kitchen to make him a chicken
sandwich, and you sit watching him in uneasy silence.
You are afraid to play the phonograph because he
does not like music; you are afraid to initiate a topic
of conversation because he resents any mention of
persons he has not met or things he does not understand; you are afraid to pick up a newspaper lest he
take it as a slight—and if you cross him he will pinch
the baby.

The fires of resistance are lit in your heart as the

sandwich comes in and he opens it with a blunt critical finger and asks for pickles and mayonnaise. Your pulse quickens in little throbs of solidarity with your unfortunate wife. You will make, you say to yourself, common cause with her and eject the tyrant. If she will do it *for* you, so much the better; but there can be no question whatever about the heartiness of your support. The danger is, of course, that in the warm fraternity of the revolt, the coziness of plans and preparations, the intimacy of secret meetings in lonely houses at night, with a reliable farmer standing guard *(Qui passe?)*, certain illusions of your wife's may be revived. The whole question of friends may be opened again; a period of anarchy may even follow in which all the ghosts of both camps will meet once more in your living room and debate the old issues; tempers will rise and you will have to fling out of the house late at night and look for a room in a hotel. In the interests of peace, you say to yourself, would it not be wiser to select in advance some common friend and avoid the interregnum? Somewhere, only recently did you not meet a couple . . . ? In vain, you try to recall their faces and their name. Memory is obstinate but you do not despair. The very dimness of your impression convinces you that you are on the right track. They are the ones. If you meet them again, you will know them at once and rush forward to meet them with a glad cry of recognition. There is only one difficulty. Supposing they are already engaged . . . ?

Your only way out of this recurrent nightmare (not counting the humane one, which is hardly worth mentioning) is for you and your wife to take the logical next step, to become the Clearys, say, of Round Hill Road. Why should you shrink from it? What have you to lose? In what do you differ from the man on the sofa?

The Cicerone

WHEN THEY first met him, in the *wagons-lits,* he was not so nervous. Tall, straw-colored, standing smoking in the corridor, he looked like an English cigarette. Indeed, there was something about him so altogether parched and faded that he seemed to bear the same relation to a man that a Gold Flake bears to a normal cigarette. English, surely, said the young American lady. The young American man was not convinced. If English, then a bounder, he said, adjusting his glasses to peer at the stranger with such impassioned curiosity that his eyes in their light-brown frames seemed to rush dangerously forward, like strange green headlights on an old-fashioned car. As yet, he felt no unusual interest in the stranger who had just emerged from a compartment; this curiosity was his ordinary state of being.

It was so hard, the young lady complained, to tell a bounder in a foreign country; one was never sure; those dreadful striped suits that English gentlemen wear . . . and the Duke of Windsor talking in a cockney accent. Here on the Continent, continued the young man, it was even more confusing, with the upper classes trying to dress like English gentlemen and striking the inevitable false notes; the dukes all looked like floorwalkers, but every man who looked like a floorwalker was unfortunately not a duke. Their conversation continued in an agreeable rattle-rattle. Its inspiration, the Bounder, was already half-dismissed.

It was not quite clear to either of them whether they were trying to get into European society or whether this was simply a joke that they had between them. The young man had lunched with a viscountess in Paris and had admired her house and her houseboat, which was docked in the Seine. They had poked their heads into a great many courtyards in the Faubourg St. Germain, including the very grandiose one, bristling with guards who instantly ejected them, that belonged to the Soviet Embassy. On the whole, architecture, they felt, provided the most solid answer to their social curiosity: the bedroom of Marie Antoinette at the Petit Trianon had informed them that the French royal family were dwarfs, a secret already hinted at in Mme. Pompadour's bedroom at the Frick museum in New York; in Milan, they would meet the Sforzas through the agency of their Castello; at Stra, on the Brenta, they would get to know the Pisani. They had read Proust, and the decline of the great names in modern times was accepted by them as a fact; the political speeches of the living Count Sforza suggested the table-talk of Mme. Verdurin, gracing with her bourgeois platitudes the board of an ancient house. Nevertheless, the sight of a rococo ceiling, a great swaying crystal chandelier, glimpsed at night through an open second-story window, would come to them like an invitation which is known to exist but which has been incomprehensibly lost in the mail; a vague sadness descended, yet they did not feel like outsiders.

Victors in a world war of unparalleled ferocity, heirs of imperialism and the philosophy of the enlightenment, they walked proudly on the dilapidated streets of Europe. They had not approved of the war and were pacifist and bohemian in their sympathies, but the exchange had made them feel rich, and they could not help showing it. The exchange had turned them into a prince and a princess, and, considering the small bills, the weekly financial anxieties that attended them at home, this was quite an accomplishment. There was no door, therefore, that, they believed, would not open to them should they present themselves fresh and crisp as two one-dollar bills. These beliefs, these dreams, were, so far, no more to them than a story children tell each other. The young man, in fact, had found his small role as war-profiteer so distasteful and also so frightening that he had refused for a whole week to go to his money-changer and had cashed his checks at the regular rate at the bank. For the most part, their practical, moral life was lived, guidebook in hand, on the narrow streets and in the cafés of the Left Bank—they got few messages at their hotel.

Yet occasionally when they went in their best clothes to a fashionable bar, she wearing the flowers he had bought her (ten cents in American money), they hoped in silent unison during the first cocktail for the Dr.-Livingstone-I-presume that would discover them in this dark continent. And now on the train that was carrying them into Italy, the European illusion quickened once more within them. They eyed every stranger with that suspicion of disbelief which, to invert Wordsworth, makes its object poetical. The man at the next table had talked all through lunch to two low types with his mouth full, but the young man remained steady in his conviction that the chewer was a certain English baronet traveling to his villa in Florence, and he had nearly persuaded the young lady to go up and ask him his name. He particularly valued the young lady today because, coming from the West, she entered readily into conversation with people she did not know. It was a handicap, of course, that there were two of them ("My dear," said the young lady, "a couple looks so complete"), but they were not inclined to separate—the best jockey in a horse race scorns to take a lighter weight. Unfortunately, their car, except for the Bounder at the other end, offered very little scope to his imaginative talent or her loquacity.

But, as they were saying, Continental standards

were mysteriously different; at the frontier at Domodossola a crowd gathered on the rainy platform in front of their car. Clearly there was some object of attraction here, and, dismissing the idea that it was herself, the young lady moved to the window. Next to her, a short, heavy, ugly man with steel-rimmed spectacles was passing some money to a person on the platform, who immediately hurried away. Other men came up and spoke in undertones through the window to the man beside her. In all of this there was something that struck the young lady as strange—so much quiet and so much motion, which seemed the more purposeful, the more businesslike without its natural accompaniment of sound. Her clear, school-teacher-on-holiday voice intruded resolutely on this quarantine. *"Qu'est-ce que se passe?"* she demanded. *"Rien,"* said her neighbor abruptly, glancing at her and away with a single, swiveling movement of the spectacled eyes. *"C'est des amis qui rencontrent des amis."* Rebuffed, she turned back to the young man. "Black market," she said. "They are changing money." He nodded, but seeing her thoughts travel capably to the dollar bills pinned to her underslip, he touched her with a cautioning hand. The dead, noncommittal face beside her, the briefcase, the noiseless, nondescript young men on the platform, the single laugh that had rung out in the Bounder's end of the car when the young lady had put her question, all bade him beware: this black market was not for tourists. The man who had hurried away came back with a dirty roll of bills which he thrust through the window. *"Ite, missa est,"* remarked the young lady sardonically, but the man beside her gave no sign of having heard; he continued to gave immovably at the thin young men before him, as though the transaction had not yet been digested.

At this moment, suddenly, a hubbub of singing, of agitated voices shouting slogans was heard. A kind of frenzy of noise, which had an unruly, an unmistakably seditious character, moved toward the train from somewhere outside the shed. The train gave a loud puff. "A revolution!" thought the young lady, clasping the young man's hand with a pang of terror and excitement; he, like everyone else in the car, had jumped to his feet. A strange procession came into sight, bright and bedraggled in the rain—an old woman in a white dress and flowered hat waving a large red flag, two or three followers with a homemade-looking bouquet, and finally a gray-bearded old man dressed in an ancient frock coat, carrying an open old-fashioned black umbrella and leaping nimbly into the air. Each of the old man's hops was fully two yards high; his thin legs in the black trousers were jackknifed neatly under him; the umbrella maintained a perfect perpendicular; only his beard flew forward and his coat-tails back; at the summit of each hop, he shouted joyously, *"Togliatti!"* The demonstration was coming toward the car, where alarm had given way to amazement; Steel Glasses alone was undisturbed by the appearance of these relics of political idealism; his eyes rested on them without expression. Just as they gained the protection of the shed, the train, unfortunately, began to move. The followers, lacking the old man's gymnastic precision, were haphazard with the bouquet; it missed the window, which had been opened for the lira-changing, and fell back into the silent crowd. The train picked up speed.

In the compartment, the young man was rolling on the seat with laughter; he was always the victim of his emotions, which—even the pleasurable ones—seemed to overrun him like the troops of some marauding army. Thus happiness, with him, had a look of intensest suffering, and the young lady clucked sympathetically as he gasped out, *"The Possessed, The Possessed."* To the newcomer in the compartment, however, the young man's condition appeared strange. "What is the matter with him?" the young man, deep in the depths of his joy, heard an odd, accented little voice asking; then the young lady's voice was explaining, "Dostoevski . . . a small political center . . . a provincial Russian town." "But no," said the other voice, "it is Togliatti, the leader of *Italian* Communists who is in the next compartment. He is coming from the Peace Conference where he talks to Molotov." The words, *Communist, Molotov, Peace Conference,* bored the young man so much that he came to his senses instantly, sat up, wiped his glasses, and perceived that it was the Bounder who was in the compartment, and to whom the young lady was now re-explaining that her friend was laughing because the scene on the platform had reminded him of something in a book. "But no," protested the Bounder, who was still convinced that the young lady had not understood *him.* He appeared to come to some sort of decision and ran out into the corridor, returning with a Milanese newspaper folded to show an item in which the words, *Togliatti, Parigi, Pace,* and *Molotov* all indubitably figured. The young lady, weary of explanation, allowed a bright smile as of final comprehension to pass over her features and handed the paper to the young man, who could not read Italian either; in such acts of submission their conversations with Europeans always ended. They had got used to it, but they sometimes felt that they had stepped at Le Havre into some vast cathedral where a series of intrusive custodians stood between them and the frescoes relating with tireless patience the story of the Nativity. Europeans, indeed, seemed to them often a race of custodians, didactic automatons who answered, like fortune-telling machines, questions to which one already knew the answer or questions which no one would conceivably ask.

True to this character, the Bounder, now, had plainly taken a shine to the young lady, who was permitting him to tell her facts about the Italian political situation which she had previously read in a newspaper. That her position on Togliatti was identical with his own, he assumed as axiomatic, and her dissident murmurs of correction he treated as a kind of linguistic static. Her seat on the *wagons-lits* spoke louder to him than words; she could never persuade him that she hated Togliatti from the *left*, any more than she could convince a guide in Paris of her indifference to Puvis de Chavannes. Her attention he took for assent, and only the young man troubled him, as he had troubled many guides in many palaces and museums by lingering behind in some room he fancied; an occasional half-smothered burst of laughter indicated to the two talkers that he was still in the Dostoevski attic. But the glances of tender understanding that the young lady kept rather pointedly turning toward her friend were an explanation in pantomime; his alarms stilled, the visitor neatly drew up his trousers and sat down.

They judged him to be a man about forty-two years old. In America he might have passed for younger; he had kept his hair, light-brown and slightly oiled, with a ripple at the brow and a half-ripple at the back; his figure, moreover, was slim—it had not taken on that architectural form, those transepts, bows, and barrel-vaulting, that with Americans demonstrate (how quickly often!) that the man is no longer a boy but an Institution. Like the young lady's hairdresser, like the gay little grocer on Third Avenue, he had retained in middle age something for which there is no English word, something *très mignon,* something *gentil,* something *joli garçon.* It lay in a quickness and lightness of movement, in slim ankles, small feet, thin, agile wrists, in a certain demure swoop of lowering eyelids, in the play of lashes, and the butterfly flutter of the airy white handkerchief protruding from the breast pocket. It lay also in a politeness so eager as to seem freshly learned and in a childlike vanity, a covert sense of performance, in which one could trace the swing of the censer and the half-military, half-theatrical swish of the altar-boy's skirts.

But if this sprightliness of demeanor and of dress

gave the visitor an appearance of youthfulness, it also
gave him, by its very exaggeration, a morbid appearance of age. Those quick, small smiles, those turns of
the eye, and expressive raisings of the eyebrow had
left a thousand tiny wrinkles on his dust-colored face;
his slimness too had something cadaverous in it—
chicken-breasted he appeared in his tan silk gabardine
suit. And, oddly enough, this look of premature senil-
ity was not masculine but feminine. Though no more
barbered and perfumed than the next Italian man,
he evoked the black mass of the dressing-table and
the hand-mirror; he reminded them of that horror so
often met in Paris, city of beauty, the well-preserved
woman in her fifties. At the same time, he was un-
questionably a man; he was already talking of con-
quests. It was simply, perhaps, that the preservation
of youth had been his main occupation; age was
the specter he had dealt with too closely; like those
middle-aged women he had become its intimate
through long animosity.

Yet just as they had decided that he was a man
somehow without a profession (they had come to
think in unison and needed the spoken word only for
a check), he steered himself out of a small whirlpool
of ruffled political feelings and announced that he was
in the silk business. He was returning from London,
and had spent a week in Paris, where he had been
short of francs and had suffered a serious embarrassment when taking a lady out to lunch. The lady, it
appeared, was the wife of the Egyptian delegate to
the Peace Conference, whom he had met—also—on
the *wagons-lits*. There was a great deal more of this,
all either very simple or very complicated, they were
unable to say which, for they could not make out
whether he was telling the same story twice, or
whether, as in a folk tale, the second story repeated
the pattern of the first but had a variant ending. His
English was very odd; it had a speed and a precision
of enunciation that combined with a vagueness of

grammar so as to make the two Americans feel that they were listening to a foreign language, a few words of which they could recognize. In the same way, his anecdotes had a wealth and circumstantiality of detail and an overall absence of form, or at least so the young lady, who was the only one who was listening, reported later to the young man. The young man, who was tone-deaf, found the visitor's conversation reminiscent of many concerts he had been taken to, where he could only distinguish the opening bars of any given work; for him, Mr. Sciarappa's stories were all in their beginnings, and he would interrupt quite often with a reply square in the middle, just as, quite often, he used to break in with wild applause when the pianist paused between the first and second movements of a sonata.

But at the mention of the silk business, the young man's eyes had once more burned a terrifying green. With his afflamed imagination, he was at the same time extremely practical. Hostile to Marxist theory, he was Marxist in personal matters, having no interest in people's opinions, or even, perhaps, in their emotions (the superstructure), but passionately, madly curious as to what people did and how they made their money (the base). He did not intend that Mr. Sciarappa (he had presented his card) should linger forever in Paris adding up the lunch bill of the Egyptian delegate's wife. Having lain *couchant* for the ten minutes that human politeness required, he sprang into the conversation with a question: did the *signor* have an interest in the silk mills at Como? And now the visitor betrayed the first signs of nervousness. The question had suggested knowledge that was at least second-hand. The answer remained obscure. Mr. Sciarappa did not precisely own a factory, nor was he precisely in the exporting business. The two friends, who were not lacking in common humanity, precipitately turned the subject to the beauty of Italian silks, the superiority of Italian tailoring to French or even

English tailoring, the chic of Italian men. The moment passed, and a little later, under the pretense of needing her help as a translator, Mr. Sciarappa showed the young lady a cablegram dated London which seemed to be a provisional order for a certain quantity of something, but the garbled character of the English suggested that the cable had been composed—in London—by Mr. Sciarappa himself. Nevertheless, the Americans accepted the cablegram as a proof of their visitor's *bona fides,* though actually it proved no more than that he was in business, that is, that he existed in the Italy of the post-war world.

The troubled moment, in fact, had its importance for them only in retrospect. A seismographic recording of conditions in the compartment would have shown only the faintest tremor. The desire to believe the best of people is prerequisite for intercourse with strangers; suspicion is reserved for friends. The young lady in particular, being gregarious, took the kindest view of everyone; she was under the impression that she was the only person in the world who told lies. The young man today fell in with her gullibility, with her "normal" interpretations of life, because he saw that they were heading for friendship with Mr. Sciarappa and felt as yet no positive objections to the idea. They were alone in Italy; a guide would be useful. Moreover, Mr. Sciarappa had announced that he was going on to Rome, where he lived with his parents, at midnight. Already he had invited them to join him for a drink in Milan in the famous Galleria; the worst they could expect was a dinner *à trois.* Therefore, he acted, temporarily, on the young lady's persuasion that their visitor was an ordinary member of the upper middle classes in vaguely comfortable circumstances, in other words, that he was an abstraction; in the same way, certain other abstract beliefs of hers concerning true love and happiness had conveyed him, somewhat more critical and cautious, into this compartment with her on a romantic journey into Italy.

But, just as it had come as a surprise to him that love should go on from step to step, that it should move from city to country and cross an ocean and part of a continent, so in Milan it was with a vague astonishment that he beheld Mr. Sciarappa remove his baggage from the taxi in front of their hotel and hurry inside ahead of him to inquire for a room. For the next three days, the trio could be seen any evening promenading, arm in arm, down the long arcade of the Galleria, past the crowded little tables with the pink, and the peach, and the lime, and the orange colored tablecloths, walking with the air of distinguished inseparables, the two tall men and the tallish young lady with a large black hat. Or at noon they could be found there, perspiring and not so distinguished, sipping Americanos, Mr. Sciarappa's favorite drink, at the café with the orange tablecloths, which Mr. Sciarappa considered the cheapest. At night, they appeared at Giannino's or Crispi's (not so expensive as Biffi's but better food, said Mr. Sciarappa), restaurants where Mr. Sciarappa made himself at home, sending back the wine which the Americans had ordered and getting in its place some thinner and sourer vintage of which he had special knowledge. The one solid trait the two friends could discover in Mr. Sciarappa's character was a rooted abhorrence of the advertised first-rate, of best hotels, top restaurants, principal shopping streets, famous vineyards; and, since for the first time in many years they saw themselves in a position to command these advantages, they found this trait of Mr. Sciarappa's rather a cross. In American money, the difference between the best and the mediocre was trifling; indeed even in Italian money, it was often nonexistent. They tried to convince Mr. Sciarappa of this, but their computations he took as an insult to himself and his defeated country. His lip would curl into a small, angry sneer that looked as if it had come out of a permanent-wave machine. "Ah, you Americans," he would say, "your streets are paved with dollars."

The two friends, after the first night, spent on bad beds in an airless room hung with soiled lace curtains moved with a certain thump into the best hotel next door. They would not have stayed in any case, for the young man had a horror of the sordid, and the best hotel proved, when you counted breakfast, to be cheaper than its second-rate neighbor. Nevertheless in the circumstances, the move had a significant tone— they hoped to fray, if not to sever, their connection with Mr. Sciarappa, and perhaps also, to tell the truth to insult him a little. The best hotel, half-requisitioned by the Allied armies, smiled on them with brass and silver insignia, freshly washed summer khaki and blond, straight, water-combed American hair; when Mr. Sciarappa came for cocktails in the same gabardine suit, he looked somehow like a man in prison clothes or the inmate of a mental institution. The young lady, who was the specialist in sentiments, felt toward him sorrow, shame, triumph.

They could not make out what he wanted of them. Whatever business had, on the train, been hurrying him on to Rome had presumably lost its urgency. He never mentioned it again; indeed, the three spoke very little together, and it was this that gave them that linked and wedded look. During the day he disappeared, except for the luncheon apéritif. He went to Como, to Genoa, and, once, in the Galleria, they saw him with an unshaven, white-haired, morose-looking man whom he introduced as his brother-in-law. In restaurants, he was forever jumping up from the table with a gay little wave of the hand to greet a party that was in the act of vanishing into the dark outdoors. Though he was a man who twitched with sociability, whose conversation was a veritable memo pad of given names, connections, ties, appointments, he seemed to be unknown to the very waiters whom he directed in the insolent style of an old customer. The brother-in-law, who plainly disliked him, and they themselves, whom he hated, were his only friends.

The most remarkable symptom of this hatred, which ate into the conversation leaving acid holes of boredom, which kept him glancing at other tables as though in hope of succor or release, was a tone of unshakable, impolite disbelief. "Ah, I am not such a fool," his pretty face would almost angrily indicate if they told him that they had spent their morning in the castle-fort of the Sforzas, where beneath the ramparts bombed by the Liberators, a troupe of Italian players with spotlights lent by the American army was preparing to do an American pacifist play. Every statement volunteered by the two friends broke on the edge of Mr. Sciarappa's contempt like the very thinnest alibi; parks and the public buildings they described to him became as transparent as falsehoods—anyone of any experience knew there were no such places in Milan. When they praised the wicked-looking Filippo Lippi Madonna they had seen in the Sforza Gallery, Mr. Sciarappa and his disaffected brother-in-law, who was supposed to speak no English, exchanged, for the first time, a fraternal, sidewise look: a masterpiece, indeed, their incredulous eyebrows ejaculated—they had heard that story before.

That Mr. Sciarappa should question their professions of enthusiasm was perhaps natural. His own acquaintance with Italy's artistic treasures seemed distant; they had had the reputation with him of being much admired by English and American tourists; the English and American air-forces, however, had quoted them, as he saw, at a somewhat lower rate. Moreover, it was as if the devaluation of the currency had, for Mr. Sciarappa's consistent thought, implicated everything Italian; cathedrals, pictures, women had dropped with the lira. He could not imagine that anyone could take these things at their Baedeker valuation, any more than he could imagine that anyone in his right mind would change dollars into lira at the official rate. The two friends soon learned that to praise any Italian product, were it only a bicycle or a child in the street, was an insult to Mr. Sciarappa's intelligence. They would be silent—and eventually were —but the most egregious insult, the story that they had come to Italy as tourists, they could not wipe away.

He felt himself to be the victim of an imposture, that was plain. But did he believe that they were rich pretending to be poor, or poor pretending to be rich? They could not tell. On the whole, it seemed as if Mr. Sciarappa's suspicions, like everything else about him, had a certain flickering quality; the light in him went on and off, as he touched one theory or another, cruising in his shaft like an elevator. And, as the young man said, you could not blame Mr. Sciarappa for wondering: was it in the character of a rich man or a poor that they stayed in the best hotel, which was slightly less expensive than an American auto-camp?

The obscurity of their financial position justified Mr. Sciarappa's anger. Nevertheless, though sympathetic, they grew tired of spending their evenings with a stranger who was continually out of sorts because he could not make up his mind whether they were worth swindling. "We did not come to Italy to see Mr. Sciarappa," they would say to each other every night as they rode up in the elevator, and would promise themselves to evade this time, without fail, the meeting he had fixed for the next day. Yet as noon came on the following morning, they would find that they were approaching the Galleria. He is waiting, they would say to each other, and without discussion they would hurry on toward the café with the orange tablecloths, where they were late but never quite late enough to miss Mr. Sciarappa.

He was never glad to see them. He rose to acknowledge them with a kind of bravura laziness of his tall "English" figure, one shoulder lifted in a shrug of ennui or resignation. He kissed the young lady's hand

and said to the young man perfunctorily, and sometimes with a positive yawn, "Hello, sit down, my dear." One of his odd little tricks was to pretend that they were not together. The young man's frequent absences of mind he treated literally, when it suited him, as if they were absences of body, and once he carried this so far as to run his fingers up and down the young lady's bare arm as the three of them rode in a taxi, inquiring as he did so, in the most civil tone imaginable, whether she found her friend satisfactory. His conversation was directed principally to the young lady, but for all that he had no real interest in her. It was the young man whom he watched, often in the mirror of her face, which never left her friend as he talked wildly, excitedly, extravagantly, with long wrists flung outward in intensity of gesture: did Mr. Sciarappa see beauty and strangeness in him or the eccentricity of money? Or was he merely trying to determine which it was that she saw?

It was irresistible that they should try to coax Mr. Sciarappa (or Scampi, as they had begun to call him, after fried crayfish-tails, his favorite dish) out into the open. The name of a certain lady, middlingly but authentically rich, who was expecting to see them in Venice, began to figure allusively, alluringly, in their conversation. These pointers that they directed toward Polly Herkimer Grabbe had at first a merely educational purpose. National pride forbade that they should allow Scampi to take them for rich Americans when a really good example of the genre existed only a day's journey away. But their first references to the flower-bulb heiress, to her many husbands, her collection of garden statuary, her career as an impresario of modern architecture, failed, seemingly, to impress Scampi; he raised his eyes briefly from the plate of Saltimbocca (Jump-in-your-mouth) that he was eating, and then returned to his meal. The language difficulties made it sometimes impossible to tell whether Mr. Sciarappa really heard what they said. They had remarked once, for example, in conversational desperation, that they had come to Italy to retrace the footsteps of Lord Byron: they were on their way from Lausanne, where he had composed "The Prisoner of Chillon" in a bedroom of the Hotel Angleterre, to Venice to visit his house on the Grand Canal. "Ah well, my dear," said Mr. Sciarappa, "if he is an English lord, you do not have to worry; his house will not be requisitioned, and you will have the use of his gondolier." There had been no way the young man could find of preventing the young lady from supplying the poet's dates, and now, it seemed, Scampi was under the impression that everyone they knew in Venice was dead. It required the largest brush-strokes to bring Miss Grabbe to life for him. By the third night, when the young man had finished a wholly invented account of Miss Grabbe's going through the customs with a collection of obscene fountain statuary, Mr. Sciarappa showed interest and inquired how old Miss Grabbe was. The next evening, at cocktails, he had an auto-pullman ticket to Venice.

He was leaving the next morning at seven. The two Americans, remembering that the flower-bulb heiress was, after all, their friend, felt appalled and slightly frightened at what they had done. They thought of dropping some note of warning into the letter of introduction which of course they would have to write. But then they reflected that if Miss Grabbe was richer than they, she was also proportionately shrewder: glass bricks only could Mr. Sciarappa sell her for that submarine architectural salon she spoke of opening in the depths of the Grand Canal. Miss Grabbe's intelligence was flighty (she had once forgotten to include the furnace in a winter house that so hugged the idea of warmth that the bathtubs were done in buff), but her estimates were sharp; no contractor or husband had ever padded a bill on her; she always put on her glasses to add up a dinner check. Men, it was true, had injured her, and movements had left her flat, but these misadventures she had cheerfully added to her capital. An indefatigable Narcissa, she adapted herself spryly to comedy when she perceived that the world was smiling; she was always the second to laugh at a pratfall of her spirit. Mr. Sciarappa, at worst, could only be another banana-peel on the vaudeville stage of her history. It was possible, of course, that he might bore her, thought the two friends, reasoning from experience; this alone she would not forgive them, yet Miss Grabbe's judgments of men were often strikingly lenient—she had been unattached when they left her in Paris.

Besides, Mr. Sciarappa was looking quite presentable this evening, even though he had not yet changed his suit. Bright, eager, intensely polite, useful, informative, he seemed once more the figure they had seen in the train corridor; some innocent, cavalier hope that had died in those long Milan evenings had revived in him, as the expectation of parting made the two friends recede from him a little and become strangers once more. The letter of introduction wrote itself out, somehow, more affectionately than the friends had planned it. "Enclosed," it said, "please find Mr. Sciarappa, who has been most helpful to us in Milan."

Signorina Grabbe was waiting alone with a gondola in the orange-lampshade glow of a Canaletto sunset when their autobus drew up, two days later, at the station. Against the Venetian panorama of white domes and pink towers, Mr. Sciarappa was so pronouncedly absent that it seemed an indelicacy to inquire after him. The two friends, whom solitude and a consciousness of indiscretion had worked up to a pitch of anxiety and melodramatic conjecture, now felt slightly provoked that Miss Grabbe had not, in this short interval, been married or murdered for her money. At the very least, they had expected to be scolded for sending her that curious envoy, but Mr. Sciarappa's arrival seemed barely to have disturbed Miss Grabbe,

who had been busy, so she said, with an inner experience. "Your friend turned up," she remarked at last,
in the tone of one who acknowledges a package.
"What on earth did you find to talk to him about?"
The young man groaned. Miss Grabbe had put her
rich, plump, practiced finger on the flaw in Mr. Sciarappa as prosaically as if he had been a piece of yard-
goods—was there nothing more to be said of him?
"We found him rather odd," the young man murmured in half-apology. "Oh, my dear," said Miss
Grabbe, raising her dyed black eyebrows, "all the men
you meet on the *wagons-lits* are like that. You must go
to the little *campos* and the *trattorias* to meet the real
Italians."

And as Miss Grabbe went on to talk, in the dipping,
swaying gondola, of the intense, insular experience she
had found, blazing as the native *grappa,* in the small,
hot squares, the working-class restaurants and dirty
churches of Venice, Mr. Sciarappa seemed indeed a
poor thing to have offered her, a gimcrack souvenir
such as one might have bought in a railway station.
The young man blushed angrily as he felt his own trip
and that of the young lady shrink to fit inside Mr.
Sciarappa's nipped-in gabardine suit. He was only
saved from despair by a memory of Miss Grabbe, as
he had last seen her in Paris, alone, with her hunter's
look, and three saucers under her vermouth glass, at a
table in a Left Bank café—"Isn't it divine?" she had
called out to him; "don't you love it, don't you hate
New York?"

Compared to Miss Grabbe, he perceived, he himself
and the young lady would always appear to skim the
surface of travel. They were tourists; Miss Grabbe was
an explorer. Looking at the two ladies as they sat facing him in the gondola, he saw that their costumes
perfectly expressed this difference: the young lady's
large black hat, long gloves, high-heeled shoes, and
nylon stockings were a declaration of nationality and
a stubborn assertion of the pleasure-principle (what a

nuisance that hat had been as it scraped against his neck on the autobus, on the train, in the Metro in Paris); Miss Grabbe's snood and sandals, her bright glass-bead jewelry, her angora sweater, and shoulder-strap leather handbag, all Italian as the *merceria*, she wore in the manner of a uniform that announced her mobility in action and her support of the native products. Moreover, her brown face had a weather-beaten look, as though it had been exposed to the glare of many merciless suns; and her eyes blazed out of the sun-tan powder around them with the bright blue stare of a scout; only her pretty, tanned legs suggested a life less hardy—they might have been going to the beach. Like Mr. Sciarappa (for all his little graces), Miss Grabbe seemed to have been parched and baked by exposure, hardened and chapped by the winds of rebuff and failure. In contrast, the young lady, with her pallor and her smile, looked faintly unreal, like a photograph of a girl whose engagement has just been announced. And the young man felt himself joined to her in this sheltered and changeless beatitude; at the same time, in the company of Miss Grabbe as in that of Mr. Sciarappa, he was aware of a slight discomfort, a sense of fatuity, like the brief, antagonized embarrassment he noticed in himself whenever, in answer to the inevitable question, he replied, with a touch of storminess, that he was traveling in Europe for pleasure.

That he and the young lady were happy became, in this context, a crime, or, at best, a breach of taste, like the conspicuous idleness of the rich. They could hardly, he remarked to himself, be expected to give up their mutual delight because others were not so fortunate; they had already settled this question with regard to steak and *cotolette*. Yet, catching Miss Grabbe's eye measuring his happiness in the gondola, he felt inclined to withdraw his feelings to some more private place, just as certain sensitive patrons of restaurants preferred nowadays to feast indoors, secure

from the appraisal of the poor. His state, as he well
knew, was of peculiar interest to Miss Grabbe: for
twenty years, Polly Grabbe had made herself famous
by coming to Europe, semi-annually, in pursuit of
love. These sorties of hers had the regularity and the
directness of buyers' trips that are signalized by a paid
notice in the Paris *Herald,* announcing to the dress-
making trade that Miss Blank of Franklin Simon is
staying at the Crillon. Under the eye of that trans-
atlantic experience, the young man felt a little discom-
fited, as if he had been modeling a housedress before
a cosmopolite audience. He had no wish to judge Miss
Grabbe, yet he felt installed in a judgment by the
dream of perpetual monogamy into which the young
lady had invited him. In an effort to extricate himself,
he inquired of Miss Grabbe very civilly, as one traveler to another, how she found the Venetian men, but
the heiress only stared at him coldly and asked what
he took her for.

   Miss Grabbe was aware of her legend; it half-
pleased her, and yet she resented it, for, at bottom,
she was naively unconscious of the plain purport of
her acts. She imagined that she came abroad out of a
cultural impatience with America; in her own eyes,
she was always a rebel against a commercial civilization. She hoped to be remembered for her architectural experiments, her patronage of the arts, her
championship of personal freedom, and flattered herself that in Europe this side of her was taken seriously.
Men in America, she complained, thought only about
business, and the European practice of making a business of love seemed to her, in contrast, the mark of
an advanced civilization. Sexual intercourse, someone
had taught her, was a quick transaction with the beautiful, and she proceeded to make love, whenever she
traveled, as ingenuously as she trotted into a cathedral: men were a Continental commodity of which one
naturally took advantage, along with the wine and the
olives, the bitter coffee and the crusty bread. Miss

Grabbe, despite her boldness, was not an original woman, and her boldness, in fact, consisted in taking everything literally. She made love in Europe because it was the thing to do, because European lovers were superior to American lovers ("My dear," she told the young lady, "there's all the difference in the *world*— it's like comparing the very best California claret to the simplest little *vin du pays*"), because she believed it was good for her, especially in hot climates, and because one was said to learn languages a great deal more readily in bed. The rapid turnover of her lovers did not particularly disconcert her; she took a quantitative view and sought for a *wealth* of sensations. She liked to startle and to shock, yet positively did not understand why people considered her immoral. A prehensile approach, she inferred, was laudable where values were in question—what was the beautiful *for*, if not to be seized and savored?

For Polly Grabbe, as for the big luxury liners and the small school teachers with their yearly piety of Europe, the war had been an enforced hiatus. Though she had wished for the defeat of Hitler and been generous with money to his victims, in her heart she had waited for it to be over with a purely personal impatience. She was among the first to return when travel was once again permitted, an odd, bedizened, little figure, alighting gallantly from the plane, making a spot of color among the American businessmen, her vulturine co-passengers, who were descending on Europe to "look after" their investments. Conditions in Paris shocked these men, deep in their business sense, and Miss Grabbe was dismayed also; her own investment had been swept away. She could not take up where she had left off: people were dead or dispersed or in prison; her past stood about her in fragments, a shattered face looming up here and there like a housewall in a bombed city; normalcy was far away. But Miss Grabbe did not lack courage. She had learned how to say good-bye and to look ahead for the next

thing. Paris, she quickly decided, was beautiful but
done for, a shell from which the life had retreated out
into the suburbs where a few old friends still persisted,
a shell now inhabited by an alien existentialist gossip,
and an alien troupe of young men who cadged drinks
from her in languid boredom and made love only to
each other. Her trip to Italy, therefore, had the character of a farewell and a new beginning, and the hotel
suite, into which she now showed the two friends, resembled a branch office which had been opened but
was not yet in full operation.

The wide *letto matrimoniale* in the bedroom, the
washstand, and the bidet with the towel over it, the
dressing-table on which were arranged, very neatly
and charmingly, Miss Grabbe's toilet waters and per-
fumes, her powders and lucite brush and comb, her
lipsticks, orange sticks, and tweezers, all had an air
unmistakably functional, to which the books and magazines, the cigarettes and pretty colored postcards set
out, invitingly, in the sitting room contributed their
share, so that it was not so surprising as it might have
been to see, when the balcony doors were opened,
the figure of Mr. Sciarappa lounging on the terrace,
like a waiting client, with a copy of *Life*.

This conception of his position, however, seemed
not to have struck Mr. Sciarappa. He was there, it
seemed, simply for the practical joke of it, for their
shrieks, for Miss Grabbe's discomfiture. He laughed at
them with candid merriment, saying, *"Caro,* I give you
a surprise." The two friends had not seen him so lively
since one night in Milan when a tired fat woman, running for a tramcar, had failed to catch it. He showed
no inclination at all to step into the role that stood
there, ready for him to try on. He had come, he said,
as a courier, proposing to take them to dinner, to the
Piazza San Marco, to Harry's Bar, where the smart
English officers went and the international set with
their electric-blue suits, blonde mistresses, heavy jaws,
and decorations from Balkan kings. With all these lit-

tle offices and services, his mind was completely occu-
pied. His original mission, Miss Grabbe, had plainly
dropped into some *oubliette* of his faculties, and the
two friends, observing him, could nearly have sworn
that his sole purpose in coming to Venice had been to
prepare a place for them, like Jesus for his disciples
in Heaven.

Dinner, however, soon restored him to his normal
state of disaffection. Once the four were seated upstairs, in the yellow lamplight at Quadri's, he was his
old self, bored, petulant, abstracted. He jumped up
from his chair with almost indecent agility to speak to
a bearded gentleman in a respectable suit of clothes,
and came back finally to announce that this was
Prince Rucellai, an illustrious Florentine nobleman
who practiced the trade of antique-dealer. In the manner of all Mr. Sciarappa's native acquaintances, the
prince at once quitted the restaurant, but Mr. Sciarappa's attention went with him out into the square,
abandoning the Americans summarily for the evening.
It was as if he suffered from some curious form of
amnesia that made him mislay his purpose halfway on
the road to accomplishment. He was in Venice and
could not remember why, and he stayed on hoping,
somehow, for a refreshment of his memory. Now and
then, during the following days, the Americans would
find him looking at them with a curious concentration,
as though their appearance might recall to him his
motive in seeking their society. From Miss Grabbe, on
the contrary, whose emeralds should have furnished
him his clue, he persistently averted his eyes.

The little bohemian heiress, in fact, was the center
of his inattention, an inattention principled and profound. From the very first night, apparently, she had
associated herself in his mind with culture, and hence,
merely by talking about them, she had fallen into the
class of objects—cathedrals, works of art, museums,
palaces maintained by the state—which, by being free
to all, were valuable, in his opinion, to none. And by

the same trick by which he substituted an empty space for the cathedral in the Piazza San Marco, he "vanished" Miss Grabbe from the table at dinner. The possibility of her buying a palazzo, which she spoke of continually, he simply declined to credit. His business interest, it would seem, was far too deep to be aroused by it, and no commission could be large enough to make him expand his idea of money to accommodate within it the living heresy of Miss Grabbe. All over Venice, volunteer real-estate agents were at work for her, the concierge at the Grand Hotel, the liftboy, a gondolier, two Communist painters in a studio across the Canal. Mr. Sciarappa only smiled impatiently whenever this project was mentioned, and once he nudged the young lady and significantly tapped his head.

Miss Grabbe, for her part, was unaware of his feelings. The first evening on the balcony, she had expressed herself strongly against him. Pointing dramatically to the blue lagoon, the towers, the domes, the clouds, the Palladian front of San Giorgio, all as pink and white, as airy, watery, clear, and neat as the bottles and puffs on her own dressing-table, she had taken the young man's arm and invited him to choose. "My dear, why do you see him? He is not our sort," she had said. "Life is too short. He will spoil Venice for you if you let him." The young man had simply stared. Mr. Sciarappa was a nuisance, but he felt no inclination to trade him for the Venetian "experience." The bargain was too sharp for his nature. If Mr. Sciarappa obstructed the European view, he also replaced it. The mystery of Europe lay in him as solidly as in the stones of Venice, and it was somewhat less worn by previous inquisitive travelers. Night after night, he and the young lady would sit up examining Mr. Sciarappa with the refined passion of connoisseurs. It was true that sometimes at the dinner-hour they would try to give him the slip, yet they felt a certain relief whenever he rose from behind a potted plant in the hotel lobby to claim, once again, their company. He had become a problem for them in both senses of the word: the impossibility of talking *with* him was compensated for by the possibilities of talking about him, and the detachment of their attitude was, they felt, atoned for by their neighborliness in the physical sphere. How much, in fact, they had come to feel that they owed Mr. Sciarappa their company, they did not recognize until the afternoon, extraordinary to them, when he was not on hand to collect the debt.

The day of the fiesta he silently disappeared. Like everyone else in Venice he had been planning on the occasion. Colored lanterns had been attached to the gondolas, floats were being decked, and rumors, gay as paper flowers, promised a night of license, masking, and folly. A party of English tourists was expected; Miss Grabbe was trying on eighteenth-century court costumes with the Communists across the Canal. Apparently, Mr. Sciarappa had set this as the date of his own liberation, for at the apéritif hour he was not to be seen, either at the hotel or, as he had stipulated, in the Piazza. The two friends connected his disappearance with the arrival of the English tourists, for at the first mention of their existence, his mind had ducked underground, into the tunnel where his real life was conducted. They had known him long enough to see him as a city of Catacombs, and to interpret his lapses of attention as signs of the keenest interest; his silences were the camouflaged entrances to the Plutonian realm of his thoughts. Nevertheless, they felt slightly shocked and abandoned. Like many intellectual people, they were alarmed by the confirmation of theories —was the world as small as the mind? They telephoned their hotel twice, but their friend had left no messages for them, and, disturbed, they allowed Miss Grabbe to go off with her maskers while they watched on the cold jetty the little gondolas chasing up and down the Canal in pursuit of the great floating orchestra which everybody had seen in the afternoon but which now, like Mr. Sciarappa, had unaccountably disappeared.

Some time later, they perceived Mr. Sciarappa alone in a gondola that was rapidly making for the pier. They would not have recognized him had he not called out effusively, "Ah, my friends, I am looking for you all over Venice tonight."

The full force of this lie was lost on them, for they were less astonished to find Scampi in a falsehood than to find him in a new suit. In dark blue and white stripes, he stepped out of the gondola; gold links gleamed at his wrists; his face was soft from the barbershop, and a strong fragrance of Chanel caused passers-by to turn to stare at them. The bluish-white glare from the dome of San Giorgio, lit up for the occasion, fell on him, accentuating the moment. The heavier material had added a certain substantiality to him; like the men in Harry's Bar, he looked sybaritic, prosperous, and vain. But this transfiguration was, it became clear, merely the afterglow of some hope that had already set for him. Wherever he had been, he had failed to accomplish his object, if indeed he had had an object beyond the vague adventure of a carnival night. He was more nervous than ever, and he invited them to join him on the Canal in the manner of a man who is weighing the security of companionship against the advantages of the lone hand. The two friends declined, and he put off once more in the gondola, saying, "Well, my dears, you are right; it is just a tourist fiesta." The two retired to their window to wonder whether the English tourists, and not themselves or Miss Grabbe, had not been, after all, the real Venetian attraction. The *Inglesi's* arrival might well have been anticipated in a newspaper, particularly since they had the reputation of being rich collectors of furniture. Mr. Sciarappa's restless behavior, irrational in a pursuer who has already come up with his prey, was appropriate enough to the boredom and anxiety of waiting. Indeed, sometimes, watching him drum on the table, they had said to themselves that he behaved toward them like a passenger who is detained between trains in a provincial railroad station and vainly tries to interest himself in the billboard and the ticket collector.

Miss Grabbe had taken very little part in all this mental excitement. So far as the two friends could see, he had no erotic interest for her. She was as adamant to his virility as he to the evidence of her money—it would have disturbed all her preconceptions to discover sex in a business suit. She received his disappearance calmly, saying, "I thought you wanted to get rid of him—he has probably found bigger fish." In general, after her first protest, she had grown accustomed to Mr. Sciarappa, in the manner of the rich. For her he did not assume prominence through the frequency of his attendance, but on the contrary he receded into the surroundings in the fashion of a piece of furniture that is "lived with." She opened and closed him like a guidebook whenever she needed the name of a hotel or a hairdresser or had forgotten the Italian for what she wanted to say to the waiter. Having money, she had little real curiosity; she was not a dependent of the world. It did not occur to her to inquire why he had come, nor did she ask when he would leave. She too spoke of him as "Scampi," but tolerantly, without resentment, as nice women call a dog a rascal. She was not, despite appearances, a woman of strong convictions; she accepted any current situation as normative and was not anxious for change. Her money had made her insular; she was used to a mercenary circle and had no idea that outside it lovers showed affection, friends repaid kindness, and husbands did not ask an allowance or bring their mistresses home to bed. So now she accepted Mr. Sciarappa's dubious presence without particular question; it struck her as far less unnatural than the daily affection she witnessed between the young man and the young lady. She domesticated all the queerness of his being with them in Venice. "My dear," she remonstrated with the young man, "he simply wants to sell us something," dissipating Sciarappa as succinctly as if he had been a Fuller Brush man at the door. It irritated them slightly that she would not see the problem of Sciarappa, and they did not guess that now, when they had given up expecting it, she would grapple with their problem more matter-of-factly than they. While the two friends slept, through the night of the fiesta she and Mr. Sciarappa made love; when he departed, in dressing-gown and slippers, she thanked him "for a very pleasant evening."

Mr. Sciarappa, however, did not stay to cement the relationship. He left Venice precipitately, as though retreating ahead of Miss Grabbe's revelations. He was gone the next afternoon, without spoken adieus, leaving behind him a list of the second-best restaurants in Florence for the young lady, with an asterisk marking the ones where he was personally known to the headwaiter. "Unhappily," his note ran, "one cannot be on a holiday forever." On a final zigzag of policy he had careened away from them into the inexplicable. Now that he had declared himself in action, his motives seemed the more obscure. What, in fact, had he been up to? It was impossible to find out from Miss Grabbe, for to her mind sex went without explanations; it seemed to her perfectly ordinary that two strangers who were indifferent to each other should spend the night locked in the privacies of love.

Sitting up in bed, surrounded by hot-water bottles (for she had caught cold in her stomach), she received the two friends at tea-time and related her experiences of the night, using confession matter-of-factly, as a species of feminine hygiene, to disinfect her spirit of any lingering touch of the man. Scampi, she said, accepting the nickname from the young man as a kind of garment for the Italian gentleman, who seemed to stand there before them, shivering and slightly chicken-breasted in the nude, Scampi, she said, was very nice, but not in any way remarkable, the usual Italian man. He had taken her back from the fiesta, where the orchestra had never been found and she had grown tired of the painters, who looked ridiculous in costume when no one else was dressed. He had pinched her bottom on the Riva and undressed her on the balcony; they had tussled and gone to bed. Upon the cold stage of Miss Grabbe's bald narrative, he capered in and out like a grotesque, now naked, chasing her naked onto the balcony, now gorgeous in a silk dressing-gown and slippers tiptoeing down the corridor of the hotel, now correct in light tan pajamas dutifully, domestically, turning out the light. For a moment, they saw him all shrunken and wizened. ("My dear, he is much older than you think," said Miss Grabbe confidentially), and another glimpse revealed him in an aspect still more intimate and terrible, tossing the scapular he wore about his neck, and which hung down and interfered with his love-making, back again and again, lightly, flippantly, recklessly, over his thin shoulder.

"Stop," cried the young lady, seizing the young man's hands and pressing them in an agony of repentance to her own bosom. "Does it shock you?" inquired Miss Grabbe, lifting her black eyebrows. "Darling, you *gave* me Sciarappa."

"No, no," begged the young lady, for it seemed to her that this was not at all what they had wanted, this mortal exposé, but that, on the contrary, they had had in mind something more sociological, more humane—biographical details, Mr. Sciarappa's relation with his parents, his social position, his business, his connection with the Fascist state. But of all this, of course, Miss Grabbe could tell them nothing. The poor Italian, hunted down, defenseless, surprised in bed by a party of intruders, had yielded nothing but his manhood. His motives, his status, his true public and social self, everything that the young lady now called "the really interesting part about him," he had carried off with him to Rome intact. He was gone and had left them with his skin, withered, dry, unexpectedly old. Through Miss Grabbe, they had come as close to him bodily as the laws of nature permit, and there at the core there was nothing—they had known him better in the Galleria in Milan. As for the affective side of him, the emotions and sentiments, here too he had eluded them. Miss Grabbe's net had been too coarse to catch whatever small feelings had escaped him during the encounter.

A sense of desolation descended on the room, the usual price of confidences. It was a relief when one of the Communist painters came in with some lira, which Miss Grabbe put in her douche-bag. The two friends exchanged a glance of illumination. Had this repository for his country's debased currency proved too casual for Mr. Sciarappa's sense of honor? Was this the cause of his flight? If so, was it the lira or his manhood that was insulted? Or were the two, in the end, indistinguishable?

The two friends could never be sure, and when they left Venice shortly afterwards they were still debating whether some tactlessness of Miss Grabbe's had set Scampi at last in motion or whether his own action, by committing him for an hour or so, had terrified him into instant removal. He was a theoretician of practice so pure, they said to each other on the bus, that any action must appear to him as folly because of the risks to his shrewdness that it involved, a man so worldly that he saw the world as a lie too transparent to fool Rino Sciarappa, who was clever and knew the ropes. As they passed through the bony Apennines, the landscape itself seemed to wear a face baked and disabused as Mr. Sciarappa's own, and thus to give their theories a geological and national cast. The terraced fields lay scorched, like Mr. Sciarappa's wrinkles, on the gaunt umber-colored hillsides; like his vernal hopes, plants sprang up only to die here, and the land had the mark of wisdom—it too had seen life. After these reflections, it was a little anticlimactic to meet, half an hour after their arrival in Florence, the face of Italian history, whose destination had been announced as Rome. "He is following us, but he is ahead," said the young man, abandoning historical explanations forever. Only one conclusion seemed possible—he must be a spy.

In Florence, at any rate, he appeared to be acquainted; he introduced them to a number of American girls who worked in United States offices and to one or two young men who wore American uniforms. All of these people, as he had once promised them in Venice, called him by his first name; yet when the dinner-hour drew near the whole party vanished as agilely as Mr. Sciarappa, and the two friends found themselves once more going to his favorite restaurant, drinking his favorite wine, and being snubbed first by the waiter and then by their impatient guide. If he was a spy, however, his superiors must at last have given him a new assignment, for the next day he left Florence, not without giving the young lady his restaurant key to Rome.

In Rome, curiosity led them, at long last, and with some reluctance, to investigate his address, which he had written out in the young lady's address book long ago, on the train, outside Domodossola, when their acquaintance had promised to be of somewhat shorter duration. As their steps turned into the dusty Via San Ignazio, they felt their hearts quicken. The European enigma and its architectural solution lay just before them, around a bend in the street, and they still, in spite of everything, should not have been surprised to find a renaissance palace, a coat of arms, and a liveried manservant just inside the door. But the house was plain and shabby; it was impossible to conceive of Mr. Sciarappa's gabardines proceeding deftly through the entrance. Looking at this yellow house, at the unshaven tenant in his undershirt regarding them from the third-story window, and the mattress and the gera-

nium in the fourth, the two friends felt a return of that
mortification and unseemly embarrassment they had
experienced in Miss Grabbe's bedroom. This house
too was an obscenity, like the shrunken skin and the
scapular, but it also was a shell which Rino Sciarappa
did not truly inhabit. By common consent, they turned
silently away from it, with a certain distaste which,
oddly enough, was not directed at Mr. Sciarappa or
his residence, but, momentarily, at each other. The relation between pursuer and pursued had been confounded, by a dialectic too subtle for their eyes.

The Old Men

TO THE young man in the hospital nightshirt, the continuous moaning of the old voice across the hall was at first a simple irritant, like the clanking of radiator pipes. Could not somebody put a stop to it? was his involuntary, impatient query. He was furious with the hospital, with the doctor, and above all with his own irrelevance in having fallen off a ladder in his friend's New England studio and landed here, at the county seat, with a broken elbow, in the private wing of an institution that, in everything but the charge *per diem,* resembled penury itself. The windy old voice perpetusually crying "Nurse, nurse!" from just across the corridor, groaning, quavering, soughing, seemed to typify everything that was antiquated and *unnecessary* in the whole situation. Despite the young man's efforts to take a more humane view, the notion that his old neighbor could be turned off with one severe twist of the wrist, like a leaking faucet, persisted in the young man's head, together with the conviction that he himself, in the old man's position, would have shown self-control. Once he had allowed himself to voice this comparative judgment, however, he was immediately filled with chagrin, for he was a just young man, of a cool but chivalrous disposition, and he recognized that there had been nothing, as yet, in his young life to test his powers of self-restraint; all he could say with positiveness was that in order to utter such vivid groans as proceeded from the opposite room he would have to be a different person—i.e., to be ailing and old.

Yet the fact that he knew himself to be, on the contrary, rosy-cheeked, gold-haired, well-favored, a graduate student of history at Harvard University, the indulged son of his parents, did not dispose of his irritation. In fact, it only quickened it by making it appear unreasonable. To grit his teeth and endeavor not to hear would have been the conventional recourse, but his native hospitality and politeness now suddenly forbade him to eliminate the suffering old man from his consciousness, even if this had been physically possible. He felt a social obligation to listen. Yet the faculty of sympathetic attention, the young man rapidly discovered, as he tried remorsefully to exercise it, is like the faculty of hearing: it ceases to reply to a regularly offered stimulus, just as one ceases to be able to hear a clock ticking in a room. He found, upon experiment, that it was possible to replenish his compassion by picturing the old man as dying (in the manner of a jaded libertine who resorts to a mental image to resuscitate the inert *fact* of love), but even this spur to fellow-feeling soon failed to prick his imagination. In a very short time, he resigned himself to the truth that he could feel sad about the old man but not really sorry, and that for every squeeze of generalized pity, there was a spurt of concrete hatred and repugnance.

"Am I a monster?" he asked himself curiously. "Or is this what everyone secretly feels toward another's ills, toward the intrusion of a foreign body into the consciousness—a reflex of distaste and censure?" In common with many of his generation who had missed the overseas war, he had kept, up to this moment, a boy's methodical piety toward the paraplegic, the refugee, the concentration-camp inmate, and even, in a peculiar way (typical also of his age and class), toward the torturer, who seemed to share somehow with the victim the distinction of participating in the actual. Now with the actual close at hand, in the form of a living sufferer, he was astonished to find it more remote from his own center of being, more irrelevant to his purposes and interests, than the sight of a plane crashing he had recently watched in a newsreel. A slight tremor of anxiety went through him: would others extrude him from their midst so casually when his time came, or was he himself deficient in the ordinary corpuscles of humanity?

A screen had been cutting off his view of the invalid across the hall, but at mealtime he gradually became aware of a process of ingestion that was going on in that room, a steady munching and salivating, which he felt rather than heard. This surprised him very much, and once, when the screen was moved, he caught a glimpse of a lump of bedclothes in the middle of the iron bedstead, which surprised him also, in the same way. There was something very active in that lump, very much alive, though how a mere convexity of bedclothes could communicate that impression, the young man could not tell.

All along, some reasoner in himself had been urging on him the idea that the old fellow was not really very sick, but the fact that such a suggestion could even occur to him was so shocking to his conscience that he had not stopped to consider it on its merits. Now, however, he sat up in bed and began to attend more objectively to his neighbor, who at present was banging feebly with what sounded like a spoon on a glass. A nurse grumbled next door in the diet kitchen; there was a rustle of starched skirts. "Use your bell, Mr. Ciccone," she commanded. A faint moan answered her; a creak of arch-preservers followed, as the nurse moved swiftly toward the bed. "Mr. Ciccone!" she cried sharply. The young man's heart gave a lurch ("Forgive me," he dumbly articulated, winging the thought after the old man, to catch him there, on the brink), but then from behind the screen came a grunt and a gurgling tobaccoey noise, like the mirth of a subterranean river-god. The old man was laughing.

The young man uttered a limp cry. Everything had abruptly coalesced: the name Mr. Ciccone, the pictorial bass with a crack in it, the tremolo and the quaver. Mr. Ciccone was acting. And instantly that collection of noises, to which the young man had been vainly striving to assign a poignant universal reality, acquired life and character. The unseen Mr. Ciccone presented himself; yellow skin, rheumy yet brilliant black eyes, white mustachios, thin liver-spotted hands, long white nightshirt. An Italian grocer, the young man conjectured, with a son in dentistry or the automobile business; a natural obstructionist and fraud, posed, in a white apron, with a mime's sense of the picturesque, against the escarole and the pomegranates, the barrels of imported almonds and walnuts, weighing out the parmigiano on the non-Detecto scales. The young man laughed joyously aloud. Mr. Ciccone was off his conscience and lodged preferentially in his heart.

From this moment, he came to wait for the groans and laments, for the plaintive tinkle of the spoon on the glass, the short puffs of indignation, the struggle against the bedpan and the hypodermic syringe. Mr. Ciccone, as he soon learned from one of the internes, was not in fact very sick; a leg injury and a mild diabetic condition had combined to put him in the hospital, where he was regarded as a "character" by the nurses on the floor. All day long, they scolded the disobedient old party, who was continually bored and mischievous but never would trust his bell to summon attention. He felt cozened by this "bell" or light, not being able to hear it ring, and preferred to rely, in any personal emergency, on his own histrionic powers, weakly crying, "Nurse, nurse!", tapping with the spoon on the glass, gasping, choking, playing dead. He was able to counterfeit extremity with such various and graphic realism that, though he had been some time in the hospital, the nurses would still rustle in alarm down the corridor ("Coming, Mr. Ciccone!"),

only to find the old man, with the covers drawn up to
his chin, chuckling at them and demanding a game of
casino or a glass of Coca-Cola. Sometimes, when a
new student relief nurse was on the corridor, Mr. Ciccone would actually get his way and would be sitting
up in bed, finishing the forbidden beverage, when the
head floor-nurse would fly in, all indignant cap and
rattling keys—"Why, Mr. Ciccone, you *know* that
Coca-Cola is bad for you"—and whisk the glass out of
the room.

Mr. Ciccone, naturally, took medicine only under
protest. He would bargain for a game of cards in exchange for good behavior, and, failing this, two or
three times a day he would put up a convincing resistance to the sedatives, enemas, milk of magnesia,
penicillin or insulin injections called for by his chart,
only stopping short of direct physical combat, and,
having concentrated a whole battery of nurses in his
room, submitting all of a sudden with an exaggerated
show of weakness as though to twit them for their display of force. After each of these submissions, he
would moan for a long time, harrowingly, so that the
delighted young man across the way could trace (as
he knew someone was meant to) the whole nefarious
course of the medicine down Mr. Ciccone's injured
gullet into his protesting stomach or through the tis-
sues of his aged buttocks up to his shuddering heart.

The young man, too, execrated the routines of the
hospital. The dreary food, dirty rooms, noise, lack of
conveniences, the understaffed and officious personnel
with its eternal "Doctor's orders" vexed his intellect
far more than his comfort, yet, on his own behalf, *as
a private patient,* he could not nerve himself to complain. Conditions in hospitals all over the country, so
he had heard, or read in an article, were nearly as
absurd as this; someone ought to speak out against
being waked up, as he was, two and a quarter hours
before breakfast, at six every morning, on the pretext

of having his temperature taken or his bandage examined, and waked up again (assuming he had been allowed to fall asleep) at three in the afternoon with a basin of lukewarm water, a toothbrush, and an order to "wash up" for the night. The idea of paying twelve dollars a day for this nonchalant and peremptory "care" was a constant insult to his acumen, but to protest on this basis was to imply that, had he been paying less, he would have had fewer grounds for objections. This, to a young man of liberal views, was not a tenable position. For purposes of social criticism, he could have wished himself a patient in the wards, where the very generalized injustice of the situation would have given him a right to speak. Shyness, the wish to appear a "good" patient, chivalry toward the nurses, all contributed to silence his criticism, but in his own eyes he was restrained, above all, by the sense that a demonstration against bureaucratic routine and authoritarian slovenliness on the part of a single patient would so plainly lack a "popular" character.

What he had seen, however, of conditions in the private wing did not inspire him to transfer to the men's ward for the mere privilege of playing the rebel there. He was determined simply to get well and be shut of this place as quickly as possible. He had been put in the hospital by his friend, and by his friend's wife, whom, as a matter of fact, he had been leaning forward to kiss when he fell off the ladder in the studio. They had sent him a bunch of bronze chrysanthemums and left him more or less to himself; he could imagine that Mrs. X regarded the fall as some sort of "judgment" for their series of desultory indiscretions; she had not, in any case, during their single stiff visit to his bedside, directed her eyes fully into his.

For this, the young man was thankful. For his own part, he had no wish to see either of the Xes again and had only feared that the accident, and the whole atmosphere of crisis surrounding it, would enclose him in a triangle by a sheer convention of the prevailing social geometry. Whatever had happened to prevent this—whether Mrs. X had "told" her husband, whether he had "guessed," or whether the accident had brought home to them what a nuisance, after all, other people (guests, in particular) really were, a common discovery of couples—the young man did not care. Throughout their visit, he himself had chattered incessantly about the hospital, Mr. Ciccone, the personal traits of the different nurses, never stopping to inquire about the farm, the pig, the projected dinner party, Mr. X's painting, while husband and wife exchanged glances, like promissory notes on a future conversation, indicating that they would never have believed, if illness and isolation had not shown them, how intensely trivial and self-centered this friend in the nightshirt was.

The solitude in which they left him, and the repudiation of their transient intimacy, gave the young man occasion to assess in his own terms the twenty-four-year-old person who, shorn of all identifying marks and validating references, was lying cranked up in the scarred hospital bed. His preoccupation with the gossip of the corridor was, he quite readily conceded, a confession of envy and inferiority. He felt a sort of jealousy of this whole *affairé* world of illness and medication from which he was excluded. He wished to know its language and be accepted by it, yet the consciousness that his injury was a minor one made him hesitate to trench upon it. He believed that the nurses looked askance at him and treated him with subtle discrimination, as though questioning the professional wisdom of the doctor in detaining him here so long. He would have liked to say that he agreed with them, that he, too, could not understand why a mere fractured elbow should require so protracted a stay in bed, to assure them that it was not of his own desire but by the arbitrary will of another that he was there presuming on their patience.

This sense of his own nothingness in contradistinc-
tion to some darker reality had been threatening him,
he now perceived, from childhood. The tone of his
mother's voice, sad, velvety, genuflectory, pronouncing
the words "They're *poor*" came back to him now with
horror. "And are we rich?" he heard himself pipe.
"No, dear, just comfortable"—the tone was of modest
complacency, tinted with social awareness. In Cambridge, among his fellows, with the Xes, even, on their
farm, he had achieved a minor entrée—he could be
found, like a point on a social graph. But here, where
no attachments secured him, where no one knew his
history or his friends, he felt himself suddenly floating,
uncircumstantiated, a mere transparency, and this
sense of himself as an absence was so compelling that
he was startled by the sight of his face, which looked
at him through its eyeholes like a Christmas mask
when they brought him in a mirror to shave by. The
mortification of being alone, unvisited, unjustified, of
having his name spelled wrong every day on the
menu he was given to check for his choice of dishes,
of having no bedroom slippers or pajamas (à la mode
enough in Cambridge but a source of daily wonder
here) had so wrought upon him that he had anticipated, without realizing it, an actual pauperization of
his features. The sight of the familiar gold forelock,
full lips, and snub nose was terribly disconcerting, as
though he looked upon himself in effigy.

To exist, he suddenly became convinced, was an
act of deliberate impersonation. Mr. Ciccone, across
the hall, being shaved with an electric razor by a party
of laughing student nurses, was a living warrant of
this; Mr. Ciccone, imitating old age in a high infirm
quaver, was both actor and *régisseur*—he had seized
his part from the director and was executing it *con
amore.* The young man listened with envy; the juve-
nile bit assigned him and, with him, his whole class and
generation of soft-voiced, accommodating extras was
too shadowy; he had no cue to rise to in the play.

What was it, he asked himself, that sustained Mr. Ciccone and, for that matter, all the lively old mountebanks of the era—Yeats, Augustus John, Freud, Einstein, Churchill? Surely not belief in the self, since the self, as those old men knew, was a joke, a nothing, a *point du départ*. Mere virtuosity perhaps, and a growing closetful of stage effects—the paunch, the wrinkle, the limp; the jowl, the shank, the bald pate. In the Santa Claus suit of old age, beneath the padding and the pillow, some spry punchinello had hold of the vital principle of artifice.

The young man had been in the hospital two or three days and was sitting up, with bathroom privileges, before a certain suspicion that had been attaching itself to Mr. Ciccone became a verified fact. Mr. Ciccone, like Homer, was not a single individual but a collaboration. There were, astonishingly, four old men on the corridor, of whom the one called Mr. Ciccone was only the ringleader—four old men, bedded in private or semi-private rooms, two of them incontinent, all insubordinate, unsubdued, sworn enemies, every one, of the bedpan, the catheter, and the needle. Antiphonally or singly, they kept up a sort of plain chant, a thin, wheezy dirge that went on, all day long in its eerie unaccentual modality:

At certain times of the day, this cry became more vociferous, when the student nurse, for example, passed through the wing with the penicillin injections. Her entry to the semi-private rooms, at the far end of the corridor, was announced by a violent hubbub: imprecations, sobbing, pleading, the occasional crash of fall-

ing furniture. The young man would lay aside his
book and wait for the authoritative creak of the head
floor nurse proceeding to the scene, the sound of feminine chiding ("Mr. Wright, you're not being thoughtful *at all*"), the shriek, and then the after-cry,
piercing, long-drawn-out, that vibrated through the
corridor as the young nurse went on to the next room,
to the women, who made no sound, and finally to Mr.
Ciccone and himself.

In the case of the two feeblest old men down the
hall, sincerity and trumpery, so far as the young man
could determine, were blended in the act of resistance.
The needle, of course, did not hurt much, but in the
lumbar regions of their spirit, *something,* plainly, was
being violated. They were childish, in the nurses'
phrase; there was a blur in their minds between actual
pain and the imagined representation of it; they did
not trouble to distinguish and acted out every fancy
with a pure, innocent sort of expressiveness. Mr. Ciccone, by contrast, was a conscious artist and a bor-
rower. Sometimes, in the afternoon, the young man
would overhear him softly rehearsing a sound effect

that he had picked up from one of his coevals, essay-
ing it again and again, tentatively, like someone practicing on a flute. Later, in the after-supper lull, the
mournful phrase, fully developed, would suddenly issue from Mr. Ciccone's room, to be taken up again by
one of the other Methuselahs, reminded by it of his
own aches and miseries, so that the whole corridor
would echo with the plaint of the old men, and the
single, stolid night nurse would clump, scolding, into

the diet kitchen, shut the door, and heat herself a cup of coffee.

This troupe of ancients, as if to confirm the young man's theories, was handled by the hospital staff, at any critical juncture, with precisely that mixture of indulgence and asperity that characterizes the plain man in his relations with the artist. On the night that the two incontinent old fellows broke a draining-tube and drank a bottle of gentian violet between them, climbed out of bed and shouted in the corridor, an orderly, like a stagehand, came whistling down the hall to subdue them. "What will they think of next?" a white-haired nurse demanded, poking her head gratuitously into the young man's room; doors slammed, lights went on, the elevator gates clashed. Only Mr. Ciccone's room remained dark and almost ostentatiously peaceful, though the young man's ear caught the sound of a dry chuckle, repeated at intervals. Yet the fact was, as the cleaning woman, shaking her head and her mop, confided to the young man in voluptuous brogue the next morning, one of those old rapscallions had just missed a date with Saint Peter.

All the while, the women patients were silent.

He had learned from one of the nurses that a woman was dying of cancer somewhere in the private wing, but only once, during his first days in the hospital, did he hear a woman's voice that was not that of a nurse or a visitor—a young woman's laugh and the sound of a door closing on it. This feminine silence began to disturb him very much; the idea that sick women of various ages and complaints were lying, blanketed, all around him, behind half-closed doors, each sheltering her unknown portion of suffering with a kind of uterine possessiveness, had the effect on him of a tactile sensation—as though he were encased in felt. He found himself with a strange, pressing desire to uncover that female suffering, to make it reveal itself to him by a sob, a gasp, a murmur, to have his ear know its contours, like a pleasure. On the fourth

night of his stay, he was awakened suddenly, out of a
deep sleep, by prolonged shrieks coming from the
darkness, a woman's voice raised again and again in
screams of such appalling vibrancy that his hair stood
up on his head. *"The cancer patient,* at last!"—the
jubilant exclamation sprang out of him, quite uninten-
tionally. He sat straight up in bed to listen, trembling
with cold and excitement. Here there was no question
of hearing or not hearing; these cries transfixed him
with horror and yet he listened to them, fascinated, in
the tingling stealth of discovery. He knew immediately
that he was not meant to hear; these shrieks were being wrung from a being that yielded them against its
will; yet in this fact, precisely, lay their power to elec-
trify the attention. "A dying woman screaming in the
night," the young man repeated musingly, as the cries
stopped, at their very summit, as abruptly as they had
started, leaving a pounding stillness, "this is the actual; the actual, in fact, is *that which should not be
witnessed.* The actual," he defined, pronouncing the
syllables slowly and distinctly in a pedagogical style,
"under which may be subsumed the street accident,
the plane crash, the atrocity, is pornography." Closing
his eyes, he sank back on a long breath of relief.

He awakened the next morning with a vivid feeling
of joy and liberation, as if during the night a responsibility had been sloughed off. He felt blithe and ready
to live, selfishly and inconsiderately, like the expressive old men; the actual no longer drew him with its
womanish terrors and mysteries, its sphinx-rebuff and
invidia. "Cast a cold eye on life, on death," he sang
out, borrowing from old Yeats's tombstone. "Horse-
man, pass by." He was positively elated, in fact, to be
young, healthy, and hungry, and, as he meant to tell
Dr. Z as soon as he appeared on his rounds, determined to go home to Cambridge on the one-o'clock
train. This elation induced in him an unusual talka-
tiveness; to the fat grumpy old nurse who came in with
the thermometer, he could not resist an allusion to

what he had heard during the night. The old nurse surveyed him tersely, shook down the thermometer without comment, unpinned her watch from her uniform, and, snapping her fingers impatiently, extended her veined hand for his pulse. "Maternity case," she finally surmised, handing him his toothbrush and the tin basin. "You won't hear a sound out of Mrs. Miller [mentioning the name of the cancer patient]. She's quiet as a lamb next door." The young man turned white at the thought of that deathy stillness so near him; he had imagined the next room to be empty, for not a sound had issued from it, and passing it on his trips down the hall to the bathroom, he had observed that the door was always shut. The next question was drawn from him by a compulsion; he did not wish to ask it and threw it out with diffidence: "She is under opiates, I suppose?"

The nurse surveyed him again with a short, measuring movement of the eye. "Brush your teeth, now," she commanded curtly. "You know we are not permitted to give out information about the other patients." She withdrew the bedpan from the commode, jerked off the towel that shrouded it, and slid it under the covers. "Put your light on when you're through," she directed. The young man sat up. "But I am allowed to go to the bathroom!" he exclaimed. "Not this morning," she said firmly. "Doctor says we are to stay in bed this morning." "But why?" demanded the young man, now thoroughly alarmed and suspicious. The nurse's creased face snapped shut. "Curiosity killed the cat," she retorted. "Doctor will be in early to see you." "I demand—" cried the young man after her, as she bustled out, leaving the door open, but he broke off, conscious of absurdity, for what he had been about to say was "I demand to see a lawyer," which was ridiculous, for he was certainly free to get up and dress and leave the hospital. The idea of flight suddenly offered itself to him as the only feasible solution. He pictured, with a return of his early-morning gaiety, the rubber-soled chase down the corridor, the escape down the fire-stairs. His imagination, however, faltered at the thought of the office: to leave without paying was unthinkable, yet would they be likely to take a check from him under such unusual conditions? He feared, all at once, to put this question to the test. He felt unequal to the imagined commotion——the painstaking verification of identity, the call to his bank in Boston——and for what purpose, he asked himself, would I do all that, for the mere assertion of my individuality? For the sake of another, he reasoned, I could conceivably do it, if it were a question of rescue or sacrifice; but for *myself?* He lay back dutifully on the bedpan and in a moment put on his light.

The nurse came in and he said coldly, "In the future, would you take the trouble to close the door when you leave the room, particularly during these intimate moments?" Yet even as he began to speak, he felt himself blushing and the final phrase, to which he had meant to impart a sarcastic intonation, was mumbled out thickly, in a tone, almost, of apology. The nurse threw the cover over the bedpan and went out, closing the door behind her with a decisive click.

An hour late, young Dr. Z appeared, all gold fillings, hair *en brosse,* smile, and rimless spectacles. "We are going to reset that elbow for you," he announced. "Anyone you want to get in touch with?" The young man opened his mouth to argue. He was free (was he not?), he reminded himself, to get up and dress and leave the hospital. He had only to refuse. The Xes, if it came down to it, could be summoned to bail him out of here. Dr. Z, after all, had no title or charter to his patronage. He had only to tell him that he preferred to have the arm reset, if necessary, in Cambridge, where he had friends and a regular physician; there was nothing in this preference that was derogatory to Dr. Z. The doctor, in his white gown, stood looking down at him, smiling rather inscrutably, as though he were very much aware of what was going on in the young man's mind. "Those friends of yours," he suggested, with a flick of the sterile glance in the direction of the dying chrysanthemums, "do you want us to give them a call?" A student nurse knocked and came in with a tray and a hypodermic needle. The young man's jaws worked and he shook his head wordlessly in reply. It was too late; in the presence of this attentive listener he could not refuse Dr. Z what suddenly, in a curious fashion, appeared to be a favor, the favor of letting him operate on him. The abominable doctor smiled again, lightly, and tapped the foot of the bed in a negligent gesture that seemed to imply a mixture of contempt and approbation, as if he had had little doubt of the outcome of this conflict between them but was nevertheless satisfied to have won.

On the way up to the operating room, being wheeled breezily along by an orderly humming *"Who?"* the young man had a sudden clear sharp sense of all that he had omitted to do to attach himself to the life of this corridor from which now, irrecoverably perhaps, he thought in panic, he was being trundled away. "Stop," he asserted faintly, raising his head on the pallet. The idea of defending himself still reached him as from a distance through the drug: Mr. Ciccone, he thought, would never have permitted this; in Mr. Ciccone, he considered tenderly, he had an ally, a veteran aider and abettor. Why, he demanded of himself, had he not taken the simple friendly course, yesterday, when he was sitting up in a chair, of offering to join his neighbor in a game of casino?

The orderly had paused to look down at him. "What's the matter, chum?" he inquired. The young man struggled up from the confining blankets. They were waiting for the elevator, he realized; it was not too late, if he were insistent, to make a date with Mr. Ciccone for this afternoon or tomorrow; the fact that this notion was absurd made it appear to him all the more urgent and necessary, all the more talismanic.

He jerked his raised head in the direction of Mr. Ciccone's room. "I must speak to the patient in Number Three," he pronounced, with an effect of hauteur and dignity. The orderly lifted shaggy red eyebrows, peered down the elevator shaft, shrugged, and consentingly set the stretcher in motion, retracing their way along the corridor. "Friend of yours?" he remarked.

In the flush of this victory over self and custom, the young man grew excited and voluble; a passing nurse turned back to look at them. "No," he said. "To tell the truth, I've never actually seen him." The orderly stared and bumped the stretcher to a standstill, but they were already opposite Number Three. The screen had been moved and the young man hastily nerved himself for the possibility that the real Mr. Ciccone might be something quite different from what he had imagined—a cantankerous misanthrope, for example, who would repulse his overture. But to his surprise the shaded room across the way into which his dilated eyes stared was empty, the bed made up and flat.

Fifteen minutes later, the young man expired under the anesthetic, before the operation proper had begun, the first case of its kind, as Dr. Z explained to Mrs. X, that he had ever come across in his entire practice, where the heart, without organic defect, sound as a bell, in fact, simply stopped beating.

II

Yonder Peasant, Who Is He?

WHENEVER WE children came to stay at my grandmother's house, we were put to sleep in the sewing room, a bleak, shabby, utilitarian rectangle, more office than bedroom, more attic than office, that played to the hierarchy of chambers the role of a poor relation. It was a room seldom entered by the other members of the family, seldom swept by the maid, a room without pride; the old sewing machine, some cast-off chairs, a shadeless lamp, rolls of wrapping paper, piles of cardboard boxes that might someday come in handy, papers of pins, and remnants of material united with the iron folding cots put out for our use and the bare floor boards to give an impression of intense and ruthless temporality. Thin white spreads, of the kind used in hospitals and charity institutions, and naked blinds at the windows reminded us of our orphaned condition and of the ephemeral character of our visit; there was nothing here to encourage us to consider this our home.

Poor Roy's children, as commiseration damply styled the four of us, could not afford illusions, in the family opinion. Our father had put us beyond the pale by dying suddenly of influenza and taking our young mother with him, a defection that was remarked on with horror and grief commingled, as though our mother had been a pretty secretary with whom he had wantonly absconded into the irresponsible paradise of the hereafter. Our reputation was clouded by this mis-

116

fortune. There was a prevailing sense, not only in the family but among storekeepers, servants, streetcar conductors, and other satellites of our circle, that my grandfather, a rich man, had behaved with extraordinary munificence in allotting a sum of money for our support and installing us with some disagreeable middle-aged relations in a dingy house two blocks distant from his own. What alternative he had was not mentioned; presumably he could have sent us to an orphan asylum and no one would have thought the worse of him. At any rate, it was felt, even by those who sympathized with us, that we led a privileged existence, privileged because we had no rights, and the very fact that at the yearly Halloween or Christmas party given at the home of an uncle we appeared so dismal, ill clad, and unhealthy, in contrast to our rosy, exquisite cousins, confirmed the judgment that had been made on us—clearly, it was a generous impulse that kept us in the family at all. Thus, the meaner our circumstances, the greater seemed our grandfather's condescension, a view in which we ourselves shared, looking softly and shyly on this old man—with his rheumatism, his pink face and white hair, set off by the rosebuds in his Pierce-Arrow and in his buttonhole —as the font of goodness and philanthropy, and the nickel he occasionally gave us to drop into the collection plate on Sunday (two cents was our ordinary contribution) filled us not with envy but with simple admiration for his potency; this indeed was princely, *this* was the way to give. It did not occur to us to judge him for the disparity of our styles of living. Whatever bitterness we felt was kept for our actual guardians, who, we believed, must be embezzling the money set aside for us, since the standard of comfort achieved in our grandparents' house—the electric heaters, the gas logs, the lap robes, the shawls wrapped tenderly about the old knees, the white meat of chicken and red meat of beef, the silver, the white tablecloths, the maids, and the solicitous chauffeur—persuaded us that prunes and rice pudding, peeling paint and patched clothes were *hors concours* with these persons and therefore could not have been willed by them. Wealth, in our minds, was equivalent to bounty, and poverty but a sign of penuriousness of spirit.

Yet even if we had been convinced of the honesty of our guardians, we would still have clung to that beneficent image of our grandfather that the family myth proposed to us. We were too poor, spiritually speaking, to question his generosity, to ask why he allowed us to live in oppressed chill and deprivation at a long arm's length from himself and hooded his genial blue eye with a bluff, millionairish gray eyebrow whenever the evidence of our suffering presented itself at his knee. The official answer we knew: our benefactors were too old to put up with four wild young children; our grandfather was preoccupied with business matters and with his rheumatism, to which he devoted himself as though to a pious duty, taking it with him on pilgrimages to Ste. Anne de Beaupré and Miami, offering it with impartial reverence to the miracle of the Northern Mother and the Southern sun. This rheumatism hallowed my grandfather with the mark of a special vocation; he lived with it in the manner of an artist or a grizzled Galahad; it set him apart from all of us and even from my grandmother, who, lacking such an affliction, led a relatively unjustified existence and showed, in relation to us children, a sharper and more bellicose spirit. She felt, in spite of everything, that she was open to criticism, and, transposing this feeling with a practiced old hand, kept peering into our characters for symptoms of ingratitude.

We, as a matter of fact, were grateful to the point of servility. We made no demands, we had no hopes. We were content if we were permitted to enjoy the refracted rays of that solar prosperity and come sometimes in the summer afternoons to sit on the shady porch or idle through a winter morning on the wicker furniture of the sun parlor, to stare at the player piano in the music room and smell the odor of whiskey in the mahogany cabinet in the library, or to climb about the dark living room examining the glassed-in paintings in their huge gilt frames, the fruits of European travel: dusky Italian devotional groupings, heavy and lustrous as grapes, Neapolitan women carrying baskets to market, views of Venetian canals, and Tuscan harvest scenes—secular themes that, to the Irish-American mind, had become tinged with Catholic feeling by a regional infusion from the Pope. We asked no more from this house than the pride of being connected with it, and this was fortunate for us, since my grandmother, a great adherent of the give-them-an-inch-and-they'll-take-a-yard theory of hospitality, never, so far as I can remember, offered any caller the slightest refreshment, regarding her own conversation as sufficiently wholesome and sustaining. An ugly, severe old woman with a monstrous balcony of a bosom, she officiated over certain set topics in a colorless singsong, like a priest intoning a Mass, topics to which repetition had lent a senseless solemnity: her audience with the Holy Father; how my own father had broken with family tradition and voted the Democratic ticket; a visit to Lourdes; the Sacred Stairs in Rome, blood-stained since the first Good Friday, which she had climbed on her knees; my crooked little fingers and how they meant I was a liar; a miracle-working bone; the importance of regular bowel movements; the wickedness of Protestants; the conversion of my mother to Catholicism; and the assertion that my Protestant grandmother must certainly dye her hair. The most trivial reminiscences (my aunt's having hysterics in a haystack) received from her delivery and from the piety of the context a strongly monitory flavor; they inspired fear and guilt, and one searched uncomfortably for the moral in them, as in a dark and riddling fable.

Luckily, I am writing a memoir and not a work of fiction, and therefore I do not have to account for my grandmother's unpleasing character and look for the Oedipal fixation or the traumatic experience which would give her that clinical authenticity that is nowadays so desirable in portraiture. I do not know how my grandmother got the way she was; I assume, from family photographs and from the inflexibility of her habits, that she was always the same, and it seems as idle to inquire into her childhood as to ask what was ailing Iago or look for the error in toilet-training that was responsible for Lady Macbeth. My grandmother's sexual history, bristling with infant mortality in the usual style of her period, was robust and decisive: three tall, handsome sons grew up, and one attentive daughter. Her husband treated her kindly. She had money, many grandchildren, and religion to sustain her. White hair, glasses, soft skin, wrinkles, needlework—all the paraphernalia of motherliness were hers; yet it was a cold, grudging, disputatious old woman who sat all day in her sunroom making tapestries from a pattern, scanning religious periodicals, and setting her iron jaw against any infraction of her ways.

Combativeness was, I suppose, the dominant trait in my grandmother's nature. An aggressive churchgoer, she was quite without Christian feeling; the mercy of the Lord Jesus had never entered her heart. Her piety was an act of war against the Protestant ascendancy. The religious magazines on her table furnished her not with food for meditation but with fresh pretexts for anger; articles attacking birth control, divorce, mixed marriages, Darwin, and secular education were her favorite reading. The teachings of the Church did not interest her, except as they were a rebuke to others; "Honor thy father and thy mother," a commandment she was no longer called upon to practice, was the one most frequently on her lips. The extermination of Protestantism, rather than spiritual perfection, was the boon she prayed for. Her mind was preoccupied with conversion, the capture of a soul for God much diverted her fancy—it made one less Protestant in the world. Foreign missions with their overtones of good will and social service, appealed to her less strongly; it was not a *harvest* of souls that my grandmother had in mind.

This pugnacity of my grandmother's did not confine itself to sectarian enthusiasm. There was the defense of her furniture and her house against the imagined encroachments of visitors. With her, this was not the gentle and tremulous protectiveness endemic in old ladies, who fear for the safety of their possessions with a truly touching anxiety, inferring the fragility of all things from the brittleness of their old bones and hearing the crash of mortality in the perilous tinkling of a teacup. My grandmother's sentiment was more autocratic: she hated having her chairs sat in or her lawns stepped on or the water turned on in her basins, for no reason at all except pure officiousness; she even grudged the mailman his daily promenade up her sidewalk. Her home was a center of power, and she would not allow it to be derogated by easy or democratic usage. Under her jealous eye, its social properties had atrophied, and it functioned in the family structure simply as a political headquarters. Family conferences were held there, consultations with the doctor and the clergy; refractory children were brought there for a lecture or an interval of thought-taking; wills were read and loans negotiated and emissaries from the Protestant faction on state occasions received. The family had no friends, and entertaining was held to be a foolish and unnecessary courtesy as between blood relations. Holiday dinners fell, as a duty on the lesser members of the organization: the daughters and daughters-in-law (converts from the false religion) offered up Baked Alaska on a platter, like the head of John the Baptist, while the old people sat enthroned at the table, and only their digestive processes acknowledged, with rumbling, enigmatic salvoes, the festal day.

Yet on one terrible occasion my grandmother had kept open house. She had accommodated us all during those fatal weeks of the influenza epidemic, when no hospital beds were to be had and people went about with masks or stayed shut up in their houses, and the awful fear of contagion paralyzed all services and made each man an enemy to his neighbor. One by one, we had been carried off the train—four children and two adults, coming from distant Puget Sound to make a new home in Minneapolis. Waving good-bye in the Seattle depot, we had not known that we had brought the flu with us into our drawing rooms, along with the presents and the flowers, but, one after another, we had been struck down as the train proceeded eastward. We children did not understand whether the chattering of our teeth and Mama's lying torpid in the berth were not somehow a part of the trip (until then serious illness, in our minds, had been associated with innovations—it had always brought home a new baby), and we began to be sure that it was all an adventure when we saw our father draw a revolver on the conductor who was trying to put us off the train at a small wooden station in the middle of the North Dakota prairie. On the platform at Minneapolis, there were stretchers, a wheelchair, redcaps, distraught officials, and, beyond them, in the crowd, my grandfather's rosy face, cigar, and cane, my grandmother's feathered hat, imparting an air of festivity to this strange and confused picture, making us children certain that our illness was the beginning of a delightful holiday.

We awoke to reality in the sewing room several weeks later, to an atmosphere of castor oil, rectal thermometers, cross nurses, and efficiency, and though we were shut out from the knowledge of what had happened so close to us, just out of our hearing—a scandal of the gravest character, a coming and going of priests and undertakers and coffins (Mama and Daddy, they assured us, had gone to get well in the hospital)—we became aware, even as we woke from our fevers, that everything, including ourselves, was different. We had shrunk, at it were, and faded, like the flannel pajamas we wore; which during these few weeks had grown, doubtless from the disinfectant they were washed in, wretchedly thin and shabby. The behavior of the people around us, abrupt, careless, and preoccupied, apprised us without any ceremony of our diminished importance. Our value had paled, and a new image of ourselves—the image, if we had guessed it, of the orphan—was already forming in our minds. We had not known we were spoiled, but now this word, entering our vocabulary for the first time, served to define the change for us and to herald the new order. Before we got sick, we were spoiled; that was what was the matter now, and everything we could not understand, everything unfamiliar and displeasing, took on a certain plausibility when related to this fresh concept. We had not known what it was to have trays dumped summarily on our beds and no sugar and cream for our cereal, to take medicine in a gulp because someone could not be bothered to wait for us, to have our arms jerked into our sleeves and a comb ripped through our hair, to be bathed impatiently, to be told to sit up or lie down quick and no nonsense about it, to find our questions unanswered and our requests unheeded, to lie for hours alone and wait for the doctor's visit, but this, so it seemed, was an oversight in our training, and my grandmother and her household applied themselves with a will to remedying the deficiency.

Their motives were, no doubt, good; it was time indeed that we learned that the world was no longer our oyster. The happy life we had had—the May baskets and the valentines, the picnics in the yard, and the elaborate snowmen—was a poor preparation, in truth, for the future that now opened up to us. Our new instructors could hardly be blamed for a certain impatience with our parents, who had been so lacking in foresight. It was to everyone's interest, decidedly, that we should forget the past—the quicker, the better—and a steady disparagement of our habits ("Tea and chocolate, can you imagine, and all those frosted cakes—no wonder poor Tess was always after the doctor"), praise that was rigorously comparative ("You have absolutely no idea of the improvement in those children") flattered the feelings of the speakers and prepared us to accept a loss that was, in any case, irreparable. Like all children, we wished to conform, and the notion that our former ways had been somehow ridiculous and unsuitable made the memory of them falter a little, like a child's recitation to strangers. We no longer demanded our due, and the wish to see our parents insensibly weakened. Soon we ceased to speak of it, and thus, without tears or tantrums, we came to know they were dead.

Why no one, least of all our grandmother, to whose repertory the subject seems so congenial, took the trouble to tell us, it is impossible now to know. It is easy to imagine her "breaking" the news to those of us who were old enough to listen in one of those official interviews in which her nature periodically tumefied, becoming heavy and turgid, like her portentous bosom, like peonies, her favorite flower, or like the dressmaker's dummy, that bombastic image of herself that, half-swathed in a sheet for decorum's sake, lent a museumlike solemnity to the sewing room and aroused our first sexual curiosity. The mind's ear frames her sentences, but in reality she did not speak, whether from a hygienic motive (keep the mind ignorant and the bowels open), or from a mistaken kindness, it is difficult to guess. Perhaps really she feared our tears, which might rain on her like reproaches, since the family policy at the time was predicated on the axiom of our virtual insentience, an assumption that allowed them to proceed with us as if with pieces of furniture. Without explanations or coddling, as soon as they could safely get up, my three brothers were dispatched to the other house; they were much too young to "feel" it, I heard the grownups murmur, and would never know the difference "if Myers and Margaret were careful." In my case, however, a doubt must have been experienced. I was six—old enough to "remember"—and this entitled me, in the family's eyes, to greater consideration, as if this memory of mine were a lawyer who represented me in court. In deference, therefore, to my age and my supposed powers of criticism and comparison, I was kept on for a time, to roam palely about my grandmother's living rooms, a dangling, transitional creature, a frog becoming a tadpole, while my brothers, poor little polyps, were already well embedded in the structure of the new life. I did not wonder what had become of them. I believe I thought they were dead, but their fate did not greatly concern me; my heart had grown numb. I considered myself clever to have guessed the truth about my parents, like a child who proudly discovers that there is no Santa Claus, but I would not speak of that knowledge or even react to it privately, for I wished to have nothing to do with it; I would not cooperate in this loss. Those weeks in my grandmother's house come back to me very obscurely, surrounded by blackness, like a mourning card: the dark well of the staircase, where I seem to have been endlessly loitering, waiting to see Mama when she would come home from the hospital, and then simply loitering with no purpose whatever; the winter-dim first-grade classroom of the strange academy I was sent to; the drab treatment room of the doctor's office, where every Saturday I screamed and begged on a table while electric shocks were sent through me, for what purpose I cannot conjecture. But this preferential treatment could not be accorded me forever; it was time that I found my niche. "There is someone here to see you"—the maid met me one afternoon with this announcement and a half-curious, half-knowledgeable smile. My heart bounded; I felt almost sick (who else could it be but them?), and she had to push me forward. But the man and woman surveying me in the sun parlor with my grandmother were strangers, two unprepossessing middle-aged people—a great-aunt and her husband, so it seemed—to whom I was now commanded to give a hand and a smile, for, as my grandmother remarked, Myers and Margaret had come to take me home that very afternoon to live with them, and I must not make a bad impression.

Once the new household was running, our parents' death was officially conceded and sentiment given its due. Concrete references to the lost ones, to their beauty, gaiety, and good manners, were naturally not welcomed by our guardians, who possessed none of these qualities themselves, but the veneration of our parents' *memory* was considered an admirable exercise. Our evening prayers were lengthened to include one of our parents' souls, and we were thought to make a pretty picture, all four of us in our pajamas with feet in them, kneeling in a neat line, our hands clasped before us, reciting the prayer for the dead. "Eternal rest grant unto them, oh Lord, and let the perpetual light shine upon them," our thin little voices cried, but this remembrancing, so pleasurable to our guardians, was only a chore to us. We connected it with lights out, washing, all the bedtime coercions, and particularly with the adhesive tape that, to prevent mouth-breathing, was clapped upon our lips the moment the prayer was finished, sealing us up for the night, and that was removed, very painfully, with the help of ether, in the morning. It embarrassed us to be reminded of our parents by these persons who had superseded them and who seemed to evoke their wraiths in an almost proprietary manner, as though death, the great leveler, had brought them within their province. In the same spirit, we were taken to the cemetery to view our parents' graves; this, in fact, being free of charge, was a regular Sunday pastime with us, which we grew to hate as we did all recreation enforced by our guardians—department-store demonstrations, band concerts, parades, trips to the Old Soldiers' Home, to the Botanical Gardens, to Minnehaha Park, where we watched other children ride on the ponies, to the Zoo, to the water tower—diversions that cost nothing, involved long streetcar trips or endless walking or waiting, and that had the peculiarly fatigued, dusty, proletarianized character of American municipal entertainment. The two mounds that now were our parents associated themselves in our minds with Civil War cannon balls and monuments to the doughboy dead; we contemplated them stolidly, waiting for a sensation, but these twin grass beds, with their junior-executive headstones, elicited nothing whatever; tired of this interminable staring, we would beg to be allowed to go play in some collateral mausoleum, where the dead at least were buried in drawers and offered some stimulus to fancy.

For my grandmother, the recollection of the dead became a mode of civility that she thought proper to exercise toward us whenever, for any reason, one of us came to stay at her house. The reason was almost always the same. We (that is, my brother Kevin or I) had run away from home. Independently of each other, this oldest of my brothers and I had evolved an identical project—to get ourselves placed in an orphan asylum. We had noticed the heightening of interest that mention of our parentless condition seemed always to produce in strangers, and this led us to interpret the word "asylum" in the old Greek sense and to look on a certain red brick building, seen once from a streetcar near the Mississippi River, as a haven of privilege and security. So, from time to time, when our lives became too painful, one of us would set forth, determined to find the red brick building and to press what we imagined was our legal claim to its protection. But sometimes we lost our way, and sometimes our courage, and after spending a day hanging about the streets peering into strange yards, trying to assess the kindheartedness of the owner (for we also thought of adoption), or a cold night hiding in a church confessional box or behind some statuary in the Art Institute, we would be brought by the police, by some well-meaning householder, or simply by fear and hunger, to my grandmother's door. There we would be silently received, and a family conclave would be summoned. We would be put to sleep in the sewing room for a night, or sometimes more, until our feelings had subsided and we could be sent back, grateful, at any rate, for the promise that no reprisals would be taken and that the life we had run away from would go on "as if nothing had happened."

Since we were usually running away to escape some anticipated punishment, these flights at least gained us something, but in spite of the taunts of our guardians, who congratulated us bitterly on our "cleverness," we ourselves could not feel that we came home in triumph so long as we came home at all. The cramps and dreads of those long nights made a harrowing impression on us. Our failure to run away successfully put us, so we thought, at the absolute mercy of our guardians; our last weapon was gone, for it was plain to be seen that they could always bring us back and we never understood why they did not take advantage of this situation to thrash us, as they used to put it, within an inch of our lives. What intervened to save us, we could not guess—a miracle, perhaps; we were not acquainted with any *human* motive that would prompt Omnipotence to desist. We did not suspect that these escapes brought consternation to the family circle, which had acted, so it conceived, only in our best interests, and now saw itself in danger of unmerited obloquy. What would be the Protestant reaction if something still more dreadful were to happen? Child suicides were not unknown, and quiet, asthmatic little

Kevin had been caught with matches under the house. The family would not acknowledge error, but it conceded a certain mismanagement on Myers' and Margaret's part. Clearly, we might become altogether intractable if our homecoming on these occasions were not mitigated with leniency. Consequently, my grandmother kept us in a kind of neutral detention. She declined to be aware of our grievance and offered no words of comfort, but the comforts of her household acted upon us soothingly, like an automatic mother's hand. We ate and drank contentedly; with all her harsh views, my grandmother was a practical woman and would not have thought it worth while to unsettle her whole schedule, teach her cook to make a lumpy mush and watery boiled potatoes, and market for turnips and parsnips and all the other vegetables we hated, in order to approximate the conditions she considered suitable for our characters. Humble pie could be costly, especially when cooked to order.

Doubtless she did not guess how delightful these visits seemed to us once the fear of punishment had abated. Her knowledge of our own way of living was luxuriously remote. She did not visit our ménage or inquire into its practices, and though hypersensitive to a squint or a dental irregularity (for she was liberal indeed with glasses and braces for the teeth, disfiguring appliances that remained the sole token of our bourgeois origin and set us off from our parochial-school mates like the caste marks of some primitive tribe), she appeared not to notice the darns and patches of our clothing, our raw hands and scarecrow arms, our silence and our elderly faces. She imagined us as surrounded by certain playthings she had once bestowed on us—a sandbox, a wooden swing, a wagon, an ambulance, a toy fire engine. In my grandmother's consciousness, these objects remained always in pristine condition; years after the sand had spilled out of it and the roof had rotted away, she continued to ask tenderly after our lovely sand pile and to manifest displeasure if we declined to join in its praises. Like many egoistic people (I have noticed this trait in myself), she was capable of making a handsome outlay, but the act affected her so powerfully that her generosity was still lively in her memory when its practical effects had long vanished. In the case of a brown beaver hat, which she watched me wear for four years, she was clearly blinded to its matted nap, its shapeless brim, and ragged ribbon by the vision of the price tag it had worn when new. Yet, however her mind embroidered the bare tapestry of our lives, she could not fail to perceive that we felt, during these short stays with her, *some* difference between the two establishments, and to take wonder and pleasure as a compliment to herself.

She smiled on us quite kindly when we exclaimed over the food and the nice, warm bathrooms, with their rugs and electric heaters. What funny little creatures, to be so impressed by things that were, after all, only the ordinary amenities of life! Seeing us content in her house, her emulative spirit warmed slowly to our admiration: she compared herself to our guardians, and though for expedient reasons she could not afford to depreciate them ("You children have been very ungrateful for all Myers and Margaret have done for you"), a sense of her own finer magnanimity disposed her subtly in our favor. In the flush of these emotions, a tenderness sprang up between us. She seemed half reluctant to part with whichever of us she had in her custody, almost as if she were experiencing a genuine pang of conscience. "Try and be good," she would advise us when the moment for leave-taking came, "and don't provoke your aunt and uncle. We might have made different arrangements if there had been only one of you to consider." These manifestations of concern, these tacit admissions of our true situation, did not make us, as one might have thought, bitter against our grandparents, for whom ignorance of the facts might have served as a justification, but, on the contrary, filled us with self-complaisance—our sufferings were more distinguished if someone acknowledged their existence, if we ourselves collaborated in them, as it were, loftily, by a privy arrangement, over our guardians' heads.

During these respites, the recollection of our parents formed a bond between us and our grandmother that deepened our mutual regard. Unlike our guardians or the whispering ladies who sometimes came to call on us, inspired, it seemed, by a pornographic curiosity as to the exact details of our feelings ("Do you suppose they remember their parents?" "Do they ever *say* anything?"), our grandmother was quite uninterested in arousing an emotion of grief in us. "She doesn't feel it at all," I used to hear her confide to visitors, but contentedly, without censure, as if I had been a spayed cat that, in her superior foresight, she had had "attended to." For my grandmother, the death of my parents had become, in retrospect, an eventful occasion upon which she looked back with pleasure and a certain self-satisfaction. Whenever we stayed with her, we were allowed, as a special treat, to look into the rooms they had died in, for the fact that, as she phrased it, "they died in separate rooms" had for her a significance both romantic and somehow self-congratulatory, as though the separation in death of two who had loved each other in life were beautiful in itself and also reflected credit on the chatelaine of the house, who had been able to furnish two master bedrooms for the emergency. The housekeeping details of the tragedy, in fact, were to her of paramount interest. "I turned my house into a hospital," she used to say, particularly when visitors were present. "Nurses were as scarce as hen's teeth, and *high*—you can hardly imagine what those girls were charging an hour." The trays and the special cooking, the laundry and the disinfectants recalled themselves fondly to her thoughts, like items on the menu of some long-ago ball-supper, the memory of which recurred to her with a strong, possessive nostalgia.

My parents had, it seemed, by dying on her premises, become in a lively sense her property, and she dispensed them to us now, little by little, with a genuine sense of bounty, just as, later on, when I returned to her a grown-up young lady, she conceded me a diamond lavaliere of my mother's as if the trinket were an inheritance to which she had the prior claim. But her generosity with her memories appeared to us, as children, an act of the greatest indulgence. We begged her for more of these mortuary reminiscences as we might have begged for candy, and since ordinarily we not only had no candy but were permitted no friendships, no movies, and little reading beyond what our teachers prescribed for us, and were kept in quarantine, like carriers of social contagion, among the rhubarb plants of our neglected yard, these memories doled out by our grandmother became our secret treasures; we never spoke of them to each other but hoarded them, each against the rest, in the miserly fastnesses of our hearts. We returned, therefore, from our grandparents' house replenished in all our faculties; these crumbs from the rich man's table were a banquet indeed to us. We did not even mind going back to our guardians, for we now felt superior to them, and besides, as we well knew, we had no choice. It was only by accepting our situation as a just and unalterable arrangement that we could be allowed to transcend it and feel ourselves united to our grandparents in a love that was the more miraculous for breeding no practical results.

In this manner, our household was kept together, and my grandparents were spared the necessity of arriving at a fresh decision about it. Naturally, from time to time a new scandal would break out (for our guardians did not grow kinder in response to being run away from), yet we had come, at bottom, to despair of making any real change in our circumstances, and ran away hopelessly, merely to postpone punishment. And when, after five years, our Protestant grandfather, informed at last of the facts, intervened to save us, his indignation at the family surprised us nearly as much as his action. We thought it only natural that grandparents should know and do nothing, for did not God in the mansions of Heaven look down upon human suffering and allow it to take its course?

The Blackguard

WERE HE LIVING today, my Protestant grandfather would be displeased to hear that the fate of his soul had once been the occasion of intense theological anxiety with the Ladies of the Sacred Heart. While his mortal part, all unaware, went about its eighteen holes of golf, its rubber of bridge before dinner at the club, his immortal part lay in jeopardy with us, the nuns and pupils of a strict convent school set on a wooded hill quite near a piece of worthless real estate he had bought under the impression that the city was expanding in a northerly direction. A sermon delivered at the convent by an enthusiastic Jesuit had disclosed to us his danger. Up to this point, the disparity in religion between my grandfather and myself had given me no serious concern, but had seemed to me merely a variant expression of our disparity in age. The death of my parents, while it had drawn us together in many senses, including the legal one (for I became his ward), had at the same time left the gulf of a generation between us, and my grandfather's Protestantism presented itself as a natural part of the grand, granite scenery on the other side. But the Jesuit's sermon destroyed this ordered view in a single thunderclap of doctrine.

As the priest would have it, this honest and upright man, a great favorite with the Mother Superior, was condemned to eternal torment by the accident of having been baptized. Had he been a Mohammedan, a

134

Jew, a pagan, or the child of civilized unbelievers, a place in Limbo would have been assured him; Cicero and Aristotle and Cyrus the Persian might have been his companions, and the harmless souls of unbaptized children might have frolicked about his feet. But if the Jesuit were right, all baptized Protestants went straight to Hell. A good life did not count in their favor. The baptismal rite, by conferring on them God's grace, made them also liable to His organizational displeasure. That is, baptism turned them Catholic whether they liked it or not, and their persistence in the Protestant ritual was a kind of asseverated apostasy. Thus my poor grandfather, sixty years behind in his Easter duty, actually reduced his prospects of salvation every time he sat down in the Presbyterian church.

The Mother Superior's sweet frown acknowledged me, an hour after the sermon, as I curtsied, all agitation, in her office doorway. Plainly, she had been expecting me. She recognized my mission; her eyes bowed to me as if I were bereaved. Touched and thrilled by her powers of divination, by her firm sense of my character, I went in. It did not occur to me that Madame MacIllvra, an able administrator, must have been resignedly ticking off the names of the Protestant pupils and parents all during the concluding parts of the morning's service. Certainly she had a faint air, when the conversation began, of depreciating the sermon: doctrinally, perhaps, correct, it had been wanting in delicacy; the fiery Jesuit, a missionary celebrity, had lived too long among the Eskimos. This disengaged attitude encouraged me to hope. Surely this lady, the highest authority I knew, could act as mediatrix between my grandfather and God; she, a plump, middle-aged Madonna, might contrive to make God see my grandfather as a special case, outside the brutal rule of thumb laid down by the Jesuit. It was she, after all, in the convent, from whom all exemptions flowed, who created arbitrary holidays (called *congés* by the order's French tradition); it was she who per-

mitted us to get forbidden books from the librarian
and occasionally to receive letters unread by the convent censor. (As a rule, all slang expressions, viola-
tions of syntax errors of spelling, as well as improper
sentiments, were blacked out of our friends' communi-
cations, so unless we moved in a circle of young
Addisons or Burkes, the letters we longed for came to
us as fragments, from which the original text could
only be conjectured.) To my twelve-year-old mind, it
appeared probable that Madame MacIllvra, the
Mother Superior, had the power to give my grandfather *congé*, and I threw myself on her sympathies.

It was the unjust and paradoxical nature of the
Jesuit's edict that affected me. I rebelled, as Augustine
and Kierkegaard had done, against the whimsicality of
God. How could it be that my grandfather, the most
virtuous person I knew, whose name was a byword
among his friends and colleagues for a kind of rigid
and fantastic probity—how could it be that this man
should be lost, while I, the object of his admonition,
the despair of his example—I, who yielded to every
impulse, lied, boasted, betrayed—should, by virtue of
regular attendance at the sacraments and the habit of
easy penitence, be saved?

Madame MacIllvra's full white brow wrinkled; her
childlike blue eyes clouded. Like many headmis-
tresses, she loved a good cry, and she clasped me to
her quivering and quite feminine bosom. She understood; she, too, momentarily rebelled. She and my
grandfather had, as a matter of fact, established a
very amiable relation, in which both took pleasure.
The masculine line and firmness of his character made
an esthetic appeal to her, and the billowy softness and
depth of the Mother Superior struck him favorably,
but, above all, it was their difference in religion that
salted their conversations. Each of them enjoyed,
whenever they met in her straight, black-and-white
little office, a sense of broadness, of enlightenment, of
transcendent superiority to petty animosities. My

grandfather would remember that he wrote a check every Christmas for two Sisters of Charity who visited his office; Madame MacIllvra would perhaps recall her graduate studies and Hume. They had long, liberal talks which had the tone of *performances;* virtuoso feats of magnanimity were achieved on both sides. Afterward, they spoke of each other in nearly identical terms: "A very fine woman," "A very fine man."

All this (and possibly the suspicion that her verdict might be repeated at home) made Madame MacIllvra's answer slow. "Perhaps God," she murmured at last, "in His infinite mercy . . ." Yet this formulation satisfied neither of us. God's infinite mercy we believed in, but its manifestations were problematical. Sacred history showed us that it was more likely to fall on the Good Thief or the Woman Taken in Adultery than on persons of daily virtue and regular habits, like my grandfather. Our Catholic thoughts journeyed and met in a glance of alarmed recognition. Madame MacIllvra's eyelids fluttered at the blank statement of my look. A moment of silence followed, during which her lips moved ever so slightly, whether in prayer or in repetition of some half-forgotten formula, I could not tell. There were, of course, she continued smoothly, other loopholes. If he had been improperly baptized . . . a careless clergyman . . . I considered this suggestion and shook my head. My grandfather was not the kind of man who, even as an infant, would have been guilty of a slovenly baptism.

It was a measure of Madame MacIllvra's intelligence, or of her knowledge of the world, that she did not, even then, when my grandfather's soul hung, as it were, pleadingly between us, suggest the obvious, the orthodox solution. It would have been ridiculous for me to try to convert my grandfather. Indeed, as it turned out later, I might have dropped him into the pit with my innocent traps (the religious books left open beside his cigar cutter, or "Grandpa, won't you take me to Mass this Sunday? I am so tired of going alone"). "Pray for him, my dear," said Madame MacIllvra, sighing, "and I will speak to Madame Barclay. The point may be open to interpretation. She may remember something in the Fathers of the Church. . . ."

A few days later, Madame MacIllvra summoned me to her office. Not only Madame Barclay, the learned prefect of studies, but the librarian and even the convent chaplain had been called in. Books had been taken down from the highest shelves; telephone calls had been made. The Benedictine view, it seemed, differed sharply from the Dominican, but a key passage in Saint Athanasius seemed to point to my grandfather's safety. The unbeliever, according to this generous authority, was not to be damned unless he rejected the true Church with sufficient knowledge and full consent of the will. Madame MacIllvra handed me the book, and I read the passage over. Clearly, he was saved. Sufficient knowledge he had not. The Church was foreign to him; he knew it only distantly, only by repute, like the heathen Hiawatha, who had heard strange stories of missionaries, white men in black robes who bore a Cross. Flinging my arms about Madame MacIllvra, I blessed for the first time the insularity of my grandfather's character, the long-jawed, shut face it turned toward ideas and customs not its own. I resolved to dismantle at once the little altar in my bedroom at home, to leave off grace before meals, elaborate fasting, and all ostentatious practices of devotion, lest the light of my example shine upon him too powerfully and burn him with sufficient knowledge to a crisp.

Since I was a five-day boarder, this project had no time to grow stale, and the next Sunday, at home, my grandfather remarked on the change in me, which my feeling for the dramatic had made far from unobtrusive. "I hope," he said in a rather stern and ironical voice, "that you aren't using the *irreligious* atmosphere of this house as an excuse for backsliding. There will be time enough when you are older to change your beliefs if you want to." The unfairness of this rebuke delighted me. It put me solidly in the tradition of the saints and martyrs; Our Lord had known something like it, and so had Elsie Dinsmore at the piano. Nevertheless, I felt quite angry and slammed the door of my room behind me as I went in to sulk. I almost wished that my grandfather would die at once, so that God could furnish him with the explanation of my behavior—certainly he would have to wait till the next life to get it; in this one he would only have seen in it an invasion of his personal liberties.

As though to reward me for my silence, the following Wednesday brought me the happiest moment of my life. In order to understand my happiness, which might otherwise seem perverse, the reader must yield himself to the spiritual atmosphere of the convent. If he imagines that the life we led behind those walls was bare, thin, cold, austere, sectarian, he will have to revise his views; our days were a tumult of emotion. In the first place, we ate, studied, and slept in that atmosphere of intrigue, rivalry, scandal, favoritism, tyranny, and revolt that is common to all girls' boarding schools and that makes "real" life afterward seem a long and improbable armistice, a cessation of the true anguish of activity. But above the tinkling of this girlish operetta, with its clink-clink of changing friendships, its plot of smuggled letters, notes passed from desk to desk, secrets, there sounded in the Sacred Heart Convent heavier, more solemn strains, notes of a great religious drama, which was also all passion and caprice, in which salvation was the issue and God's rather sultanlike and elusive favor besought, resisted, despaired of, connived for, importuned. It was the paradoxical element in Catholic doctrine that lent this drama its suspense. The Divine Despot we courted could not be bought, like a piece of merchandise, by long hours at the prie-dieu, faithful attendance at the sacraments, obedience, reverence toward one's superiors. These solicitations helped, but it might well turn out that the worst girl in the school, whose pretty, haughty face wore rouge and a calm, closed look that advertised even to us younger ones some secret knowledge of men, was in the dark of her heart another Mary of Egypt, the strumpet-saint in our midst. Such notions furnished a strange counterpoint to discipline; surely the Mother Superior never could have expelled a girl without recalling, with a shade of perplexity, the profligate youth of Saint Augustine and of Saint Ignatius of Loyola.

This dark-horse doctrine of salvation, with all its worldly wisdom and riddling charm, was deep in the idiom of the convent. The merest lay sister could have sustained with spiritual poise her end of a conversation on the purification through sin with Mr. Auden, Herr Kafka, or *Gospodin* Dostoevski; and Madame Mac-Illvra, while she would have held it bad taste to bow down, like Father Zossima, before the murder in Dmitri Karamazov's heart, would certainly have had him in for a series of long, interesting talks in her office.

Like all truly intellectual women, these ladies were romantic desperadoes. They despised organizational heretics of the stamp of Luther and Calvin, but the great atheists and sinners were the heroes of the costume picture they taught as a subject called history. Marlowe, Baudelaire—above all, Byron—glowed like terrible stars above their literature courses. Little girls of ten were reciting "The Prisoner of Chillon" and hearing stories of Claire Clairmont, Caroline Lamb, the Segatti, and the swim across the Hellespont. Even M. Voltaire enjoyed a left-handed popularity. The nuns spoke of him with horror and admiration mingled: "A great mind, an unconquerable spirit—and what fearful use they were put to." In Rousseau, an unbuttoned, middle-class figure, they had no interest whatever.

These infatuations, shared by the pupils, were brought into line with official Catholic opinion by a vareity of stratagems. The more highly educated nuns spoke of the polarity of good and evil—did not the knowledge of evil presuppose the knowledge of God, were not the satanic poets the black apostles of the Redeemer? A simple young nun, on the other hand, who played baseball and taught arithmetic to the sixth and seventh grades, used to tell her pupils that she personally was convinced that Lord Byron in his last hours must have made an act of contrition.

It was not, therefore, unusual that a line from the works of this dissipated author should have been waiting for us on the blackboard of the eighth-grade rhetoric classroom when we filed in that Wednesday morning which remains still memorable to me. *"Zoe mou, sas agapo"*: the words of Byron's last assurance to the Maid of Athens stood there in Madame Barclay's French-looking script, speaking to us of the transiency of the passions. To me, as it happened, it spoke a twice-told tale. I had read the poem before, alone in my grandfather's library; indeed, I knew it by heart, and I rather resented the infringement on my private rights in it, the democratization of the poem which was about to take place. Soon, Madame Barclay's pointer was rapping from word to word: "My . . . life . . . I . . . love . . . you," she sharply translated. When the pointer started back for its second trip, I retreated into hauteur and began drawing a picture of the girl who sat next to me. Suddenly the pointer cracked across my writing tablet.

"You're just like Lord Byron, brilliant but unsound."

I heard the pointer being set down and the drawing being torn crisply twice across, but I could not look up. Trembling with excitement and a kind of holy terror, I sank back in my seat. Up to this moment, I had believed shallowly, with Napoleon, that the day of one's First Communion was the happiest day of one's life; now, in the glory of this sentence, I felt that petit-bourgeois notion give a sudden movement inside me and quite distinctly die. Throughout the rest of the class, I sat motionless, simulating meekness, while my classmates shot me glances of wonder, awe, and congratulation, as though I had suddenly been struck by a remarkable disease, or been canonized, or transfigured. Madame Barclay's pronouncement, which I kept repeating to myself under my breath, had for us girls a kind of final and majestic certainty. She was the severest and most taciturn of our teachers. Her dark brows met in the middle; her skin was a pure olive; her upper lip had a faint mustache; she was the iron and authority of the convent. She tolerated no infractions, overlooked nothing, was utterly and obdurately fair, had no favorites; but her rather pointed face had the marks of suffering, as though her famous discipline had scored it as harshly as one of our papers. She had a bitter and sarcastic wit, and had studied at the Sorbonne. Before this day, I had once or twice dared to say to myself that Madame Barclay liked me. Her dark, quite handsome eyes would sometimes move in my direction as her lips prepared an aphorism or a satiric gibe. Yet hardly had I estimated the look, weighed and measured it to store it away in my memory book of requited affections, when a stinging penalty would recall me from my dream and I could no longer be sure. Now, however, there was no doubt left. The reproof was a declaration of love as plain as the sentence on the blackboard, which shimmered slightly before my eyes. My happiness was a confused exaltation in which the fact that I was Lord Byron and the fact that I was loved by Madame Barclay, the most puzzling nun in the convent, blended in a Don Juanesque triumph.

In the refectory that noon, publicity was not wanting to enrich this moment. Insatiable, I could hardly wait for the weekend, to take Madame Barclay's words as though they had been a prize. With the generosity of affluence, I spoke to myself of sharing this happiness, this honor, with my grandfather. Surely, *this* would make up to him for any worry or difficulty I had caused him. At the same time, it would have the practical effect of explaining me a little to him. Phrases about my prototype rang in my head: "that unfortunate genius," "that turbulent soul," "that gifted and erratic nature."

My grandfather turned dark red when he heard the news. His forehead grew knotty with veins; he swore; he looked strange and young; it was the first time I had ever seen him angry. Argument and explanation were useless. For my grandfather, history had interposed no distance between Lord Byron and himself. Though the incestuous poet had died forty years before my grandfather was born, the romantic perspective was lacking. That insularity of my grandfather's that kept him intimate with morals and denied the reality of the exotic made him judge the poet as he judged himself or one of his neighbors—that is, on the merit of his actions. He was on the telephone at once, asking the Mother Superior in a thundering, courtroom voice what right one of his sisters had to associate his innocent granddaughter with that degenerate blackguard, Byron. On Monday, Madame Barclay, with tight-drawn lips, told her class that she had a correction to make: Mary McCarthy did not resemble Lord Byron in any particular; she was neither brilliant, loose-living, nor unsound.

The interviews between my grandfather and Madame MacIllvra came to an end. To that remarkable marriage of minds the impediment had at last been discovered. But from this time on, Madame Barclay's marks of favor to me grew steadily more distinct, while the look of suffering tightened on her face, till some said she had cancer (a theory supported by the yellowness of her skin) and some said she was being poisoned by an antipathy to the Mother Superior.

C. Y. E.

NEAR THE CORNER of Fourteenth Street and Fourth Avenue, there is a store called Cye Bernard. I passed it the other day on my way to the Union Square subway station. To my intense surprise, a heavy blush spread over my face and neck, and my insides contorted in that terrible grimace of shame that is generally associated with hangovers. I averted my eyes from the sign and hurried into the subway, my head bent so that no observer should discover my secret identity, which until that moment I had forgotten myself. Now I pass this sign every day, and it is always a question whether I shall look at it or not. Usually I do, but hastily, surreptitiously, with an ineffective air of casualness, lest anybody suspect that I am crucified there on that building, hanging exposed in black script lettering to advertise bargains in men's haberdashery.

The strangest part about it is that this unknown clothier on Fourteenth Street should not only incorporate in his name the mysterious, queerly spelled nickname I was given as a child in the convent, but that he should add to this the name of my patron saint, St. Bernard of Clairvaux, whom I chose for my special protector at a time when I was suffering from the nickname. It is nearly enough to convince me that life is a system of recurrent pairs, the poison and the antidote being eternally packaged together by some considerate heavenly druggist. St. Bernard, however, was, from my point of view, never so useful as the dog that

144

bears his name, except in so far as he represented the contemplative, bookish element in the heavenly hierarchy, as opposed, say, to St. Martin of Tours, St. Francis Xavier or St. Aloysius of Gonzaga, who was of an ineffable purity and died young. The life of action was repellent to St. Bernard, though he engaged in it from time to time; on the other hand, he was not a true *exalté*—he was, in short, a sedentary man, and it was felt, in the convent, I think, that he was a rather odd choice for an eleven-year-old girl, the nuns themselves expressing some faint bewilderment and concern, as older people do when a child is presented with a great array of toys and selects from among them a homely and useful object.

It was marvelous, I said to myself that day on the subway, that I could have forgotten so easily. In the official version of my life the nickname does not appear. People have asked me, now and then, whether I have ever had a nickname and I have always replied, No, it is funny but I do not seem to be the type that gets one. I have even wondered about it a little myself, asking, Why is it that I have always been Mary, world without end, Amen, feeling a faint pinch of regret and privation, as though a cake had been cut and no favor, not even the old maid's thimble or the miser's penny, been found in my piece. How political indeed is the personality, I thought. What coalitions and cabals the party in power will not make to maintain its uncertain authority! Nothing is sacred. The past is manipulated to serve the interests of the present. For any bureaucracy, amnesia is convenient. The name of Trotsky drops out of the chapter on the revolution in the Soviet textbooks—what shamelessness, we say, while in the meantime our discarded selves languish in the Lubianka of the unconscious. But a moment comes at last, after the régime has fallen, after all interested parties are dead, when the archives are opened and the old ghosts walk, and history must be rewritten in the light of fresh discoveries.

It was happening to me then, as I sat frozen in my seat, staring at the picture of Miss Subways, February 1943, who loves New York and spends her spare time writing to her two officer-brothers in the Army and Navy. The heavy doors of the mind swung on their hinges. I was back in the convent, a pale new girl sitting in the front of the study hall next to a pretty, popular eighth-grader, whom I bored and who resented having me for a deskmate. I see myself perfectly: I am ambitious, I wish to make friends with the most exciting and powerful girls; at the same time, I am naive, without stratagems, for I think that I have only to be myself. The first rebuffs startle me. I look around and see that there is a social pyramid here and that I and my classmates are on the bottom. I study the disposition of stresses and strains and discover that two girls, Elinor Henehan and Mary Heinrichs, are important, and that their approval is essential to my happiness.

There were a great many exquisite and fashionable-looking girls in the convent, girls with Irish or German names, who used make-up in secret, had suitors, and always seemed to be on the verge of a romantic elopement. There were also some very pretty Protestant girls, whose personal charms were enhanced for us by the exoticism of their religion—the nuns telling us that we should always be especially considerate of them because they were Protestants, and, so to speak, our guests, with the result that we treated them reverently, like French dolls. These two groups made up the élite of the convent; the nuns adored them for their beauty, just as we younger girls did; and they enjoyed far more réclame than the few serious students who were thought to have the vocation.

Elinor Henehan and Mary Heinrichs fell into neither category. They were funny, lazy, dangling girls, fourteen or fifteen years old, with baritone voices, very black hair, and an insouciant attitude toward convent life. It was said that they came from east of the mountains. Elinor Henehan was tall and bony, with horn-rimmed glasses; Mary Heinrichs was shorter and plump. Their blue serge uniforms were always a mess, the collars and cuffs haphazardly sewn on and worn a day or so after they ought to have been sent to the laundry. They broke rules constantly, talking in study hall, giggling in chapel.

Yet out of these unpromising personal materials, they had created a unique position for themselves. They were the school clowns. And like all clowns they had made a shrewd bargain with life, exchanging dignity for power, and buying with servility to their betters immunity from the reprisals of their equals or inferiors. For the upper school they travestied themselves, exaggerating their own odd physical characteristics, their laziness, their eccentric manner of talking. With the lower school, it was another story: we were the performers, the school the audience, they the privileged commentators from the royal box. Now it was our foibles, our vanities, our mannerisms that were on display, and the spectacle was apparently so hilarious that it was a continual challenge to the two girls' self-control. They lived in a recurrent spasm of mirth. On the playground, at the dinner-table, laughter would dangerously overtake them; one would whisper to the other and then a wordless rocking would begin, till finally faint anguished screams were heard, and the nun in charge clapped her clapper for silence.

What was unnerving about this laughter—unnerving especially for the younger girls—was its general, almost abstract character. More often than not, we had no idea what it was that Elinor and Mary were laughing at. A public performance of any sort—a recital, a school play—instantly reduced them to jelly. Yet what was there about somebody's humble and pedestrian performance of *The Merry Peasant* that was so uniquely comic? Nobody could tell, least of all the performer. To be the butt of this kind of joke was a singularly painful experience, for you were never in a position to turn the tables, to join in the laughter at your own expense, because you could not possibly pretend to know what the joke was. Actually, as I see now, it was the intimacy of the two girls that set their standard: from the vantage point of their private world, anything outside seemed strange and ludicrous. It was our very existence they laughed at, as the peasant laughs at the stranger from another province. The occasions of mirth—a request for the salt, a trip to the dictionary in the study hall—were mere pretexts; our personalities *in themselves* were incredible to them. At the time, however, it was very confusing. Their laughter was a kind of crazy compass that was steering the school. Nobody knew, ever, where the whirling needle would stop, and many of us lived in a state of constant apprehension, lest it should point to *our* desk, lest we become, if only briefly, the personification of all that was absurd, the First Cause of this cosmic mirth.

Like all such inseparable friends, they delighted in nicknames, bestowing them in godlike fashion, as though by renaming their creatures they could perform a new act of creation, a secular baptism. And as at the baptismal font we had passed from being our parents' children to being God's children, so now we passed from God's estate to a societal trolls' world presided over by these two unpredictable deities. They did not give nicknames to everybody. You had to have some special quality to be singled out by Elinor and Mary, but what that quality was only Elinor and Mary could tell. I saw very soon (the beginnings of wisdom) that I had two chances of finding an honorable place in the convent system: one was to escape being nicknamed altogether, the other was to earn for myself an appellation that, while humorous, was still benevolent; rough, perhaps, but tender. On the whole, I would have preferred the first alternative, as being less chancy. Months passed, and no notice was taken of me; my anxiety diminished; it seemed as though I might get my wish.

They broke the news to me one night after study hall. We were filing out of the large room when Elinor stepped out of the line to speak to me. "We have got one for you," she said. "Yes?" I said calmly, for really (I now saw) I had known it all along, known that there was something about me that would inevitably appeal to these two strange girls. I stiffened up in readiness, feeling myself to be a sort of archery target: there was no doubt that they could hit me (I was an easy mark), but, pray God, it be one of the larger concentric circles, not, oh Blessed Virgin, the red, tender bull's-eye at the heart. I could not have imagined what was in store for me. "Cye," said Elinor and began to laugh, looking at me oddly because I did not laugh too. "Si?" I asked, puzzled. I was a new girl, it was true, but I did not come from the country. "C-Y-E," said Elinor, spelling. "But what does it mean?" I asked the two of them, for Mary had now caught up with her. They shook their dark heads and laughed. "Oh no," they said. "We can't tell you. But it's very, very good. Isn't it?" they asked each other. "It's one of our best."

I saw at once that it was useless to question them. They would never tell me, of course, and I would only make myself ridiculous, even more Cye-like, if I persisted. It occurred to me that if I showed no anxiety, they would soon forget about it, but my shrewdness was no match for theirs. The next day it was all over the school. It was called to me on the baseball field, when the young nun was at bat; it was whispered from head to head down the long refectory table at dinner. It rang through the corridors in the dormitory. "What does it mean?" I would hear a girl ask. Elinor or Mary would whisper in her ear, and the girl would cast me a quick glance, and then laugh. Plainly, they had hit me off to a T, and as I saw this my curiosity overcame my fear and my resentment. I no longer cared how derogatory the name might be; I would stand anything. I said to myself, if only I could know it. If only I had some special friend who could find out and then tell me. But I was new and a little queer, anyway, it seemed; I had no special friends, and now it was part of the joke that the whole school should know, and know that I wanted to know and not tell me. My isolation, which had been obscure, was now conspicuous, and, as it were, axiomatic. Nobody could ever become my friend, because to do so would involve telling me and Elinor and Mary would never forgive that.

It was up to me to guess it, and I would lie in bed at night, guessing wildly, as though against time, like the miller's upstart daughter in Rumpelstiltskin. Outlandish phrases would present themselves: "Catch your elbow," "Cheat your end." Or, on the other hand, sensible ones that were humiliating: "Clean your ears." One night I got up and poured water into the china basin and washed my ears in the dark, but when I looked at the washcloth in the light the next morning, it was perfectly clean. And in any case, it seemed to me that the name must have some more profound meaning. My fault was nothing ordinary that you could do something about, like washing your ears. Plainly, it was something immanent and irremediable, a spiritual taint. And though I could not have told precisely what my wrongness consisted in, I felt its existence almost tangible during those nights, and knew that it had always been with me, even in the other school, where I had been popular, good at games, good at dramatics; I had always had it, a kind of miserable effluvium of the spirit that the ordinary sieves of report cards and weekly confessions had been powerless to catch.

Now I saw that I could never, as I had hoped, belong to the convent's inner circles, not to the tier of beauty, nor to the tier of manners and good deportment, which was signalized by wide moiré ribbons, awarded once a week, blue, green, or pink, depending on one's age, that were worn in a sort of bandolier style, crosswise from shoulder to hip. I could take my seat in the dowdy tier of scholarship, but my social acquaintance would be limited to a few frowzy little girls of my own age who were so insignificant, so contemptible, that they did not even know what my nickname stood for. Even they, I thought, were better off than I, for they knew their place, they accepted the fact that they were unimportant little girls. No older girl would bother to jeer at them, but in me there was something overweening, over-eager, over-intense, that had brought upon me the hateful name. Now my only desire was to be alone, and in the convent this was difficult, for the nuns believed that solitude was appropriate for anchorites, but for growing girls, unhealthy. I went to the library a great deal and read all of Cooper, and *Stoddard's Lectures.* I became passionately religious, made a retreat with a fiery missionary Jesuit, spent hours on my knees in adoration of the Blessed Sacrament, but even in the chapel, the name pursued me: glancing up at the cross, I would see the initials, I.N.R.I.; the name that had been given Christ in mockery now mocked me, for I was not a prig and I knew that my sufferings were ignoble and had nothing whatever in common with God's. And, always, there was no avoiding the communal life, the older girls passing as I crept along the corridor with a little knot of my classmates. "Hello, Cye."

Looking back, I see that if I had ever burst into tears publicly, begged for quarter, compunction would have been felt. Some goddess of the college department would have comforted me, spoken gently to Elinor and Mary, and the nickname would have been dropped. Perhaps it might even have been explained to me. But I did not cry, even alone in my room. I chose what was actually the more shameful part. I accepted the nickname, made a sort of joke of it, used it brazenly myself on the telephone, during vacations, calling up to ask a group of classmates to the movies:

"This is Cye speaking." But all the time I was making plans, writing letters home, arranging my escape. I resolved that once I was out of the convent, I would never, never, never again let anybody see what I was like. That, I felt, had been my mistake.

The day I left the Mother Superior cried. "I think you will grow up to be a novelist," she said, "and that can be a fine thing, but I want you to remember all your life the training you have had here in the convent."

I was moved and thrilled by the moment, the prediction, the parting adjuration. "Yes," I said, weeping, but I intended to forget the convent within twenty-four hours. And in this I was quite successful.

The nickname followed me for a time, to the public high school I entered. One of the girls said to me, "I hear you are called Cye." "Yes," I replied easily. "How do you spell it?" she asked. "S-I," I said. "Oh," she said. "That's funny." "Yes," I said. "I don't know why they called me that." This version of the nickname lasted perhaps three weeks. At the end of that time, I dropped the group of girls who used it, and I never heard it again.

Now, however, the question has been reopened. What do the letters stand for? A happy solution occurred to me yesterday, on Fifteenth Street and Fourth Avenue. "Clever Young Egg," I said to myself out loud. The words had arranged themselves without my volition, and instantly I felt that sharp, cool sense of relief and triumph that one has on awakening from a nightmare. Could that have been it? Is it possible that that was all? Is it possible that Elinor and Mary really divined nothing, that they were paying me a sort of backhanded compliment, nothing certainly that anybody could object to? I began to laugh at myself, affectionately, as one does after a long worry, saying, "You fool, look how silly you've been." "Now I can go back," I thought happily, without reflection, just as though I were an absconding bank teller who had been living for years with his spiritual bags packed, waiting for the charges against him to be dropped that he might return to his native town. A vision of the study hall rose before me, with my favorite nun on the platform and the beautiful girls in their places. My heart rushed forward to embrace it.

But, alas, it is too late. Elinor Henehan is dead, my favorite nun has removed to another convent, the beautiful girls are married—I have seen them from time to time and no longer aspire to their friendship. And as for the pale, plain girl in the front of the study hall, her, too, I can no longer reach. I see her creeping down the corridor with a little knot of her classmates. "Hello, Cye," I say with a touch of disdain for her rawness, her guileless ambition. I should like to make her a pie-bed, or drop a snake down her back, but unfortunately the convent discipline forbids such open brutality. I hate her, for she is my natural victim, and it is I who have given her the name, the shameful, inscrutable name that she will never, sleepless in her bed at night, be able to puzzle out.

III

III

was private, as twilight it was; you could tell from
the old green rowboats drawn up on the shore and the
little fishing hut and the kayak that the place must
belong to somebody. But you could not refuse them
even when they paid you the courtesy of asking. The
young mothers were accustomed to reply, in that soft

new people swam there. Whereupon the new people,
already dressed in bathing suits, would park their car
at an awkward angle and, pantomiming thankfulness

The Appalachian Revolution

IN JULY, the first week, the psychiatrists came. A
heavy black car with a black-and-orange license plate
appeared on the dirt road to the lake, known as Mirror Lake on the road map but always spoken of by
the natives and the "old" summer people as Poor
Farm Pond. The car hesitated for a moment at the
trampled clearing in the bushes where a number of
dusty station wagons and shabby sedans and convert-
ibles and a trailer were already parked. On the small
strip of muddied beach at the road's left, a group of
young matrons and their children sat, not moving; behind the bushes, in the meadow, a young couple, sun-
bathing, raised their heads and let them drop back in
disgust. A curtain twitched in the trailer. In the water,
a rowboat manned by a small, curly-haired boy came
to a halt as the rower stared darkly at the automobile,
whose engine made the only sound in the bristling silence. It was as if Poor Farm Pond were holding its
breath, beseeching the intruders to pass on. But the
big car was deaf to entreaty; a mop of gray hair protruded from the window by the driver's seat and
nodded with commanding emphasis to another car,
behind. The horn tooted, "Doctor, here is the place."

On the beach, the young mothers sighed and
reached for their cigarettes. The new cars always hesitated and always concluded this was the place. If
(unlike these latest arrivals) the occupants were well
mannered, they called out to ask whether the beach

was private, as evidently it was; you could tell from the old green rowboats drawn up on the shore and the little fishing hut and the kayak that the place must belong to somebody. But you could not refuse them, even when they paid you the courtesy of asking. The young mothers were accustomed to reply, in their soft, anxious, scrupled voices, that the beach *was* private but that the owner would not mind, probably, if the new people swam there. Whereupon the new people, already dressed in bathing suits, would park their car at an awkward angle and, pantomiming thankfulness, heat, exhaustion, plunge into the water, stirring up the bottom, while the children looked on coldly and angrily, sometimes groaning aloud, until the mothers shushed them. "Why did you tell them they *could,* Mother, for heaven's sake!" the adolescent girls would wail when the newcomers had struck out for the middle, and the young matrons, noble Romans, would answer with simple dignity, "You must remember, it doesn't belong to *us* either, dear."

But this statuesque reminder did not express the felt truth, which was that the beach did belong to Us, for the group of young mothers had been coming here ever so long, with the owner's permission—since Mother's or Grandmother's day, in many cases, right back almost to the time when the tall, tumbling house up the road, with its old raspberry patch, had been the town poor farm. And it was they, the young mothers and their husbands and occasional house guests, who had made the place a beach. Before they came, the bottom had just been mud and slippery brown leaves, like the rest of the lake's margin; they had imported the sand. Every summer, they conscientiously laid down a new load of it, and every summer, on the first warm weekend, one of the husbands and some of the prep-school boy cousins would go and find the old raft, at the other end of the lake, where it had drifted to during the winter, and tow it back to the beach and moor it, so that the children could dive.

So they did have the right to say no, as the children begged them to do, but they did not have the temerity or the cruelty to, especially since Lodestone Pond, where the natives and the French Canadians from the nearby granite town had been swimming from time immemorial, had been taken over by the beavers.

There were other places, admittedly, even now, for the public to patronize, but either they were marshy or stony or froggy or had bloodsuckers or you had to pay to park there or pay to be rowed out to the middle. This spot on Poor Farm Pond, thanks to the work that had gone into it, was something pretty enviable in a region where the swimming was nothing to boast about. There was really quite a problem. The young mothers and their husbands had discussed it until they were sickened by the subject. *Their* mothers, the grandmothers, crisply advised them to take action— buy the place and put up "No Trespassing" signs and a fence. But that, smiled the young mothers sadly, was a different generation talking. Few would criticize the grandmothers for putting up "No Trespassing" signs, or even a fence, because the grandmothers, like the children, did not know any better; they had not gone to Vassar or Bryn Mawr. And in any case the owner, who was elderly and deaf and peculiar, had no inclination to sell. A year ago, one of the husbands had approached him with a tentative offer, but the old man had misunderstood. "Use it, use it!" he had shouted benevolently in his flat, deaf voice. "You folks have always used it." And whenever he drove by, on a Sunday, in his new Buick, and saw a crowd of people in the water, he smiled and nodded like a Maecenas. If he had ever swum himself, he might have seen the hardships of having twenty or thirty strangers and their dripping dogs crowd onto two hundred and fifty square feet of specially imported sand, but, like so many of the old-timers, Mr. Bascomb was wary of the water. It was in winter he used the pond; the fishing hut on the shore belonged to him, and every winter he pulled it out to the pond's center, cut a hole through the ice, and, protected from the elements, fished through the hut's open bottom. This was his asserted reason for refusing to sell, even though the would-be buyer, a Washington lawyer, had assured him that he could retain, in the deed, the right to fish from the shore lot and the right to keep the hut there. The real reason, observed the grandmothers, was that the old man was land-proud; he liked to know that the "old" summer people and the man with the trailer, who kept a grocery store across the mountains, were beholden to him every year for their swimming.

"Money talks," opined the local real-estate man, counselling a higher offer. But the young mothers firmly shook their heads; if old Mr. Bascomb was really disinclined to sell, it would not be fair to tempt him with an appeal to his baser nature. It would surely hurt the old man to come by on his Sunday drive and see a place barred that had always been open; even the grandmothers conceded this, when pressed by their daughters. There was a tacit covenant in the region governing change, property rights, and the relations between the summer people and the natives, though the old ladies, who were supposed to be its custodians, were growing more and more wayward and forgetful of their duties. *Quis custodiet ipsos custodes?* angrily cried a Swarthmore classics professor when his mother-in-law "surprised" her grandchildren by damming up her brook to make a swimming pool for them. You did not make swimming pools in Minster; the spirit of the place frowned on it. Here in this secluded corner of a northern state, with its spruce forests and mountain panoramas and round red cow barns and abandoned quarries and bears and wildcats and beavers, there was a tradition of pioneer simplicity and frugality of which the summer people were supposed to be proud. There were no estates or country clubs; there was not, as yet, even a cocktail set, properly speaking. The summer ladies baked and put up jellies

and preserves, sharing their recipes with the farm
women; the children went blueberrying and raspberry-
ing, and sold Kool-Aid on Sundays and holidays at
roadside stands under the maple shade. There was a
dairy cooperative and an electrical cooperative and a
cooperative store; the gaunt little towns, with their
cheese factories, had pallid fairs and barbecues and
lawn fêtes and Fourth of July displays. The whole
valley was different from the other side of the mountain range, where there were winter ski resorts and
summer tourist hotels and gentlemen-farmers and
Black Angus cattle. The summer people even dressed
differently. The old ladies—widows of clergymen and
college professors and lawyers—still wore white straw
hats and printed lawn dresses; the husbands wore old
clothes, and the young mothers, for the most part,
blouses and skirts and moccasins. They came to the
beach with liberal magazines and serious books borrowed from the library at the state capital and discussed world events and local oddities while keeping
an eye on the children in the water. The "difference"
of the place rested responsibly on their minds; they
were anxious to preserve it, as an heirloom, for their
children, like one of Grandma's quilts. They had a
cupboard language of place names, unknown to the
mapmakers, for the ponds, brooks, and mountain
peaks: harsh names that had been passed on to them
by the old-timers, quaint names that had been coined
by the children—Bloodsucker Pond, Quag Pond, Hunger Brook, Sodom Marsh, Niggerhead, Dogface, the
Dark Tarn, Sliding Pools. They knew the wildflowers
and the birds and the snakes. Some of them had taken
a geology course at college, and, sitting to dry on slabs
of limestone, they talked eagerly of regional forma-
tions—Ordovician, pre-Devonian, metamorphic rock,
the mica schist in the gorges.

And the place *was* beautiful—"beyoutifull," as the
two psychiatrists, alighting from their big black cars,
now informed their womenfolk. The mop-haired psy-

chiatrist took a stand on the narrow strip of sand, surveyed the birch-fringed lake, and addressed his colleague. "I like the background," he stated, in an authoritative foreign voice, while the young mothers, a few feet away, but disregarded, as if by a stage convention, faintly grimaced at each other. "It's like a picture." Indeed it was. Like many northern lakes, with green waters reflecting the near birch and the long ridge of spruce trees rising sharply from the far shore, it resembled a picture on a calendar; one could imagine an Indian maiden and her lover in a birch canoe drifting across the canvas. But from the vantage point of the young mothers and their huddle of curious children, the psychiatrists themselves and their wives and female secretaries ("Right away, Doctor") were now in the picture also.

From their cars they brought out rainbow-striped beach towels and two large tan blankets, a portable radio, the New York *Times,* sun-tan oil, Noxzema, and two inner tubes. The two older women, disrobed, displayed mountains of white flesh and bulging veins spilling out of very tight new bathing suits, one lavender, one black; they wore white cut-out fancy sandals on short, fat white feet. While the two younger women oiled themselves and lay down, shoulder straps dropped, to sun themselves on towels, the rest of the party spread the blankets, turned on the radio, opened the newspaper. Twirling the dial, the reclining fat women sought a news program, found dance music, household hints, a French-language broadcast from Canada, a ball game; they propped their waved heads on their palms to appraise the frowning young mothers in their decorous bathing suits, who had reopened their books and magazines and were pointedly trying to read. The smaller psychiatrist, who had a bald head, thickly wrinkled brown skin, and bowed legs, impatiently switched off the radio ("Please! We are here to enjoy Nature") and began to tell his colleague about a flattering letter he had once received from

Stekel. His colleague answered with an anecdote about Ferenczi. The men's voices were loud and heavily stressed; each repeated the other's final line, chorus-like, on a rising note: "I had a letter from Stekel." "So? You had a letter from Stekel?" And then, to the lavender-suited woman, who wore a hearing aid: "Martha, he had a letter from Stekel." The lake magnified this dialogue, as it did every sound; ordinarily, you could hear a fish jump half a mile away or an old Victrola playing in a house on the ridge.

The young mothers rattled their magazines. In sheer self-defense, they declared afterward, they started a show conversation of their own, talking in high, strained voices of impersonal, mannerly things, till the children took it as a game and began to shout commonplaces at each other. *"Nice day!"* they bellowed. *"Looks to me like rain!"* "Sh-h-h!" duteously murmured the mothers, coloring. "These people will think you're copying them." "Mother, who *are* they?" whispered a pig-tailed girl, under cover of the radio, which had been turned on again. In this region, every stranger was supposed to be known, or at any rate identifiable. "They're psychiatrists, I think, dear," whispered back her mother, unplaiting the child's wet braids. "That's a sort of doctor that fixes your soul when it's sick." This explanation was uttered on a sweet, pensive, "understanding" tone that made the other mothers squirm. "How ridiculous," said a boy, with a scornful glance at the soul doctors. "It's not ridiculous; it's a science," reproved his mother. "It's not a science, it's a pseudo science—isn't it, Mother? That's what you and Daddy think," said another boy. "Hush," said his mother, equably. "Manners! We will talk about it when we get home." "But, mother, where do they *come* from?" persisted the first child, irritably pulling her long hair away from her parent's hands. "New York, silly—you can see it on their license plates," said the second boy. "I can see *that,*" said the girl. "I mean up here, in Minster." And the mothers' widened eyes appealed to each other. "I know that, too," said the same sturdy boy calmly as the mothers turned to stare at him. "They're staying at Meade Farm." "Ah-h-h," cried the mothers softly. Meade Farm was a boarding farm fifteen miles away, in the next township, that advertised "Cultured Surroundings" in the *Saturday Review*. "Are you sure?" "How did you find out?" "I listened," answered the boy simply. "You only have to listen to find out everything about them." The mothers smiled fondly among themselves; this eight-year-old was the brightest of all their progeny, and every mother loved him as if he were a communal holding. "But why do they come *here?*" demanded a hoarse twelve-year-old. "Nobody from Meade Farm has ever come here before." The mothers smiled wanly. "Somebody must have told them about it."

There it was: what could you do? It was foolish to imagine you could keep Poor Farm Pond and this special beach a community secret forever and yet, alackaday, these psychiatrists were the first rank outsiders to find their way along the dusty network of back roads and "discover" it, as they were now proclaiming to each other in blaring, self-commendatory tones. ("I am a water witch, eh, Doctor?" the mop-haired man chuckled.) Everybody else who had come here either was local, like the granite workers and the townspeople from the state capital, or had some thread of connection with one of the original summer families. If you did not know them, they knew a friend or a friend of a friend. The young mothers could not but feel, forlornly, that they were witnessing the end of an epoch as they watched the frizzle-headed psychiatrist, who had sloping shoulders and breasts like a woman, don a black bathing cap and stride into the water with one of the inner tubes. Soon he was shouting, through the megaphone of his hands, that the water was wonderful and splashing himself to demonstrate it, like a man in a shower. The small brown psychiatrist fitted on a nose clip and followed him, and finally the whole party was in the water, with the inner tubes and a ball; the two immense older women floated in the inner tubes; the men tossed the ball back and forth to each other; the secretaries lay sunning on the raft.

It did not occur to them, probably, that they were monopolizing the water—this was the kindest explanation and the one that had to be given the children, who were looking on with poison-steeped eyes, like little savages seeing the white man preëmpt the happy hunting ground. One atavistic little girl, in fact, picked up her homemade bow and arrow and, pointing it at the bathing party, glanced around, grinning boldly, for approval; her mother seized her wrist, slapped it, and confiscated the toy. But the children could not be quelled. One and all, they were refusing to swim while these *awful* people were in the water. They were unmoved by the force of example—"Come, Mummy will swim with you," announced one resolute matron—and coldly indifferent to the argument, usually decisive for them, that they would hurt the people's feelings. On the other hand, despite whispered cajolery, they declined to leave and go and take a dip in Granny's pool or be driven to a pothole, ten miles off, made by a waterfall on Dogface—a mossy, cold, green balsamy, hidden spot that was saved for special treats. The older children simply sat, wrapped in dirty towels, and stared adamantly at the strangers, while the younger ones, not comprehending, began to whimper. The mothers gazed at each other pregnantly. The children's attitude seemed a judgment handed down from on high; it absolved them of responsibility. They did not wish to be snobbish or over-fastidious, God knew, but there was a limit. They consulted their wristwatches; they shrugged. Grasping towels, children, sneakers, reading matter, they rose in panoplied purpose and picked their way to their cars, past the psychiatrists' outspread gear. It was only three-thirty, and the sun still lay warm on the violated pond.

"There is a limit, Pick," said Margaret Callaway to her husband, striding into her house with a retinue of weeping children behind her. Tall and olive-skinned, with a long, aristocratic nose and a shock of black short hair, she confronted her husband with the air of an avenging queen. "The children mutinied," she announced. "All of them. Ours and everybody else's." And she recited what had happened, crisply, while the children bated their sobs to listen to the account of their grievance.

"The children simply copied your attitude," said Pickman ("Pickles") Callaway, an industrial consultant, when he had heard. "I *knew* you would say that," answered his wife, between her teeth. "I *knew* it, I knew it. But, Pick, I promise you I didn't say a word —not a word." Her vocal cords had got tight, producing a strained noise; the children looked up at her curiously. "You didn't have to say a word," said Pickles, in a more sympathetic tone. "You obviously *looked* volumes. Kids are animals," he added, stroking a small, crew-cut head. "They felt you stiffen up the way a dog feels it when a human being is afraid."

Margaret slumped into a chair. "You are right," she said desolately. "I was wrong." She vented an exhausted sigh. To be *in the right* was Margaret's consuming ambition, to which all meaner aims had been sacrificed. She was a sincerely moral person, as Pickles Callaway, who had no morals, was always discovering to his surprise. Poor Margaret (as he privately styled her) had been renowned as a big brain at college; she had inherited a tidy wad from a Massachusetts millowning family; she had a successful husband, three beautiful children, a knack for household management, troops of friends; two winters before, she had had a tremendous nervous breakdown, which was all that was needed, Pickles once remarked (in a jest oft repeated in Minster), to complete the picture of the all-round woman of the year. Yet her accomplishments and sensibilities galled her, like handicaps imposed in the race for perfection. Margaret was a thoroughbred, the grandmothers averred, and with her distant, alarmed gaze and flaring nostrils and restive gait, she had the strained look of a blood mare carrying extra weight. Like all the Minster matrons, she worried a great deal about her privileges, which obliged her, she knew, to make allowances for those who had not had them. At the same time, the shortcomings of others seemed to her a sort of *unfairness,* a drain on her resources of understanding that was bleeding her white. Her mind, Pickles complained, was like a civics textbook, and Minster had served her for a model of what she believed possible.

It was Margaret, preëminently, who had been the conscience of Poor Farm Pond, the watchdog of the *genius loci.* She had been outraged by the plan to buy the shore lot from old Mr. Bascomb; she had grown heated in defense of the granite workers who came to the pond on Sundays in trucks and cars that blocked the parking space. It was not much of a sacrifice, she pointed out, in her high-pitched Bostonian voice, for the summer people to give up Poor Farm Pond one day in the week to men who worked six days at heavy labor. The fact that she had voted Republican in the last two Presidential elections (in the interests of the national welfare and public harmony, relinquishing her own preference for the Democratic candidates) gave this pro-labor statement of hers an air of disinterested equity that silenced all opposition. Wives whose husbands flew up just for the weekend—unlike fortunate Pick, who took the summers off—were free, she cheerily suggested, to drive the extra miles to the waterfall, where they would be rewarded by a wonderful view. And to demonstrate the feasibility of this she had started a series of prodigious Sunday-lunch mountain picnics, to which everybody brought a covered dish.

And last year, when parties of high-school students from the state capital, twenty miles away, began to come to the pond on Saturday afternoons, late, and sometimes Sundays, too, and leave beer cans and paper plates and candy wrappers behind them, Margaret had remained staunch and organized a work detail with her children to clean up the beach on Monday mornings. The other mothers were grateful to Margaret's superior energy; the fact that Margaret outdistanced them in her zeal for local democracy, as in everything else, allowed them to praise her without emulation. "She enjoys it; let her do it," decreed the husbands when the other mothers voiced a qualm. But this, alas, was false. Margaret believed in the force of example and was always perplexed when other people did not follow her lead; she did not understand how anybody could see the *right thing* and not desire, urgently, to imitate or surpass it. She did not really enjoy the cleanup; picking up dirty papers with a pointed stick, she felt lonely and a little absurd, as if her friends' absence were a subtle criticism. And the children, usually so compliant, hated this early-morning chore. Sometimes, too, they found things in the bushes that led them to ask premature questions. This, in turn, showed Margaret that she was making a grave mistake. The children were learning to hate the public-high students who left this jetsam behind them; she had perhaps found the surest way of turning her children into snobs and disgusting them with sex as well. Therefore, this year, every Monday, Margaret rose quietly, before the children were awake, and drove in her jeep down to the pond to clean the beach herself. Pickles Callaway, who once accompanied her, promptly declared that the whole idea was masochistic. "Delegate power, my dear," he commanded. "Make the other gals help you. They swim here, too."

But this was cavalier husband talk. Pick in his heart knew better: the other girls were not Margaret. Even her best friends, Ginny and Adelaide, after two Mondays of it, would be shirking and sending their husbands to try and overcome Mr. Bascomb with an offer of more money. If Margaret wished to preserve the tradition, she would have to clean the beach herself. There was no other solution, Pickles had to admit as he felt Margaret stir every Monday morning in the bed beside him. You could not get the town to clean the beach, because the town did not own it; you could not get old Mr. Bascomb to do it; and you could not leave it littered. You *could* set up a trash can with a sign, "Please dump here," but this would invite the inference that the beach was public—an inference nobody, not even Margaret, wanted the community to draw, for despite everything, despite the weekend incursions and the trailer and old Mr. Bascomb's attitude, the township itself still understood that this peninsula jutting into Poor Farm Pond "belonged" to the summer people who had brought the sand and the raft. The Minster youngsters used the swimming holes in the brooks and another part of Poor Farm Pond, a reedy shallow cove round the bend where a man had rowboats to rent. And when the granite workers came on Sunday—whole enormous families of them, with a long picnic table on their truck—they, too, understood that the place had a prior claim on it and treated it with respect. They were shy, nice, traditional people who sent to ask permission for their children to use the rowboats and always left them in good order, pulled up on the beach. Even the high-school students were well aware that this was the summer people's preserve and never came when the young mothers were there but waited till the last station wagon had driven off before starting their parties. Sometimes, on a weekday, a pair of young lovers would come walking, hand in hand, up the road, carrying their bathing suits to change in the meadow, but lovers had special rights everywhere—the whole natural world "belonged" to them.

This was democracy, the summer colonists consoled themselves whenever they were tempted to look back with longing to a time when they had had the pond all to themselves. It was not ideal but it worked; given tact and mutual forbearance, you could always find a modus vivendi. And in dreamy moods, some of the mothers looked upon Poor Farm Pond as a sort of parable for today, the kind of thing you saw with pictures in the Sunday-magazine section: everybody pulling together—America. They had a lump in their throats when they thought of their own and everybody else's goodness. That is, until now.

The republic had fallen. This, in effect, was the news the desolated young mothers carried home to their husbands that evening—carried, however, with a certain triumphant ceremony, as if on a flashing salver. Margaret and Ginny, Adelaide and Charlotte —they all marched into their dwellings and set down the news with a thud. The gentlest, softest, creamiest mother recounted the details of the invasion with a glittering intensity quite unlike her normal self. And each young woman had an air of speaking as a corporate body, attesting incontrovertible truths. When the puzzled husbands remarked, reasonably, that the psychiatrists were not likely to put in an appearance *every* day, the wives tossed their heads. Psychiatrists, they declared, were clock men; they would be there every afternoon, punctually, at two. Furthermore, they would summon their colleagues to share their discovery, this summer or the next. Psychiatrists vacationed in swarms, often surrounded by their patients; this was a well-known fact, and Ginny Marx could instance, from her own experience, a lonely beach in Massachusetts that had been *completely* taken over by them. Their profession had made them overbearing (of course, there were exceptions); they methodically pulped every experience like an orange-juice extractor. And they might as well be armadillos for all the feeling they had for the feelings of other people.

The husbands scratched their heads, astounded by the knowledge their wives appeared to have of the characteristics of psychiatrists in general and by the wealth of simile and metaphor these particular psychiatrists had tapped. "They're against Nature, Pick," said Margaret Callaway, with a breathless seriousness, when the children had been tucked into bed, and the two sat, with the Silex between them, in the small, sparsely furnished sitting room. "The children felt it, I tell you. Jonathan stared at them as if they were some of the space people he sees in his comic books. That's exactly how they looked in the water, with the black bathing cap and the inner tubes; they're contrary to Nature. Everything about them is synthetic and sleazy, like some horrible new fabric. One of them has skin that looks like imitation crocodile leather."

"They're probably no more unsightly than some of the locals," observed Pickles calmly. Margaret leaned forward and spoke almost in a whisper. "Pick, they're different, I tell you. I've been thinking about it; I'm sure I'm right. They've *chosen* to look the way they do. I shouldn't blame them for an accident or a deformity—you know that—but they've *chosen* to be ugly and dissonant."

Pick blinked his light-green eyes. As a scientist of sorts, he was irked by positive assertions. He was a homely man himself—small, slight, lantern-jawed, with thick, rather sensual red lips and heavy black-rimmed glasses. Partly for business reasons, he had stylized himself as an impersonal, scientific observer and dressed the part, as he conceived it; in the country, he wore Bermuda shorts cut down from old flannels, ribbed, heavy knee socks, and a soft white shirt, sleeves rolled up to the elbow, baring tan, wiry arms, on one of which flashed a very expensive French wristwatch that told the day of the week, and the month and year, and the moon phases, as well as the time of day. Out-of-doors, he carried a German camera and binoculars in leather cases on shoulder straps. To human life and technology, his subject, he had fashioned an attitude of strict, gloomy accuracy; his own bias was conservative, but he did not shirk the facts. To him, as he sometimes told his clients, man was chiefly an animal, obedient to certain biological and technological laws. At the same time, Pickles was a humorist, and the moral consciousness of Minster was a source of wry entertainment to him as he sat in his box seat, watching, with a critical, erudite eye. Behind the mask of imperturbability, he was peppery and eccentric, like a boyish little old man—exactly the same now, said the grandmother, as when Ginny's brother had brought him home from prep school, a wizened State of Maine boy on a scholarship, bright as paint in his studies, full of the devil, and a convinced, logical tory even then.

For two summers now, with detachment, he had watched his wife fighting her anxious shadow-battle with the problem of Poor Farm Pond. It did not surprise him that she had finally reached the breaking point. He was not a heartless man, but he regarded Minster as a pocket of old-fashioned individualism that could not long resist the encroachments of mass society. Margaret's "solutions," he perceived, were typically anachronistic: she relinquished the pond on Sundays at a time when the forty-eight-hour week was already a thing of the past. She reckoned, as he could have told her, without the expansion of leisure, and supposed she could contain the problem within the limits of the region, though it was not a regional question, as he would presently seek to show her: mechanized man was leisured man, wherever you found him —the industrial revolution had unleashed the crowd. But it was interesting that she was now reacting, like all old cultures, with a violent xenophobia. The psychiatrists, as *he* saw them, advancing on Margaret's pond, were the prophets of universal leisure, teaching the glad gospel of play, bidding nerves relax—their trademark, of course, was the couch. And nothing, he agreed, was more horrible to *homo faber,* that vanishing American, than the sight of other men sprawling, relaxed and unbuttoned, in a state of nature.

"Pick," said Margaret, urgently, interrupting his thoughts. Pickles quirked an eyebrow. She laced her long fingers; two jagged lines of worry appeared between her dark, somewhat protruding eyes. "I'm afraid of myself," she announced. "I didn't know until this afternoon that I had so much hatred in me. Pick, such a power of hatred!" She raised her eyes and looked straight at him. "Pickman, I have to tell you. I wanted to kill those six people." Pickles was shocked and irritated; it seemed to him she presumed on their marriage to make him such a grotesque and unseemly confidence. "And not because they gate-crashed our beach. That was just an excuse. I wanted to kill them because they *were the way they were.* Can you understand that? To make them see themselves, for one second, reflected from my eyes?" The dilation of her mare eyes unnerved Pickles; he did not like the urgent rolling look of complicity with which she was now regarding him, as though she expected him to share her murderous fantasies. As a proclaimed conservative, he had been, before this, the recipient of a number of confessions from liberals to the effect that they too loathed their fellow-man; Pickles, who was a stranger to all strong emotion, found the implication insulting.

"Nonsense," he said sharply. "You've been playing good little girl too long. You and your friends are acting a silly charade you pleasantly call democracy—a dangerous charade, let me tell you. The common man is no fool—face it, my dear. He doesn't like to be patronized. He can spy out a moral aristocracy in its simple last year's bathing suit." He lit a cigarette. "A moral aristocracy," he repeated. "Bred in the convents of Vassar and Bryn Mawr and Radcliffe. Holding its summer court at Minster, waving its sceptre over Poor Farm Pond. A very pretty pastoral—Arcadian. But this is the twentieth century. What right have you to try to be better than the common herd and to teach your children to be better? No right, in a universal democracy; the people won't stand for it. Why should they? I agree with them. This moral superiority is an insufferable ostentation—an exercise of privilege that derogates the common man."

Pickles glared mettlesomely at his wife, who was now sitting, downcast and submissive, her arms clasping her knees, in her flowing chambray skirt. "Why, Pick, you sound like a radical," she murmured, doubtfully smiling. But Pickles shook his head. He believed, as she ought to know, in private property and individual rights. He considered the idea of equality the most pestilential idea ever to have entered human thought —an idea that could only culminate in murder, as she herself had just demonstrated. There were only two kinds of equality that a rational man could accept: equality before the law and the career open to the talents. Social equality was an absurdity; there could never be equal shares of the things men valued. "Face facts, my dear. You can't share Poor Farm Pond or anything else you care about. Either you have it or they do. I've got nothing against these psychos, personally, but there's not enough water to go around. You gals have been a long time seeing that."

"But that's just *it*," cried Margaret. "We *have* seen it." She leaned forward with a pleading smile. "Pick, how *can* we say no to a car full of hot people when there isn't another place in miles?" "You have your own kids to think about," retorted Pickles. "What are you going to do—pack them off to camp so as to leave the pond free for the hoi polloi?" "Oh, Pick, you're exaggerating." Margaret gave a nervous laugh, as if he had paid her a compliment. "I'm facing facts," said Pickles. "That's what's in the cards. You've waited too long as it is. John Q. Public has got his foot in your pond." Margaret nodded glumly, seeming to give up all at once. "It's my fault, I see it," she sighed. "I assumed the leadership." Pickles said nothing. "If only," she murmured, "there were some other solution, some place that was just as nice for *them* to go." "That," said Pickles brusquely, "is their worry." "Oh dear, oh dear," said Margaret. "We always come back to that. *Think,* Pickles, *think,*" she adjured him. "If you think of something, I promise we'll do anything you say."

All over Minster, that night, thinking caps were on. Something would have to be done, nearly everybody conceded; today's episode was the last straw. Aside from anything else, it was bad for the children to have all this buzz about psychiatry. "It's nothing, Mother," "*Please,* Mother!" exclaimed the young matrons with acerbity when the grandmothers telephoned, abrim with curiosity and counsel. One typical old lady wished to know whether the two men were Freudians or whether they belonged to the new interpersonal school—it made all the difference, a friend in Brookline had told her. "How should *I* know, Mother? Go to bed, Mother," wearily replied her daughter. "We will talk about it tomorrow." "I hope to goodness you're going to do something finally," and "You've brought this all on yourselves," affirmed the old voices. "*Yes,* Mother, yes," sighed the young voices. They had heard this same judgment from the children (*"We* think you try to be much too good, Mummy"), and though the mothers smiled, it alarmed them to see the youngsters deducing, critically, that goodness did not pay.

Next day, the dire effect on the children sprang to every mother's thoughts. Thanks to the party lines, the whole township was astir. All afternoon, the road to Poor Farm Pond was dusty with unwonted traffic as the community turned out to take a peek at the psychiatrists, who, sure enough, were spread out on the tiny strip of beach with their blankets and their radio, just as the young mothers had described them. It was awful, declared the young mothers, alighting resolutely from their vehicles and proceeding to the waterside as if nothing had happened; the psychiatrists themselves were bad enough, but the way people came to stare at them, as if they were animals in a zoo, made you ashamed for Minster. And the children were lapping it all up, sitting in a long line on their haunches and giggling and declining to go in the water, till one of the mothers, strapping Charlotte Husted, bodily dumped her two in, while the psychiatric party clucked and frowned. What were you going to do? Adelaide Currier, a warm-spoken, lively brunette, announced that *she* was going to take *her* children to swim on Dogface every day until the excitement blew over, but everybody knew Adelaide would not hold to it; you could not run a household—even a slapdash one like Adelaide's—and drive more than twenty miles for a swim every day. And then there was the idea Ginny Marx had, of talking it over with the psychiatrists in a friendly way and asking them to leave the beach to the children after nap-time every afternoon, but everybody knew Ginny would never have the nerve. How could you explain to them delicately a thing they did not feel for themselves?

And they were here for the whole month. Mrs. Currier, Adelaide's mother-in-law, briefly settled this question by calling up the landlady at Meade Farm, who was on the Valley Fair Committee with her. So it was not just a temporary annoyance, which was what everybody had been half hoping; it was the heart cut out of the summer—and the next summer and the next, in all probability. A long-range solution would have to be found, said Margaret Callaway, briskly, in the post office, quoting Pickles. Minster was now facing a problem that had been gripping most of northern New England; a farming area was being converted into the site of a vacation industry that was overturning all the old values. The problem was really worldwide, she explained to a group of mothers as the tobacco-stained old codgers who hung around the post office edged up to listen: it would be the fate of all obsolete civilizations to become the tourist meccas of the civilizations that replaced them. Minster was feeling the effects of a technological revolution that was just as unsettling as a geological upheaval like the

Appalachian Revolution, which had metamorphosed the mountain ranges.

A long sigh rose from around the postboxes. According to Pickles, then, there was no escape, the young mothers queried, absently opening their mail; the postmistress's rubber stamp stayed poised in the air as she listened. But Margaret shook her head. A strange, new exaltation had appeared in her. Her nostrils quivered; her faraway gaze had taken on a focus of conviction. Pickles was thinking, she said proudly. He was looking at the problem scientifically, in terms of the new situation, and was very near an answer. The mothers exchanged looks. Any "solution" of Pickles' would have in it something caustic; he would want to rub salt in the community's wounds as he applied iodine to his boys' feet when they had cut them. The grandmothers doted on Pickles, but the young mothers had never approved of him since he went into business; they thought him selfish and a snob.

And yet their own ideas were terribly shaken, they had to confess. They were distressed by the froth of ill will that rose in their breasts whenever they so much as thought about Poor Farm Pond. Instead of hating the intruders, they ought to pity them, they supposed, for being noisy, ugly, and self-satisfied, which was probably the result of conditioning. "Imagine looking like that!" murmured Ginny to Adelaide with a shudder. "Imagine *being* like that!" retorted Adelaide. "I *won't* pretend to be sorry for them; they have free will just like the rest of us." And absurd arguments began to break out, at parties, about free will, and whether people could help their appearance. One or two of the husbands, plain men, were so irritated by these conversations that they were actually threatening to sell their houses and move away from Minster if the swimming problem was not settled, once and for all, this summer.

Nothing was the same. Starting with the psychiatrists, many new species of summer people began to be seen in Minster. A bright-red British car with a New York license plate was sighted flashing by on the back roads; slim, tanned, painted, smart women were glimpsed driving about with the real-estate agent, poking into old farmhouses. And all through July—for the first time in history—cars with streamers saying "Ausable Chasm," "Howe Caverns," "Desert of Maine" drew up at the parking place at Poor Farm Pond and parties of tourists settled down for an outing, with dogs, potato chips, Cracker Jacks, shampoo soap, insect repellent, beer, and all the rest of it. It was unaccountable. Minster had not been written up, so far as anybody could find, in the newspapers or travel magazines. It was as though the news had got about telepathically, as messages fly between birds. One afternoon—an ominous touch—a tall lean coveralled native with pale shifty eyes came with his lean pale-eyed son and a fishing rod and "borrowed" the Curriers' rowboat; and the psychiatrists had the gall to complain to their landlady (Mrs. Currier had it direct) that "Mirror Lake" was getting spoiled: "We are writing a few friends to join us for a rest—here is so nice and quiet. And now comes a crowd. What can you do? It is America."

Even the animals, apparently, had tuned in on the news. The eeriest thing—one afternoon, late, at sunset, when the pond was finally deserted, Adelaide Currier came down with a towel for a swim, and as she sat drying her legs, she heard an unusual sound in the water, not a fish jumping but a beaver swimming. She saw his black tail slapping the surface near the farther shore. And, looking more closely, along the far edge, green and still, under the shadow of the ridge, she noticed for the first time a little paling of dry branches. Her heart nearly stopped beating. Everybody in Minster knew what the beavers meant.

"Lodestone!" she cried five minutes later, panting across the Callaways' lawn in her white towelling robe and beach slippers. "The beavers have come over from Lodestone!" She fell into a deck chair. "They're building, along the far shore. I saw it." The Callaway children came running out of the house. Pickles set down his highball leisurely, and got up to make her one at the trestle table. "That is very interesting, Adelaide," he observed with a smile, glancing at his wife and children. "You actually saw the beaver?" Adelaide nodded. Then and there, as she said later, she should have guessed something queer was up. *"Very* interesting," repeated Pickles, in his most mystifying young-fogy manner. Adelaide was irritated. She stared from Pickles to Margaret. "You're taking it so calmly," she protested. "You'd think you'd never seen Lodestone." The three children looked at their parents and burst into giggles. "We saw it yesterday!" cried the youngest, gleeful, and dove under the table. "Then you *know* what it means," said Adelaide, sternly. "It's nothing to laugh about." "No," agreed the children, but their lips were twitching. "What *is* this?" she demanded. "Pickles, what are you up to? What were you doing at Lodestone?" All the Callaways smiled enigmatically. "A good question," said Pickles.

And, in fact, Adelaide's puzzlement was well founded. With the coming of the beavers, Lodestone Pond had reverted to wilderness, and the remote little village of Lodestone, five miles up the valley, had dried up and died of neglect. Nobody from Minster ever went there any more, except to show it to visitors as a curiosity. Today, there was nothing left of the village but a paintless church and a post office that sold a few dust-coated packaged provisions to the half-savage natives who lived in the hills on derelict farms, with fierce mongrel dogs and wild, inbred children. Civilization had crept away from Lodestone and left it —rumor declared—to incest and bestiality. The faded old homemade signs, indicating "Lodestone" with a pointer, in frail, spidery lettering, could still be seen nailed to trees along rutted back roads that had once borne a Sunday traffic of picnickers from the granite town and the cheese town and the state capital. But when they fell down, nobody replaced them; the stony mountain roads were nearly impassable to modern, low-slung automobiles, and dogs rushed out of unkempt farmyards, barking amazedly at the rare car that came through, usually with an out-of-state plate and a shaken, scarified driver, who emerged full of sociological questions—questions that won only the briefest retorts from the Minster natives, for Lodestone Pond and the whole infertile scrubby valley round it had the name of a place accursed.

It had not always been so; the grandmothers could remember a time when Lodestone was the dearest spot in the region, with strawberry festivals and church suppers and a music school and a little local band playing in the picnic grove. And, actually, there was nothing supernatural about what had happened. The beavers had done it. The tree-shaded pond had vanished, like a sunken ship: there was only a noisome still swamp, with dead birch and poplar trunks, stripped of bark, rising like masts or spars from the scummy surface. At one end of the swamp, amid the reeds and yellow water lilies, a remainder of the old diving raft still floated, with its tower. And you could see where the picnic grove had been, by the rope swing still hanging from the big arm of a dying giant maple that stood in a foot of slimy water. Whenever weekend visitors were driven over to see Lodestone, a cry of horror went up as the station wagon drew up on the little peninsula and the deathly sight was disclosed.

Outsiders found it hard to understand how the beavers could have done it. They had read in their school natural-science courses that beavers lived in streams and built dams there. They had never heard, they said, awe-struck, of beavers taking over a whole lake. Somebody (most often Pickles Callaway, for whom the place had a fascination) would then have to show them, with a geodetic map and binoculars, precisely what the beavers had done. Offering the binoculars,

Pickles would point out the brook that had originally
been dammed by the beavers, and explain how, to
make their dams and underwater lodges, they had cut
down small birch and poplar and dragged them to the
lake's outlet. This obstruction had had the effect of
flooding the pond, which had overflowed its borders
and killed the surrounding vegetation. The tall dead
trees they saw had once been on dry land—they could
find it on Pickles' map. Dammed up, the pond had
become a spreading marsh; reeds and water lilies had
sprung up in the stagnant water, and scum had slowly
covered it. With knitted brows, the visitors would pass
the binoculars back and forth, note the interlacing of
twigs, branches, and sapling trunks, sawed by the ro-
dent teeth. And in the end they never saw how Pickles
could take it so coolly. Facing the ruined pond, fend-
ing off the mosquitoes and gnats, sniffing the unwhole-
some air, they all claimed to feel something vast and
unjustifiable in the magnitude of the destruction, as if
Nature, in her ordinary business, could never have
encompassed such a thing. "The industrious beaver,"
they would murmur, the implication making them solemn for the rest of the afternoon. They could not help
sensing that the quality of this devastation was human; the decapitated tree trunks made them think of
mutilated cities. There was something at once purpo-
sive and purposeless in the display of technology before them. "The means," Margaret always remarked,
in her sharp, high, querulous bird voice, "have literally
swamped the end."

And she told a story that had been told her by the
old music teacher in Lodestone—that it was a summer
person who was responsible for what had happened to
the pond. The beaver had disappeared from the region
until a man from New York had come and bought
property and imported a pair of beavers to dam up his
brook and make him a natural swimming pool. The
beavers had escaped and settled in the outlet of Lodestone. Nobody but Margaret put credence in this tale.

The beavers, said the grandmothers, had first come to Lodestone *years* ago, before there were any summer people, except themselves, in the neighborhood. The story was a native fabrication, scoffed Pickles; no summer person could ever have been that thrifty.

Except Pickles, emended Adelaide, now, on the terrace, turning her bright hazel eyes from one grinning Callaway face to another. Pickles, she said to herself, had always had a mean, frugal streak, just like the man in the story. Adelaide was angry; she hated having mysteries made. "Shall we tell her?" wondered Pickles aloud, tilting his narrow head sidewise. Margaret and the children eagerly nodded.

."We drove over to inspect the property," he said, with a sharp look at Adelaide over his glasses. "Margaret bought Lodestone yesterday."

Adelaide's gasp resounded throughout the community. This, at last, was the fruit of Pickles' thought, and truly it was a stroke of genius, Minster acknowledged—tactful, diplomatic, and remarkably public-spirited. "I believe it will last our time," Pickles said with modest pride, at a lap supper Margaret gave to explain the idea to their friends. And Pickles had arrived at the idea, emphasized Margaret excitedly, via the social sciences. Using the historical method, he had asked himself (Pickles nodded confirmation) what was the proximate cause of the problem of Poor Farm Pond. The basic cause was, of course, as they all recognized, the social and technological revolution, whose trend, in the long run, was irreversible. But the immediate tendency could be checked or diverted elsewhere, depending on secondary factors. In this case, the secondary factor, or proximate cause, had stared Pickles in the face, the minute he sat down to think: the problem of Poor Farm Pond had come to a head two years ago, when the last, forlorn camp on the shore of Lodestone had been given up and the pond had finally been abandoned to the beavers. The tradition or unwritten law regarding swimming rights

had rested on the assumption that there were two
ponds to swim in: one for the natives and transients
and one for the "old" summer people—separate but
equal. The beavers had destroyed this assumption.

Ergo, concluded Pickles, to restore the status quo
ante you had only to eliminate the beavers.

The main point, which everybody saw at once, murmuring assent to Margaret, was that there was no human component to reckon with. That was the beauty
of Pickles' scheme. Nobody swam at Lodestone now.
There could be nobody, therefore, to complain that
the summer people had displaced them, as there
would have been, inevitably, at Poor Farm Pond,
even if Mr. Bascomb had been brought to terms. In
this light, all the manifest objections to Lodestone—
the sinister and forsaken character of the lake, the
stagnant smell, the evil repute the place bore with the
natives—became positive assets. Nobody wanted Lodestone, which meant that the land could be bought
up dirt-cheap, for the taxes. Much of it, Pickles had
discovered, had already been taken over by the bank
in Graniteville, through mortgage foreclosures. The
bank was delighted to arrange for Margaret to get the
whole thing for a song. The bank president, in fact,
had nearly wrung her hand off when the deeds were
signed, congratulating her on a public service. He
seemed to think, actually, that the reclamation of the
pond would put the whole village of Lodestone back
on its feet.

Clearing out the beavers, continued Margaret,
should not present too much difficulty. Not nearly as
much as some people were saying who had not gone
into the matter. They were protected for most of the
year, of course, but you could trap them during the
open season; Pickles and some of the other men might
come up for a weekend beaver hunt during the winter. The main thing, however, would be to knock out
their dams and lodges with a bulldozer and a dredger
—in this state, no conservationist statute could stop

you from doing that on your own property. The beavers could shift for themselves, since they were supposed to be very adaptive. The worry would be to not let them get reëstablished in Lodestone after you had driven them out; it might be fun for the children to set up a beaver patrol. Besides the bulldozer and dredger, there would be a few other expenses, for removing the dead trees and landscaping and replanting the shore. It would be nice if the people who were going to be using Lodestone, the "old" summer people and their friends, would get together and share the costs and the labor, just as they had always done with the sand at Poor Farm Pond.

And the people who put up the money (*or* the labor, either one) could form a little club—nothing pretentious, just a diving raft and a few bathhouses, since Lodestone was pretty far from home for some of the colonists, and maybe later on a tennis court and a hall for barn dances. You would not have to call it a club, said Margaret, quickly, cutting into the murmur that rose from all sides of her long dining room. If the word "club" struck a false note in Minster, you could call it "Lodestone Associates," or something of that kind. And it would not have to be snobbish; anybody could buy shares and join—more like a subscription library, really, than a club.

"*Any*body?" said Ginny, sharply. Everybody knew what she was thinking, but there had never been a trace of anti-Semitism in Minster. "Anybody we *knew,* I suppose," said Charlotte, with a hesitant look around. "Does that go for the natives?" demanded Bill Husted, in a rather truculent tone. Margaret's hand, as if alarmed, went to her olive brow; she turned to Pickles for help. "Let's be realistic," urged Sam Marx in his soft, sweet, husky voice. "The natives won't come into such a project. It's a question of economics." Pickles nodded. "Right. Let's put it this way. They can join if they want to but they won't." "Oh," said Janet Wheeler, a Girl Scout leader, in a booming voice, "I think it's disgusting to put it on a basis of economics. I thought we were going to *share*." "Don't be absurd, Janet," said Adelaide. "The natives are *farmers;* they work twelve hours a day." "And they don't swim, anyway," said Ginny. "I predicted this," said Pickles glumly to Margaret as the whole room began to talk at once.

Margaret shook her head. The whole thing, she declared, rapping for order, was eminently *fair*. The public, including the natives, would get Poor Farm Pond—why should they want Lodestone? Everybody stood to profit. And the old summer people had the right to protect themselves against today's migratory population by joining together and pooling their resources. Naturally, if the consensus of opinion should be against a club, she and Pickles stood ready to bear the expense themselves and invite their friends to swim with them. But it seemed to her that it was more democratic if everybody did it together; nobody would feel, then, that they were presuming on the Callaways' hospitality.

The assembly, uneasily dispersing, had to agree that Pickles' proposition was logical. To form a club, as they pointed out to each other during the ensuing days, was only to vest in legal form that membership, one of another, that had always been the essence of Minster. The belongingness they all felt, among themselves, the young mothers acknowledged, had always had its focus on the peninsula at Poor Farm Pond. It was there plans were made, world affairs argued, magazines and newspapers shared; a *de-facto* club already existed, which Lodestone Associates would merely incorporate formally. There would be no real difference, except in the name. Or would there?

"You're ungrateful fools in my opinion," said old Mrs. Hathaway, Ginny Marx's mother, "if you don't take Pickles' offer while the taking's good." She sat on her side porch, serving dandelion wine (with just a tincture of raspberries) to a conclave of dubious young mothers. Across the road, the children were diving in the pool she had dammed up. "You've lost nearly the whole month of July already," she said sharply. "If I were Pickles, I'd withdraw the offer and teach you all a lesson." "We *can't* be taught a lesson, apparently," said Adelaide Currier, from the steps, with a humorous sigh. "Then you're not going to do it!" cried Mrs. Hathaway. The young mothers sighed together, swaying like willows on the porch: *"We don't know."* "Look, Mrs. Hathaway," said Charlotte. "You've been here longer than anybody else. Don't you think this club will make a line between the summer people and the natives? That's what Bill and I keep coming back to." "There's a line right now," said the old lady. "There always has been. And there've always been some that cross it." "Mother!" cautioned Ginny. Adelaide mixed a good deal with the natives, came up early in the spring and stayed late in the fall; she was also rumored to be very friendly with a tall telephone linesman, who came sometimes in his high boots to the pond, late in the afternoons. Still, cross it or not, the line was there. The summer women did not drink with the natives, but the summer men did, getting out a bottle and glasses with punctilio when the plumber or the carpenter came. The summer women did not wear shorts in public, because the farm women disapproved. The summer children did not speak of their winter boarding schools, except in terms of sorrow, to the native children they played with, or of money or city entertainment. Even Adelaide's flirtation came within the rules, for the rumored meetings were out-of-doors and casual; she did not invite the man to her house. And, of course, she could not take him to a club.

"Our equality's really based on pretense," said Ginny. "We pretend we don't have a winter life or any life that's different from theirs. Come September, we die down like the vegetation." "Like Persephone, we go back to Hades," said Adelaide, who hated the city.

"That's the point, I think, Mother," cried Ginny. "If we have the club, we'll be flaunting the other side of our lives, the winter side. I can't help it; it seems tasteless to plump a clubhouse down in plain sight of people we see every day, in the store and the post office, who won't be able to come to it." "Perhaps they won't want to," said Mrs. Hathaway. Ginny shook her head. "That isn't the point," she insisted. "Even if they wanted to, they couldn't." Mrs. Hathaway shrugged; she had seen it before. Girls who married Jewish husbands were always touchy on these questions, even when there was no reason.

"There's another thing," said Charlotte. "What if we don't like somebody and he has the money for the shares?" "*Exactly!*" cried Adelaide. "You know how it will all end? *We'll be letting in those damned psychiatrists.* After having spent thousands of dollars. The last state of the man will be worse than the first." Rueful laughter shook the porch swing. "You don't have to let them in," said Mrs. Hathaway placidly. Ginny's big round china-blue eyes glared at her mother. "You tell us, Mother, please, how we're going to keep them out," she said sarcastically. "On what basis, do you suggest?" "Why, simply because you don't care for them socially," replied Mrs. Hathaway. "That's the basis of every club's membership policy. A club is like your home; you're not required to give a reason for not inviting people to it. Not yet, at any rate." The young women exchanged looks. "I'm sorry, Mrs. Hathaway," said Charlotte, acting as spokesman. "That may be all right for the Chilton Club, but it just won't do for the country, where you see people every day. You can't practically say in so many words, 'We don't like you.'"

Three young bosoms, gingham, linen, chambray, exhaled a common sigh. Mrs. Hathaway's voile print underwent a convulsion. "Then what is the point of a club, girls?" "Exactly," said Adelaide mournfully. "For people like us, maybe there isn't any point. We couldn't say no to anybody. You see, we *are* incorrigible." She flashed her most winning smile, demure and repentant, on the old lady, and held out her glass. "But you're willing and able to say no to Pickles?" rapped out Mrs. Hathaway, setting down the pitcher. The three heads, fair, dark, and chestnut, denied the charge. "We feel Pickles is trying to rush us," said Ginny. "We aren't sure yet in our own minds. We do see the advantages. A club would keep out transients." "But there's another thing, Mrs. Hathaway," said Adelaide. "What's going to happen to the beavers when Pickles drives them out of Lodestone?" Mrs. Hathaway's eyes closed for an instant, as if in silent prayer. "My dear," she remonstrated, in a kindly, concerned voice that seemed to belong to a gentler old lady, "you can't worry your head about the fate of the beavers. You must leave that much to Providence." "It's not the beavers themselves, Mrs. Hathaway," proffered Charlotte. "It's where they'll go. They'll be all over the countryside, like a plague. Pickles can't trap them all, in one open season. He admits that himself." "Adelaide saw one in Poor Farm Pond, Mother," put in Ginny. "Stuff!" said Mrs. Hathaway. "Adelaide doesn't know a beaver from an otter." "No, truly," protested Adelaide. "I could tell by the tail. It's going to be a terrible thing if they pour into Poor Farm. Everybody in Minster will be furious with us."

"I shouldn't be at all surprised," observed Charlotte, "if the town raised our taxes." The old lady's brows shot up, but she recovered herself. *"Girls!"* she said firmly. "You sound like children. Why, it would take the beavers years to come all the way over from Lodestone. They'll settle down in some stream over there and mind their own business." "It seems to me," said Adelaide, "that Pickles will never be shut of them if they *don't* come over to Poor Farm. They must be an enormous colony by now. You'd think Pickles, since he's so clever, would have given that some thought." The old lady considered. "Have you spoken to him about it?" she demanded. "Yes, of course," said Adelaide. "And what did he say?" Adelaide looked rueful. "He just laughed. He says everybody has a private obsession that's working against the club, and mine is the beavers. He and Margaret are getting pretty annoyed with us. Every day, somebody meets him in the post office with a new objection. Some of them, I admit, are pretty farfetched." "Including yours, my dear," said Mrs. Hathaway, rising. "If I see Pickles, I shall tell him what I think of the lot of you. You deserve to have a stick of dynamite put under you." She made her way into the house. "Mother is dying to have the club so she can start blackballing people," confided Ginny, with a giggle. "The Historical Society has never given her any scope."

On the last day of July, Pickles looked steadily at Margaret. "They're not going to do it," he announced. They were sitting alone on the terrace, at twilight. Their friends had been avoiding them for the last few days; the older children had gone with the Husteds to the state beach over the mountains, where there were lifeguards and twenty-foot diving towers; the youngest was in bed, tearful, because he was too little to stay up so late and drive home after dark. Every child, practically, in Minster had been in the dumps for weeks; the Husteds had packed theirs off to camp, where they could have all the swimming they wanted, right outside their tent. "And yet, damn it," cried Pickles now, "their fool parents won't raise a finger." "Perhaps they'll still do it," said Margaret. Pickles shook his head. "I know them," he said. "Once the psychiatrists go and Minster gets its beach back, they'll forget there was ever an emergency." "Well," said Margaret bravely, "we can still fix up Lodestone. We can afford it, Pick." "It's not the money," said Pickles. "It's the principle. This whole damned community has lost the will to survive."

And, of course, on the first of August, the psychiatrists were gone. It was like a miracle, almost. The other invaders were gone, too, as if obedient to a signal. The young mothers, in their skirted bathing suits, were back on their slabs of limestone; the children were in the water; the rowboats plied back and forth; the old raft buckled as divers hurtled off it. The pond was still, save for the plash of oars and the swash of the raft and the shrieks and gurgles of the children. Pages turned in the liberal weeklies; a clear voice quietly read aloud a dispatch from Yugoslavia in the New York *Times*. Knitting and four back numbers of the *New Statesman* came out of a wicker basket. Everything seemed precisely as it had been a month before, as it always had been. At four o'clock, a truck drove up, and it was the telephone linesman; handsome as a bronze and very tall, he nodded tersely to Adelaide and did a perfect jackknife from the raft. Dragonflies dipped; a fish jumped; firs rustled. As the sun descended toward the ridge, a murmurous rippling arose, like a sigh, from the shaded far shore. It can never change, really, the young mothers reflected, because *we* are the same.

But it was on the very next afternoon—the second of August, two days after the psychiatrists had gone—that Ginny Marx, walking up to the raspberry patch with her two small children, saw the creature cross the road. There could be no mistake; it was a beaver. The children saw it, too, and it looked just the way a beaver was supposed to look—reddish brown and lowslung, something like a large rat, but with webbed hind feet. It hurried across the road in the direction of Poor Farm Pond, and Ginny let out a little cry. A moment later, coming from the other direction, Pickles Callaway drove up in his new station wagon—on his way, he said, to the post office. Ginny and the children excitedly climbed in. They had just seen a beaver, they all attested, heading for Poor Farm Pond. Pickles raised a skeptical eyebrow. They had beavers on the brain, he said, scoffing; it was probably just a woodchuck. But Ginny and the children all shook their fair heads. It was a beaver; they had just seen one in the Natural Science Museum at the state capital.

And a minute later, while they were still arguing, the children made a curious discovery. Under one of the back seats was a canvas case with holes for ventilation. "What is it?" they asked, edging it out with their sandalled, dusty feet. Ginny, turning to rebuke them, caught a funny, boyish flicker of Pickles' light-green eye, magnified by the big lens. The thing under the seat was a cat carrier, empty.

Naturally, Ginny acknowledged, breathless, when Pickles, bold as brass had let her off at the beach, you could not *prove* what had been in it. "But of course we *know*," said Charlotte, tucking her chestnut hair into her bathing cap. "How long do you suppose he's been doing it?" "From the very first, I imagine," said Adelaide. "The one I saw must have been his maiden effort." Ginny shook her head. "Perhaps it was the other way round. Perhaps that one came there naturally and gave him the idea." Adelaide dimpled. "So like Pickles," she murmured. "He saw the historical trend and lent it a helping hand." "Dreadful," pronounced Charlotte. "Do you think Margaret knows?" Adelaide slowly shook her head. "Impossible," she said. "Inconceivable." "But *why,* Mummy, *why?*" whispered Adelaide's eight-year-old beauty, who had been sitting in the water, eavesdropping. *"Why* is Mr. Callaway putting beavers in our pond?" The mothers looked helplessly at each other. "Hush," said Adelaide. "You're not to speak of it." "Is it because he's mad at us?" "In a way, I suppose, dear," said her mother. "It's a sort of joke on us. Run away now and swim." The child obeyed. "Joke?" cried Charlotte. "Why, *I* think he's doing it to pressure us into joining his club." Adelaide and Ginny shook their heads. "No," said Adelaide. "Pickles doesn't care any more where we swim; he's washed his hands of us. I don't blame him. In fact, you know, I rather admire him. He had to dispose of the beavers, and this was simple, ingenious, and anti-social. He made us a present of them. Pickles is an actionist; none of *us* would have had the nerve. And for that matter," she added, "I don't suppose he's even doing anything illegal. Is it illegal to transport a beaver in a station wagon across a town line?" There was a ripple of reluctant laughter. "*I* think it's criminal," said Charlotte, rather feebly, immersing herself in the lake.

Ginny and Adelaide sat staring into the clear green water—deep, much deeper than Lodestone, and fated, it almost seemed, like something beautiful in a fairy tale, to create trouble and perplexity. All at once, the Currier rowboat came to a stop. The oarsman, nine-year-old Henry Currier, had heard a peculiar sound. "Hey!" he called. "Hush," said Ginny. Everybody stiffened, as if playing a game of statues.

Across the pond, near the far shore, two lustrous beavers were swimming. Their flat tails made a distinctive noise as they slapped the water. "*Beavers,* children!" softly cried Charlotte, her face suddenly aglow. She stood like a classic water nymph, pink and plump, in her ample bathing dress, up to her waist in the water. The rowboat veered about; the little girls on the raft stood up and shaded their eyes. "I see them, I see them," proud voices called in shrill succession. "Mother, they're *darling*." "Look at their little heads!" The young mothers caught their breaths; the gleaming round heads moving along the green surface *were* charming, and behind each beaver was a shining silver-white wake. At the same time, in the late-afternoon light, the line of newly cut gray branches was quite plainly visible, etched against the dark bank.

The rowboat drew up, with businesslike strokes. "Can we row over and investigate them? *Please?*" Henry Currier had a crew of three aboard. The young mothers' eyes consulted; each face had a look of consternation. "Very well," said the mothers. The rowboat made off swiftly, with its four tense explorers.

Ginny ran her tongue over her lips. "Henry," she called, "if you see their house, don't disturb it. Just investigate and report back." Her fair neck flushed. "We can trap them later on," she explained to the other young mothers. "After the children are gone." "We won't be here in the winter," whispered Charlotte. "Perhaps the town could do it," murmured Adelaide. "They could get a permit or something. Or maybe old Mr. Bascomb could trap them."

The eyes met again, and dispersed to the moving boat. "*Much* the best," said Charlotte, settling down to a backstroke and thereby closing the subject.

The Hounds of Summer

The village had an inn with thirteen rooms, running water, and a bath for general use, two boarding houses, a post office, two dark provisions stores, an open-air vegetable stand, a meat market, a bakery, a fish store, a milk store, a drygoods store, and a newsstand which sold soap flakes, toilet paper, stamps, Italian cigarettes, matches, and the provincial edition of the *Nazione* of Florence, supplemented for the summer trade by the *Corriere della Sera, La Stampa,* and *Il Girono*. There was a pay telephone in a booth and at the inn, and this *posto pubblico* was the only telephone in Porto Quaglia, except for the doctor's, so they said. Telegrams came down by bicycle from the hill town of Acquafredda, where there was a telegraph office, a *municipio,* and a police station. There was only one frigidaire, they said, in Porto Quaglia, not counting the one in the inn, and one bathroom with hot water. There was no cream to be bought in the dairy store, and the milk had to be boiled. The dentist drove over from Sarzana, the nearest market town, to pull teeth in the patient's parlor or kitchen, and in summer he brought along his bathing suit, to get double value from the trip: there were *cabine* to rent at the public beach, and a small bar selling coffee, Campari soda, *gelati* in paper cups, bottled fruit juice, and vermouth. In short, the village was poor. The villagers spoke an ugly Italian and many of them had lost most of their teeth. The older women wore dark-blue dotted

cotton house dresses and had hair of that peculiar
metallic iron gray found among poor Italians and sug-
gestive of rust.

It was a fishing village, *un petit hameau de
pêcheurs, un piccolo villaggio di pescatori.* That was
how those who went there for their vacations found
themselves describing it to their hairdressers, manicur-
ists, pedicurists, concierges, postmen, train and air
companions en route from London, Rome, Paris,
Milan. True or false?

True because Porto Quaglia was in fact populated
by fishermen whose thin brown nets like hair nets
were spread out to dry in the sun behind the white-
washed houses, and there was no other industry in the
village except for the desultory transport of marble
from the nearby mountains above Carrara, which was
carried out in boats and barges equipped with giant
cranes, grappling hooks, pulleys, and winches that appeared to spend the whole month of August condemned like Sisyphus to dump five or six blocks of
gray stone on the waterfront and then reload them.
Porto Quaglia's little harbor had once had a fleet of
sailing vessels that carried marble from Carrara as far
as Marseilles, but then Carrara had built its own harbor at Marina di Carrara, and the sons of the Porto
Quaglia mariners became barmen on the United States
and Italian Lines. At any rate, Porto Quaglia today
was simply a fishing village, and yet to say so to your
manicurist or your B.B.C. producer was a lie.

Partly because the words *"hameau de pêcheurs,"*
et cetera, implied something colorful—a picturesque
fishing fleet heavy with dragging nets like dark bridal
veils; orange sails, red sails, yellow sails, marked with
crescents and suns; bright-blue boats with an eye
painted on the prow pulled up on the beach; old men
mending their gear. A few old men did occasionally
mend their gear but not where they could be observed;
there were no sails except the white ones of small
pleasure boats; and it was rare to see a fishing trawler,

even on the horizon. The prized local catch was *muggine*—a special kind of white mullet, they said, that lived only in the tidal reaches of the bamboo-fringed River Quaglia, on which the village bordered. Yet *muggine* was hardly ever to be found in the fish store, which sold chiefly sole and red mullet that were suspected of coming from somewhere else along the coast. Fishing, such as it was, was practiced secretively as a rule. At night sometimes you would hear a lone rowboat push off from a wooden landing, then the plash of oars or the sound of an outboard motor. In the dead stillness of noon, you would see a man or a boy standing in a rowboat casting a white furled hand net into the river with a beautiful circling, swooping motion; this net was called "the hawk" and it struck into the glassy green water like a gauzy bird of prey. But often the man proved to be the doctor from Carrara in white duck trousers, who had learned the hawk in middle age; he was the "other" doctor, married into the local hill gentry, and had a tennis court, a telephone, a frigidaire, and at least one bath with hot water, which were never counted in the inventory, probably because *he* was not counted, out of courtesy to the indigenous doctor, who had a monopoly on the sick of Porto Quaglia. The boy in the rowboat with the net was always the same boy; he cast it again and again without catching anything, giving a tranced sense of time suspended like the giant black cranes forever groping for the gray marble.

Yet the fact that Porto Quaglia did not conform to a touristic image of a fishing village was not exactly the reason for the feeling that the description was false. Had it looked like Collioure or Concarneau or Chioggia or Provincetown, there still would have been something wrong—indeed wronger. The inauthenticity of the description lay in the describers. That is, if a native of Porto Quaglia described his home as a fishing village, he would be telling the truth, but in the mouth of, say, a Milanese publisher these words became horribly fraudulent. To a local fisherman Porto Quaglia was self-evidently a fishing village, but to a Milanese publisher it was *"un piccolo villaggio di pescatori."* Those quotation marks, which sprang up around the words quite without the publisher's volition, were the source of all the trouble.

Similarly with the word "unspoiled." It was true that Porto Quaglia was not yet spoiled, comparatively speaking, yet only a very unaware summer visitor, perhaps an Englishwoman, would try saying this to a native, whose whole interest lay in having it spoiled as fast as possible. There is something suspect in a laudatory remark that cannot be made in the presence of those being lauded. "Unspoiled," moreover, had grown those quotation marks as the old women in Porto Quaglia grew tufts of iron-gray whiskers. But how else would you describe Porto Quaglia, without going into detail, except as a fishing village on the Ligurian coast that had not yet been completely spoiled by tourists?

This was the first slight embarrassment for the kind of person who came to Porto Quaglia—the difficulty of stating, in brief form, where he was going without making it sound like the kind of place that would attract someone quite different from himself—say, an editress of *Vogue* or another Milanese publisher. It was no solution to reply "I'm going to Porto Quaglia," for this led to "Where is Porto Quaglia?" and "Should I know about it?," all of which ended in a description of P. Q. as a simple fishing village on the Ligurian coast.

The only remedy, it was decided at lunch at the Buonsantis' (he was a tall bald Italian employed at UNESCO in Paris: she was small and French and translated philosophic and economic texts), would be for Porto Quaglia to be "put on the map," like Portofino or Portovenere or Port Said. But if your concierge or your hairdresser already knew about Porto Quaglia, so that the mere name produced a ready-made description like a pop-up toaster, then the reason for going there would have vanished. The reason for going there was that nobody knew about it. But of course everybody wants to go to a place no one knows about (except those in the know), though for varying motives, which is why the words "simple fishing village" have been as abused as a pinewoods in which there is now a Camping. Those who, like the Buonsantis and their guests, had been attracted to Porto Quaglia by the absence of yachts, luxury hotels, motorboats, water skiers, skin divers, golf, casinos, shops, cocktail lounges, night clubs, sports cars, and other amenities were refugees from a banal summer life, but it was impossible, they agreed, to escape from a cliché of action without being stamped with a cliché of speech, like an exit permit. The world will allow you to go to Porto Quaglia as long as it has Porto Quaglia's "number."

Fifteen people, the usual complement, were eating lunch at a long table under a trellis covered with trumpet vines in the Buonsantis' garden, which looked out onto the main street and the river, where a few masts of small boats could be seen. The garden contained a flagged terrace of varicolored marbles, a grape arbor, a sour-cherry tree, some trampled lawn, two large ornamental palms, and two Christmas trees, symmetrically planted. There was also a "fantasy" table, made of stone in the shape of a large mushroom and surrounded by little painted stone toadstools. On the balcony rail of the apartment above, facing the river, hung some striped towels and damp bathing suits. In the green midday shimmer the luncheon party, which was still peeling figs and drinking wine, resembled a scene by Renoir, the more so because they were speaking French. French was the prevailing language among the summer people at Porto Quaglia, who were know to the natives as *"i francesi,"* whatever their nationality. Today the group included Mme. Buonsanti's father, the two Buonsanti children, a French engineer, his wife—a child psychologist—and their three children, a Roman editor and his wife, a Livornese professor of history on loan to Columbia University, and an American journalist and his wife, who were staying at the inn. Three bicycles, a surf mattress, and a rubber boat leaned against the wall of the house, and some beach chairs were sprawled near the table; the double doors were open into the principal room of the Buonsantis' apartment, where a great many straw hats were piled on top of the sideboard and a chessboard was set up for play on the glass-covered dining table. More "French" kept arriving and pulling up chairs. The women and girls were wearing summer cotton dresses, and the men striped jerseys with khaki shorts or long blue or white canvas trousers. They were still discussing what to call Porto Quaglia.

"You French are so frightfully analytical," said an English labor lawyer, who was opposed to what he called "blood sports" and had appeared at the end of lunch, in cleated shoes and with a sweater tied round his hips, to take the Buonsanti children on a mountain hike. "My wife and I don't find it at all embarrassing to say we're going to a fishing village. I mean, why not face facts?" He then translated his remarks into French.

"If you faced facts," said the Roman editor tartly, "you would say you were going to a summer resort."

"Une petite station balnéaire," agreed Mme. Buonsanti, laughing.

"Plage modeste," added her husband.

Everyone laughed, thinking of the dusty town beach where none of the *"francesi"* swam except when the sea was rough and a boat could not land at the White Rock or Raven Point or one of the many coves and grottoes farther up the coast. One reason that Porto Quaglia remained "unspoiled" was that the snobbish causal tourist saw only the *page modeste* at the end of the village and immediately turned his Alfa Romeo around and shot off to Lerici or Forte dei Marmi. To sit in the café outside the inn and watch this happen while eating an ice-cream cone was one of the children's amusements on dull mornings when the boats had not yet come to take them bathing and the family outboard motor was *"en panne."*

The White Rock was the chief lure and secret beauty of Porto Quaglia. Parties of bathers were taken there every morning by the fishermen in little yawls with inboard motors; informal excursions ran several times before noon from the pier in front of the inn, and regular passengers were picked up at the rickety little wooden landings along the river, off the single main street. Starting at ten o'clock, cries began to ring out from the bank as the fishing boats with little triangular colored flags in their rigging were sighted. "Pierino!" "Paolo!" "Romeo!" *"Venga, venga!"* Or "Wait, wait! I am coming. *Aspetti!* Wait for me, Pierino!" Or *"Jean, où est Jean? Où est le matelas?"* "Irene, have you got the basket?" "My glasses! I forgot my glasses!" "Carlo! *Dov'è il tuo cappillo?"* *"Dov'è Michel? Où est Marc?"* *"Son già partiti? Con Romeo?"* With thermos bottles of cold water, baskets of cheese and fruit, baskets and bags of bathing equipment, with surf mattresses, pails and shovels, yellow and red and white and blue inflated tubes, beach umbrellas, nets containing books and newspapers, the boats were finally packed and headed for the White Rock. Fifteen minutes later, the landing was accomplished, the older children swimming to shore and returning like a school of fish to hover alongside and seize the bags and baskets as they were lifted over the bow and offer a hand to the women in their dresses and beach gowns as they climbed down the unsteady ladder, while the men, having leapt to shore, formed a human chain along which the younger children were passed. Nearly every day someone or something fell overboard in the excitement of landing: a straw hat, a book, a pair of glasses, shoes, a middle-aged newcomer—or all of these together in one parcel. This had happened yesterday morning to the whiskered American journalist, thought by the children to resemble Uncle Sam, and François, the twelve-year-old Buonsanti boy, had jubilantly taken a picture of it with his new camera.

Starting at one o'clock, the boats reappeared at the White Rock, at Raven Point, at the various *scogli* and small pebbly beaches, to bring the bathers back for lunch. Naturally, irritations sprang up from time to time between the boatmen or between the boatmen and the passengers, who would complain that Romeo or Paolo had forgotten them and taken a party of new people in preference. But those who were left behind on the jetty would always appear at Rocca Bianca, rowed by an old man or a little boy, and some came in the old man's rowboat by preference, disapproving of the motor sailboats and the oil they spread on the water. Some of the young people came by threes and fours in rowboats rented for the summer or given them for Christmas or a birthday, and one family had an outboard motor. Sometimes the older children, in pairs or accompanied by François in his rowboat, would swim back to Porto Quaglia and arrive late and panting for lunch, or they would walk back in a party over the marble cliffs, though this was considered dangerous by their parents.

The White Rock was really a mass of rocks and cliffs of pure milk-white marble that formed a towering point jutting into the sea. Above it, on a steep mountain flank, grew ilex and pine and wild olive trees. The water around it was a pale green and exceptionally clear. If you swam way out beyond your depth you could still look down to the white marble shelving that extended along the sea floor like a vast bath for sea horses or Tritons. Along the shore it formed deep caves. The sea at this point was seldom quiet and gave the impression of washing itself, like laundry, by beating against the rock and rinsing itself as it ran in and out of the cool caves. Blue-green and violet marbles were not uncommon along this stretch of coast, but white was freakish; it was as though a vein of sculptor's marble had escaped from its mountain prison miles off in the Apuan Alps and raced underground to burst into the sea in a great release of energy, so that to imaginative bathers this marine spot was like a temple full of glittering forebodings or polished memories of statuary—nymphs and dolphins and Venuses rising from the spray. For some reason, doubtless connected with the marble, the water here and in the nearby coves was cooler than is usual in the Mediterranean, and there were no jellyfish.

Farther along, at the beach called Raven Point and at the lonely beach called Judgment Day by the summer people, because it looked like the scene of a Tintoretto "Last Judgment," there were mussels and purple sea urchins clinging to the dark rocks. The children collected them; the men opened them with pocket knives, and the bathers shared them at midday, along with the cheese, figs, grapes, pears, peaches brought in the individual baskets, to stave off hunger, before Pierino or Romeo or Paolo came to take everyone home for a two-o'clock lunch. Like a backdrop to this watery, summery scene bobbing with small craft and bright swimming tubes, the Carrara mountains came into view as the boats rounded into Porto Quaglia's harbor—pale brown, like canvas, in the blue distance, patched with what appeared to be snow fields, streaked with crevasses and awesome glaciers, all made of white marble—a realm of Titans, Michelangelo Land. In the intermediate distance, in the green-forested hills above the Quaglia, were belfried Tuscan hill towns that caught the gold of the afternoon sun in their medieval clocks, towers, and ramparts. It was like an illustrated history lesson: the children's eyes travelled thoughtfully from the remote white fissures of the quarries, which had been opened in Roman times, down to picture-book Castelnuovo, where Dante had stayed, down to the stone artillery nests, so near you could almost touch them, that the Germans had made in the last war.

Except on Sundays, when trippers came from Sarzana and Acquafredda, the "French" usually had the White Rock to themselves, and the strangers, principally English, who from time to time "discovered" Rocca Bianca while staying at the inn or in a *pensione,* were adopted by the "French," offered fruit and cheese, the loan of a child's pail or surf mattress, invited to play chess in the evenings or join in political discussions in the café outside the inn. The English, henceforth known as *"francesi"* to the boatmen and shopkeepers, reciprocated with ice creams, lifts to Sarzana or Marina di Massa for shopping, invitations to drive to Lucca or Pisa. Sometimes, when the "French" went to Raven Point or Judgment Day, a smart motorboat with water skis would come whizzing up from Lerici, disgorging Roman writers, society women, publishers, who were staying at the Hotel Doria or the Hotel Byron or the Hotel Shelley e delle Palme. A different world, as different as the blue Lerici waters from the green waters of Porto Quaglia, a world of palms, villas, and esplanades, but this world too was accommodated. Joint dinners were arranged at a mountain inn known for its *prosciutto* and sheep cheese or else in the port of Lerici, where the guests would eat *spaghetti alle vongole* or plates of *datteri,* those brown polished date-shaped mussels that grew only on the soft stone of Portovenere, where they were said to burrow holes like cliff swallows. Or the Roman writers and publishers would come to dinner at the inn at Porto Quaglia, telephoning ahead of time to the *posto pubblico* to order *muggine ai ferri* and to recommend that the waiters wear jackets. But the boy waiters in the inn at Porto Quaglia did not have jackets; the only smartening up they could do was to roll down their shirtsleeves and take the pencil from behind their ear. *"Un piccolo villaggio di pescatori,"* the host at dinner would explain to the troop he had brought with him, bestowing a tender, fatherly smile on the café where the "French" were playing chess as if nothing had happened.

There was no fear that these Romans would "discover" Porto Quaglia, for they believed they already knew it, like the inside of their pocket: "Byronian scenery," they explained. Still, word was getting around, as Mike, the American journalist, was saying to Hélène Buonsanti, lowering his voice slightly, as though passing on a piece of confidential information.

"Qu'est-ce qu'il dit, maman?" said Laure, the fourteen-year-old Buonsanti girl alertly. All the children were on the *qui vive* for any threat to their summer home, and they understood by instinct when it was being talked about, even in a foreign tongue.

Mme. Buonsanti's father, Dr. Bernheim, shook his gray locks and checked his granddaughter with his eyes, which were generally half closed, as if inattentive, like the ear of a confessor. His lids now dropped again, and his hand cradled his chin, but the tilt of his head betrayed the fact that he was following closely what the American said.

"Yep," continued Mike, "the word's getting around, I'm afraid, Hélène." He coughed and moved his chair closer to his little hostess, still talking under his breath, but since he was in the habit of raising his voice when speaking English to a foreigner, the effect was of an arresting stage whisper. Everyone at the table turned to listen. "I read about it in New York," he shouted, sotto-voce. "Last winter. In *Harper's Bazaar*. A highbrow fashion magazine. They said Porto Quaglia was where the French left-wing intellectuals went for the summer."

"How stupid!" said Hélène Buonsanti coldly. "The French left-wing intellectuals! *Écoute, Arturo. Figure-toi.*"

"Mais c'est vrai, maman!" said Laure. *"C'est vrai, maman,"* said François, grinning. *"C'est vrai, n'est-ce pas, Catherine?"* He turned his bright, demure black

eyes to the engineer's oldest daughter, who was fifteen and humorless.

"*Tais-toi, François!*" flashed his mother. The children made fun of spectacled Catherine, because in her *lycée* she had organized a circle of *Filles des Obscurs Intellectuels de Gauche.* "*C'est dégoutant,*" Hélène burst out, banging her fist on the table.

"Why does it make her so mad?" demanded Mike, of the table at large. "Why does it make your daughter so mad?" he added, shouting at the doctor.

Hélène calmed herself. "It is the same as 'fishing village,'" she explained in her slow English. "It is true when the children say that we here are intellectuals of the left. But if someone says it in a fashion magazine it is a silly lie."

Arturo Buonsanti was laughing. "*Mais c'est merveilleux!*" he cried. "Eh, Hélène? Next summer when your hairdresser asks you where you are going for your vacation, you can answer that naturally you are going where the French intellectuals of the left go."

"*Et les juifs, et les juifs, papa!*" chanted Laure, jumping up from her place and putting her arms around her father's neck. A few days before, someone had noticed that the greater part of the summer people were either Jewish, half Jewish, a quarter Jewish, or, like Arturo Buonsanti, married to someone Jewish. This *trouvaille* still enchanted the children, like a meadow full of four-leaf clovers. "*Pauvre papa,*" murmured Laure, hugging him. "*Tu n'es pas juif; mais moi, je le suis!*"

Arturo Buonsanti was chuckling. "*Modeste station balnéaire, très fréquentée par les juifs.*"

"Oh, I say," protested the British lawyer, "that would be liable to misinterpretation, wouldn't it?"

"Gives the wrong picture, I agree," said Mike. "Sort of a Miami Beach." He laughed nervously. Both he and the Englishman were embarrassed by the children's freedom with the "racial" topic, which their parents seemed positively to encourage, like premature talk about sex. Mike, in particular, had an uneasy notion that he was being led on by this permissive atmosphere into making what might sound (to Jews) like an anti-Semitic remark. The other day at the café, for instance, they had teased him without mercy because he had refused to believe that everyone present was Jewish. "But you don't *look* Jewish, any of you."

"Il cherche le nez," François had murmured, watching the American stare at each face in turn.

"Hey!" Mike had retorted. *"Vous avez tort, mon garçon. J'aime les juifs.* I'm not Jewish, but my wife is. Aren't you, darling?" The children had burst into giggles. They loved to tease Mike, because he was good-humored, said *"vous"* to them, and was exactly like their idea of an American. Even Catherine had asked him gravely whether all Americans ate with their feet on the table—she had seen it in the films. So that now, when Catherine and her cronies passed him eating breakfast at the café, he would quickly put his feet on the table and, for good measure, his spoon in his coffee cup, to the amazement of the waiters, whom he tried to include in the joke with a series of broad winks. The result of this charade was that Elisabeth, another American, who lived above the Buonsantis, was asked by the innkeeper whether all Americans ate with their feet on the table.

Mike's wife failed to find the story amusing. She was irritated by these nonchalant and observant children, whom she had overheard chiming "Don't you think so, darling?" in what she uncomfortably recognized as her husband's voice. It was obvious, she told Mike, that these European children had been indoctrinated with anti-Americanism. Their good manners offended her too—always *"Bonjour, Monsieur," "Bonjour, Madame,"* instead of "Hi, Mike," "Hi, Irene," the way she was used to in America. She was touchy about being American and touchy about being Jewish. She had a rather large nose, which she was touchy about too. "That little boy," she said, "was making fun of my beak." She could speak quite coarsely when she wished to. " *'Il cherche le nez.'* "

Mike shook his head. "No, no," he said. "He was riding *me*. As a matter of fact, honey, when he caught me I *was* looking for the nose. I have to admit it."

Irene resented Porto Quaglia. She was sorry she had ever saved that clipping from *Harper's Bazaar*. It was not a *real* fishing village; there were no real intellectuals, like Sartre or Françoise Sagan; there was nothing to buy; and though they had been here only a short time, she was pressing Mike to go to Ischia. "I like it here," Mike kept repeating, but Irene's dissatisfaction was slowly convincing him; like an echo, he too began to criticize the *pensione* at the inn: spaghetti twice a day and fish with too many bones in it.

"Vous n'aimez pas la nourriture italienne," Hélène Buonsanti said kindly to Irene. She meant, Irene retorted, that Americans only liked steak and fried potatoes. *"Mais non,"* Hélène protested, determined to make peace. *"Le steak et les frites sont tout à fait français."*

Mike interposed that no one liked Italian cooking better than he and Irene, but why couldn't they get real filet of sole at the inn? *"Without bones,"* he emphasized. Hélène had had her cook fillet the soles for lunch, over the objections of Arturo, who said that they would be flavorless. Mike was a popular figure, and everyone saw regretfully what was happening. To please his wife, he would soon have to leave Porto Quaglia, and he was foxily seeking a reason for leaving without regrets. Yet no one at the table was prepared for the undercurrent of antagonism that had made itself felt, like a sudden cold tug, just now, at the end of lunch, when he began playing with the notion that Porto Quaglia's days were numbered. "Yes, Hélène," he went on easily, "it's just a question of time, I'm afraid. *Une question de temps.* Irene and I went exploring this morning. We got a boy to row us across to that big beach on the other side of the river."

A look of understanding passed along the table. "*Lo spiaggione*," whispered a pretty girl to a young architect from Turin. "*Parla dello spiaggione*." "*La grande plage, grand-papa*," said Laure to Dr. Bernheim. "*Oui, mon enfant. J'ai compris*," said the doctor, nodding sadly.

"*Quelle horreur!*" said Mike. "Wasn't it, darling? *Ruinée, eh, Arturo? Kaput!*"

The host, who resembled a sage because of his prematurely bald head, knitted his brows and agreed. "*J'ai raison, eh?*" said Mike, looking around him. No one dissented. Until the previous year they had been in the habit of going across the Quaglia and walking half a mile down a path through a thicket of bamboo to *lo spiaggione*—a big wild sandy beach on the other side, on the open Mediterranean, where there were rollers to ride and where the children could build sand castles. This had been a regular alternate to the White Rock. But the tide of humanity coming up the coast from Viareggio, with its flotsam of night clubs, cheap hotels, neon-lit seafood restaurants, had finally overtaken Punta Sabbia, as the settlement across the river was called, and a Camping that had been planted there two years ago was literally the last straw. The *grande plage* was now covered with straw huts, bamboo huts, loose straw, tents, candy wrappers, ice-cream cartons, rusty cans, broken bottles, old automobile tires, watermelon rinds, not to mention the lengthening row of *cabine* and rented umbrellas; to reach the water in many places it was necessary to pick one's way through refuse and human bodies as in a game of stepping stones. The advent of the campers, moreover, had created a serious sanitary problem, and the refuse had bred flies and mosquitoes. This summer only the children had been across to the big beach; the grownups did not speak of it any more, as if it were someone who had died in a horrible way or

lived on upstairs in a special room like an insane relation in the last century. The *grande plage,* which
had been an essential feature of the Porto Quaglia
agenda, like the yearly boat trip to Portovenere or the
climb up Monte Morello, was resolutely ignored. No
one cared even to remember the indignant meetings
of the summer before last, when they had tried to
save *lo spiaggione:* the open letter to the mayor of
Acquafredda protesting the sanitary conditions on the
other side of the river, the manifesto to the Belle Arti
at La Spezia calling attention to the despoilment of
the bamboo and the *pineta,* the photographs of Before
and After they had sent to *Il Mondo* and *Italia Nos-
tra.* The ruin of the *spiaggione* was accepted, and
there were those who, last summer, had claimed to see
a virtue in the necessity, pointing out that what had
happened on the other side would be a lesson to the
elements in Porto Quaglia that wanted to see it "developed." Mass tourism, they declared, could not be
stopped; the hope was to divert it, and Punta Sabbia
ought to be welcomed as a human dump, where all
the undesirables collected in one place, without any
compulsion being exercised but according to a kind of
natural zoning law. This summer, though, these arguments, once half persuasive, had been put away regretfully, like last year's faded bathing suits and
rusted bathing caps; they did not seem to fit any more.

"Mais c'est tout à fait différent!" said the Roman
editor sharply, breaking the gloomy silence that had
fallen on the table. "The *spiaggione* is sand, good for
pitching tents. Here we are on rock and stones."

" 'It can't happen here,' eh?" said Mike.

"But, Francesco, what about the new Camping at
the *bivio?*" gently put in the editor's wife. This was a
very small Camping, of only a few tents, at the fork
two miles away where the road from Sarzana divided,
the main branch going south toward Carrara and a
long spur following the river to Porto Quaglia, where
it ended.

"It is at the *bivio*," her husband said impatiently. "They do not come here to swim: they go to Punta Sabbia." And he went on to reiterate his theory that Porto Quaglia could not be "developed" because it was not on a through road. "People looking for pleasure don't like to be at a dead end. They are afraid of being bottled up. They are restless. Everyone today is restless—especially the Italians." This theory, which he had been propounding for five years with increasing conviction, served as usual to pacify the doubters; his disgust with the tendency of modern life, familiar to readers of his editorials, made him all the more credible as a forecaster—an optimist they would not have relied on. In the same way, the whole community, including the children, trusted him as a weather prophet because he distrusted the weather.

Just then, down the marble walk under the grape arbor, came the Irish poet Frank O'Hare. He was the night-owl of Porto Quaglia, a big pale deep-chested man with a fringe of gray hair; he rented a house from a fisherman, never swam or sunned, and was seldom seen in daylight, though he was generally dressed only in bathing trunks, as he was now. To see him saunter down the walk in broad afternoon was a sign of trouble, as though an evening bat had flitted across the palm trees; if he came by day, it was to "have a word" with Dr. Bernheim, and everyone now jumped to the conclusion that his pregnant wife or one of his five children must be "under the weather" again. But he wore a large smile and carried a chessboard. "I've come for a game with Arturo," he explained, shaking hands all around and accepting a glass of whiskey, which Hélène had run into the house to procure. O'Hare was the chess champion of Porto Quaglia—a title he held from having beaten Hélène's father three out of five at the end of the previous summer. This was only his second year at Porto Quaglia; he spoke no French and hardly a word of Italian, but he was extremely sociable and knew all the gossip of the village, which he picked up at the "pub" over a glass of beer (he did not drink wine) and from his private sources among the fishermen and maids. "Have ye heard the news?" he said now, and at once everyone guessed that this was the reason for his visit. "The Germans have discovered Porto Quaglia."

A long cry of dismay went up in the garden. O'Hare raised a hand to hush it. This morning, he went on, folding his arms, he had gone into Sarzana to get some medicine for Sean, whose foot was infected again ("I'd like a word with you later, if I may, Doctor." *"Papa—"* *"Oui, ma fille, j'ai compris"*), and while he was there he had stopped in at the travel agency, where they sold the bus tickets, to pass the time of day. There he had found a young German pair inquiring for a purse the girl had left on a bus from La Spezia; the long and short of it was that he had acted as translator for them (the boy had a little English) and had asked them, by the bye, what they were doing in Sarzana. They told him that a tourist bureau in Frankfurt had recommended Porto Quaglia.

"Oh, là là!" said Arturo Buonsanti. *"Oh, là là!"* said the engineer. *"Oh, là là!"* cried all the children.

"Qu'est-ce qui se passe?" called a woman's voice with an American accent from the balcony above.

"C'est les allemands, Elisabeth!" shouted the children. *"Ils sont à Sarzana. Ils ont découvert Porto Quaglia."* A shriek answered.

The Buonsantis' cook, Anna, rushed out from the kitchen. *"Cosa, signora? Cosa?"*

"I tedeschi, Anna," said Hélène. *"Sono arrivati qui."*

Anna shielded her eyes and peered out to the street, along the green tunnel of the arbor. *"Dove? Dove sono, professore?"* She turned to Arturo. *"All' albergo?"*

Arturo reassured her. *"Non é vero, Anna. Almeno é un po' esagerato."* But he too, behind his smile, was very much taken aback. *"Oh, là là!"* he repeated to himself.

Down the outside staircase trooped the families who rented the second-story apartments—Mme. Brée, wakened from her after-lunch nap, was wearing a frilly cotton dressing gown, and her children's hair was tousled. Fat Margherita from the house next door, who took boarders, appeared in a parting of the hedge; from the house behind, young Dr. Livio, from Rome, came buttoning his white shirt. Little Anne, the engineer's youngest, hopped on a bicycle to go tell her friend Suzanne down the street. O'Hare stood clasping an oar and embroidering the tale for the group clustered around him while Hélène and Elisabeth, the American, acted as interpreters.

"You'd think it was an air-raid alarm," said Mike, guffawing.

"They were here in these hills," replied the professor of history, chidingly. He nodded his head at the green hills behind the house. "In '44. Fighting the Partisans, who were hiding in the woods on Monte Morello. Anna remembers."

"That was a tragedy," said the Roman editor. "This is farce."

Mike's wife interrupted. "Those people in Sarzana —were they West Germans or East Germans?" "West, of course," said the editor irritably. "They are from Frankfurt." "I don't think we should be prejudiced against the West Germans," declared Irene in a virtuous tone.

"I quite agree," said the British lawyer. "I bear no prejudice against the present generation of Germans —West *or* East. I loathe prejudice of any kind. As I loathe blood sports. That's the thing I hold against your lamented compatriot, Hemingway—" "Sh-h-h," Mike said to him. "I want to hear this."

"They won't be coming here after all," O'Hare was saying. "They'll wait for the purse to turn up and then go on to Pisa."

The lawyer frowned suspiciously, hearing a note of mischief in the poet's bland tone. "What did you tell them about Porto Quaglia?"

O'Hare grinned. "Well, I painted the picture a bit black, you might say. They asked about the bathing, and of course I was bound to tell them that I'd been here a month and hadn't had a bathe yet. Not so much as a sunbathe." A gleeful laugh rang out. The Irishman's white torso and limbs were not a testimonial to Porto Quaglia as a summer resort, and the others began to joke about posting him at the *bivio* as a deterrent, like a quarantine sign.

"Very funny," said the editor tartly. "It would be very amusing no doubt to see O'Hare turning back the Huns. A Ste.-Geneviève at the gates of Paris— perhaps our poet can be cannonized. But it is not a joke, what he has told us. Porto Quaglia is on a tourist map of Italy published in Germany as a vacation guide!"

The poet nodded. "I saw it. With my own two eyes. Porto Quaglia is there, big as life, with a star."

"But how?" cried the pretty girl, who was the daughter of the history professor. "It is not even on the Esso map. How did the Germans find out about it?"

"They have their ways," said her father darkly, at which everyone burst out laughing.

"Ils ont leurs espions!" cried the children delightedly.

And now it was remembered that a pair of fat middle-aged blond strangers had been seen one day the previous summer on the marble rocks at Rocca Bianca, but though they had been heard to speak German, they had been given the benefit of the doubt, for they might have been refugees. And only a few weeks before, Anna the cook had brought the news that Germans had been reported in the new Camping at the *bivio*. But two possible Germans on the rocks, two more in a Camping had not been seen as significant; now these isolated cases suddenly "made sense," like the first seemingly unrelated deaths in what would prove to be the outbreak of an epidemic. There had always (that is, for several years) been Germans across the river, which the poet had one night fancifully compared to the Rhine, with the Germans on one side and the French on the other. But now, it seemed, scouts had crossed the frontier, and an invasion was beginning against which Porto Quaglia had no defenses. The French would be mowed down as by a Panzer division. The local inconveniences that had protected Porto Quaglia from prosperous Italians and Americans would make no difference to the Germans, who never seemed to take baths while travelling and were not particular about iced drinks. Porto Quaglia, in fact, would yield without a murmur to the German soul, which vacationed with quotation marks in its rucksack ready to fasten around *"ein kleines Fischerdorf."*

"Ja, ja, wunderschön!" savagely mimicked François in his cracking voice, hoarse as a crow's from the onset of puberty.

The grownups nodded. They agreed that it was just a question of time till the dread signs *"Zimmer"* would be posted outside the homes of the simple fisherfolk of Porto Quaglia. *"Zimmer und Frühstück," "Lebensmittel"*—they had seen these signs move up the coast, as though the Angel of Death had passed by marking the villages, one by one, for liquidation.

Mike's wife spoke up. "I think you're setting your kids a very bad example. You should teach them to judge Germans as individuals." Hélène whirled around. "Do they come here as individuals or as a mass? With a map from headquarters like an army? Do you meet German tourists as individuals or in busloads?"

"Écoute, Hélène," chided her husband. *"Frank vient de rencontrer deux individus à Sarzana."*

"The first swallows, though," observed O'Hare.

"We've got them in Killarney—all the old Nazi boyos. The new landed gentry. Hitler's chief of protocol. They've closed off the beaches to the Irish poor."

"*Tu vois?*" exclaimed Hélène.

"*Franchement, je les déteste,*" said the engineer's wife calmly. "If Germans come here, I will not come back."

"Do you mean that seriously?" asked Mike. "You mean if one German comes here you won't come back? Supposing Mayor Brandt comes here next year for his vacation?"

"*Soyez sérieux, Mike,*" interposed Arturo. "Mayor Brandt is not the question. *Vous le savez bien. Nous parlons du touriste moyen.* The ordinary tourist."

"Let them go to Pisa!" burst out Hélène. "Let them go to Florence! *Là il y a l'histoire, les monuments! L'histoire, les monuments appartiennent à tout le monde.* To everybody. *Mais Porto Quaglia nous appartient à nous.*"

"So it belongs to you. How interesting," said the British lawyer in a courtroom manner. "I should think it belonged to the fishing people."

"It belongs to the fishing people first," said Hélène. "Next it belongs to us." "By what right?" said the lawyer. "By the right of use," said Hélène. "Is that not a right in English law? We have been coming here now for ten years; our children have grown up here. We have rights here; we belong here. Why should Germans come and push us aside? As they do always in queues. I have seen them in Paris. Because I am small, they try to push me aside."

"You should see them in Killarney," eagerly put in the poet, and everyone began to recount some personal experience of German effrontery.

The lawyer raised his voice. "And if the fishing people want their trade? Will you forbid Pierino or Romeo to take them to Rocca Bianca? Perhaps you'd like to institute some racial laws here to prevent that?" "Hear, hear!" said Irene.

Hélène raised her small tanned face anxiously to her tall husband. *"Aide-moi, Arturo."*

"Il a raison, Hélène," Arturo said mildly. *"Sur le plan légal."*

"Hell," said Mike suddenly. "Can't Hélène say what she thinks about German tourists without being attacked as a racist? I'm on her side. Lafayette, we are here!" He laughed at his own weak joke to break the tension.

Spots of color appeared in the Englishman's cheeks; he and Mike were not congenial, having already had disputes about prizefights and the execution of Caryl Chessman. "And what about the Americans?" he said to Hélène in a trembling voice. "Personally, if we must speak in these terms, I prefer the Germans to the Americans."

"No!" said Hélène, with violence. "The Americans do not come where they are not wanted. They are more sensitive, even the worst. They go where there are other Americans. To Harry's Bar."

"What they do as tourists doesn't interest me," retorted the lawyer. "Unlike you, Mme. Buonsanti, I try to think politically. On that level, I can assure you, the Americans are not wanted in Europe. I can't speak for the keepers of public houses, but I can promise you that the English people don't want the sensitive Americans with their nuclear toys. Nor the Scots, nor the French, nor the Italians, nor even the Germans—if their governments consulted them. 'Go home, Yankee,' is what the Europeans really feel. Try talking to the fishing people here. If your American friends"—he glanced around him—"were sensitive, they'd clear out. No wonder the Germans are welcomed by the plain folk. At least there are no German military bases outside Germany!"

Irene was the first to speak. "You can thank the Americans for that!" "I prefer to thank the Russians," said the lawyer.

"You are so rude," said Hélène, wheeling on him,

"that I would think you were probably a German. You look like a German." Her blazing eyes surveyed his mountain-climbing costume. "I do not believe you are an Englishman."

"*Ma fille,*" said her father warningly. "*Calme-toi.*" And he rose, small and peaceable in his open-throated tan sports shirt, to put his arm around her and lead her to a chair. As he did so, they all saw the blue tattoo, like a laundry mark, on his plump sunburned forearm: his number at Auschwitz. Everyone drew a sharp breath. Nearly all of them had at least glimpsed it before—on the White Rock, while the doctor lay sunning, at table, during a chess session. But generally they tried not to look at it, even the smaller children, out of courtesy to the doctor, as if it were a deformity, and the doctor himself made this easier by his habitual meditative posture, chin sunk, arms folded on his lap. Now they stared at the number, at the lawyer, at Hélène.

"Here," said the Irish poet suddenly to the children, reaching into the pocket of his bathing trunks. "Go get yourselves ice creams." He treated children to ice creams with the same absent abandon that he treated or tried to treat grownups to drinks. "Have a whiskey" or "Have an ice cream" was his customary greeting, according to age. But the children this time refused to budge; instead, the lawyer turned, picked up his stick, and marched down the walk without speaking.

At once Hélène was remorseful. "*J'ai trop bu à déjeuner,*" she confessed.

O'Hare and Arturo began to play chess at one end of the table, while the doctor watched; he had learned the game in Auschwitz. The children lingered round the table, as if feeling cheated at the way the discussion had been terminated by the unexpected appearance of Dr. Bernheim's "number," like a card produced from his sleeve. Everyone was silent, pursuing his own train of thought.

"*Tu l'as fait exprès, Maurice,*" Arturo declared suddenly to his father-in-law, looking up from the board with a chuckle. "He did it on purpose, O'Hare."

"What?" said the poet.

"Showing his number. To help his daughter."

The old man indicated a chess move with a silent finger. *"Peut-être,"* he said imperturbably.

"You know, *maman,"* exclaimed Laure, raising her head, "I think you were right. I think he *is* a German."

"Mais oui, mais oui!" shouted François, his eyes sparkling. *"Maman a parfaitement raison!"* And the little boy assured them that the Englishman had paled when the word "spy" was mentioned. *"C'est lui, j'en suis sûr, qui a dénoncé Porto Quaglia aux allemands. Il a pâli, comme ça."* He gave a wild start, shuddered, and tried to make his small brown face blanch. The other children watched this performance agog. The adults, impressed for a minute by the boy's conviction, quickly regained their balance. *"Mais non, mais non!"* they cried soothingly.

"It's just that he doesn't like Americans, François," Mike explained. "You can understand that, can't you?" And he made a funny face. "He thinks they eat with their atom bombs on the table."

"What are you trying to cover up?" demanded Irene. "François is old enough to know that that man's a Communist!"

The "French" protruded their lower lips and doubtfully shrugged their brows; Arturo glanced up from the chessboard. *"Je ne crois pas,"* he said soberly.

"La Voix de la Raison a parlé," announced the editor, clapping his friend on the shoulder.

"Mais en tout cas ce n'est pas une injure," mildly pursued Arturo. And the others began to argue as to whether it was an insult to call a person a Communist.

"Anyway, he's not a Communist, honey," said Mike, intervening. "It's not that simple. He's an overexcited unilateral disarmer." "But why should that make him pro-German?" someone demanded. *"Mais il n'était pas pro-allemand,"* objected someone else.

The Irishman had been concentrating on the chessboard, ignoring the conversation. He captured a rook with his knight. "I'll tell ye what it is," he said abruptly, tilting back in his chair. "This fellow is a German who passed for English during the war years in England to keep on the good side of his neighbors. Get him to show ye his passport. I'll wager he was born in Hamburg."

"C'est plutôt un juif allemand qui s'est fait anglais," murmured the doctor. *"Mais tu es fou, papa!"* cried Hélène.

"Favole!" said the editor. "You are telling each other fairy stories. The truth is simple. This Englishman would like to be unprejudiced, but he is not, unfortunately. Hélène would like to be prejudiced, but she is not, fortunately." He rose to leave. "Meanwhile," he added, with a grimace, "the real Germans are advancing." Mike and Irene rose too.

Irene approached Hélène. "I'm sorry I attacked you about the Germans coming here. I forgot about your father."

Hélène started to reply hotly, *"Ce n'est pas à cause de mon père,"* but then she gave it up, realizing that she could not explain in English to Irene what she felt toward these new Germans, and that if she were able to explain it in French, Irene would not understand. *"Merci,"* she said simply, instead.

The summer, after this, was not the same. The only immediate consequence was that for a few days Hélène and the English lawyer stopped speaking when they met. But Hélène would not allow this to continue, for it would have ended in the creation of factions. There had never been factions in Porto Quaglia, and Hélène, therefore, when the time came, invited the lawyer and his family as usual to François' birthday party—the great social event of the season, for which cakes were baked in Parma and sent over the mountains by bus. The English accepted, and the quarrel was patched up.

The party was just like the parties of other years, except that it was too much like them—too defiant of change. The littlest girls dressed up in costumes representing, this year, the great sirens—the Queen of Sheba, Cleopatra, the Lorelei, Brigitte Bardot—and were made up by one of the painters; François shinned up a palm tree; everyone came, old and young, maids and nurses. As usual, the first goodbyes of the season were said, for François' party was in the middle of August—after that, traditionally, the first departures took place. Yet the fact was these gay promises—"See you next year," "*All' anno prossimo*," "*À bientôt*"— were tinged this year with uncertainty, wan like the flickering light of the Chinese lanterns hung from the trumpet vines and fir trees. Everyone looked at everyone else, wondering which would be the defector, which family would send postcards next year with "*auguri*" for François and love to everyone from Provence or Elba.

From the day of O'Hare's discovery, the "French" had been living in a state of apprehension, which they tried not to show each other. The blue buses that came nearly every hour from Sarzana and La Spezia were covertly watched, and no one went into Sarzana without casting a supervisory glance over the main square, to note what strangers were about. At the sound of an unfamiliar horn along the road, walkers would stop to listen anxiously, expecting a big German tourist bus to appear around the next curve. The yearly expedition to Portovenere, which included a swim from the boat in a blue grotto and lunch outdoors on an island under a tree with a swing, was repeatedly postponed on various excuses, as though the "French" were afraid to leave Porto Quaglia unguarded, lest they come back and find it violated. None of these actions was planned; no one watched on purpose stationed in the café. It was just that now automatically even the chess players glanced up at the sound of a car or a bus braking, whereas before nobody had paid any attention unless waiting for a friend or a package. The effect of the alert was most noticeable on the children, who roamed about the village in bands, were reluctant to go blackberrying on Monte Morello, and swam in expeditionary forces beyond Raven Point to reconnoitre the coves and grottoes. As if enlisted by this *esprit de corps,* Mike and his wife had stayed on.

The only person not privately on the watch for Germans was their herald, O'Hare, who again was invisible in the daytime and was said to be writing a verse play on Marlowe and the School of Night. And at night peace returned to Porto Quaglia. Just before dusk the old ladies, mothers of the Italians among the "French," appeared on the road, walking with sticks, in pairs or leaning on the arm of a servant or a daughter-in-law. The emergence of *le mamme,* white-haired, talcum-dusted, woolly-shawled, like soft, powdery moths heading for the café, was the sign that traffic had stilled and Porto Quaglia was safe for the night; the buses had stopped running, and few cars passed. Across the river, the last rays of the sun, already hidden from the village behind Monte Morello, touched the windows of the golden hill towns, which sparkled and beaconed as though they had been turned into mica embedded in the green hills. After this, O'Hare, the owl, cruised into the café.

At night Mamma Nature took possession of Porto Quaglia. After supper the children thronged up and down the waterfront picking out the stars, which seemed very near and bright. Sometimes the poet would join them in front of the café and teach them the English names—a game that caused much laughter, incredulity, and wonder. To think that what little Anne's star book called the Great She Bear was known as the Big Dipper to the English, and La Chaise was Cassiopeia's Chair.

"Ye won't find Orion's Belt, Frankie," O'Hare would remind François. "Not till the autumn."

"Ah oui, vous voulez dire Le Bâton de Jacob."

"Jacob's Rod, is it?"

"Mais non, c'est Les Trois Rois!"

"Mais si," Catherine would speak up. *"Le Bâton de Jacob et Les Trois Rois sont la même constellation n'est-ce pas, Monsieur O'Hare?"*

"Here's a good one," the poet would interject. "Do ye know what the English call Sirius? Orion's Hound." This pleased the children in the same way as penetrating the foreign disguises of the pieces on their fathers' chessboard: was it true, they would ask the poet, that the English called the *fou* the "bishop"? And the Italians called him *"l'alfiere."* The chessboard had its own constellations, said the Irishman, and the fixed moves of the pieces were like the fixed courses of the stars; it was a very old game—as old as the hills.

When the children had gone to bed, the moonlit village was still, except for the faint sound of dance music coming from across the river, from the restaurant Il Pilota, near the house of Romeo, the boatman. The honky-tonk sound floating across the river seemed bathed in frontier innocence, and the menace of Punta Sabbia, just beyond, was reduced to the melody of an old jazz tune. In former years the "French" would have themselves rowed across on a Friday or a Saturday to dance, but now no one went, not even the young people, but the music still continued, as old as the hills itself, as if nothing had changed.

In the daytime this illusion could not be maintained. The sighting of the Germans in Sarzana had served to call attention to a fact that had been half escaping notice: the White Rock was filling up with bathers. Each day there were new ones. Arriving in their boats, the "French" would discern dark figures, tiny in the distance in the white glare of the cliff, which made them look like people in an overexposed photograph; disembarking, the "French" would often find their places

preempted: Dr. Bernheim's special shady corner under an overhanging cliff, François' lookout post on the
highest rock, Hélène's hollow. Another umbrella
would be standing in the crevice where the engineer's
wife had always planted hers: in the cave where they
were in the habit of changing they would find a fat
man asleep or a couple embracing. Romeo, Pierino,
and Paolo were continually chugging back and forth
with strangers aboard whom they deposited—strangers
from no one knew where, since they were not staying
at the inn or at either of the two boarding houses. And
as if this were not enough, new motorboats and even
small cruisers began appearing from the other direction and discharging passengers.

All these people, materializing seemingly from thin
air, behaved as if they belonged here, as if they had
"always" been coming to the White Rock, which they
treated in cursory fashion, like a row of *cabine* with
showers. They did not exclaim over the beauty of the
spot but at once put on diving masks and flippers and
began to swim. Or launched their children in tubes
and themselves on surf mattresses. Or slung cameras
round their necks and started photographing—"action" shots of a group splashing each other in the water. This matter-of-fact behavior and the way they
ignored the "French," who outnumbered them, gave
the August mornings the quality of a dream sequence.
It was as if the "French" collectively had become invisible; the others crossed by them, climbed over
them, talked past them, as if they were not there at all
in reality but were only figments of their own imagination. If they spoke, they felt they would be inaudible,
like someone trying to shout in a dream, and in fact
they became remarkably silent. Only their eyes spoke.
Some of the strangers, who for the most part were extremely ugly, brought food with them and ate lunch at
midday, scattering grape skins and peach pits and sa-
lami rind and crusts of bread on the marble and
throwing empty Chinotto bottles into the sea. Large

horseflies appeared on the White Rock. On the green water there was an iridescent film of gasoline.

These strangers varied from day to day, but they did not have a marked individuality; rather, they seemed a species whose children, summoned in raucous authoritarian voices, were all named "Umberto" or "Massimo." "They will go away after Ferragosto," the editor prophesied, but the fifteenth of August passed and the shriek "Umberto!" "Massimo!" was still heard on the White Rock like the perpetual crying of gulls.

And one day, at last, Germans came; Romeo had brought them from the Camping at Punta Sabbia. First there were two, then four, then a whole boatload, many of them middle-aged—the men old enough to have been in the S.S. or, to judge them more charitably, to have manned those very pillboxes just around the point that had cowed the area with their artillery till the Americans took Viareggio. Yet now that they were here, in the too too solid flesh, the "French" banished these memories, just as they tried not to look at the number on Dr. Bernheim's arm. In actuality, the Germans from the Camping, it was admitted, were no worse than the invaders who had preceded them; the invaders were all "Germans," in the sense of a foreign species with the power of rapid multiplication, as the invaded were all "French."

But as if to illustrate the complexity of the subject, Irene was accosted one morning toward the end of the month by an Italian crone, the grandmother of some Umberto or Massimo and their little sister (never summoned) Marisa or Silvana. *"Sprechen Sie Deutsch?"* said the old woman, seizing Irene by the skirt of her beach gown as she tried to pass on the rocks. And when Irene refused angrily to answer her, she continued to gabble at her in German, eager, no doubt, said the editor, to renew conversations she had enjoyed in the old times with the Nazis. Soon afterward Hélène had a similar wounding experience in the post office when she went to buy stamps. *"Franco-bolli, per favore,"* she said, pushing her postcards through the window and starting to make a remark about the weather.

"Per la Germania?" interrupted the employee. *"Deutschland?"*

Hélène was outraged. The woman had not even troubled to *look* at the postcards. Or at her. They were for France, Hélène pointed out. She was not German; she was the Signora Buonsanti. But the employee, who was new, it seemed, did not recognize her. *"Cento lire,"* she said, counting out stamps for the postcards and handing them back for Hélène to lick.

"Après dix ans c'est un peu fort," declared Hélène, seating herself with a thump in the café.

Arturo gave his genial laugh. *"Comme c'est beau!"* he said. *"Per loro adesso siamo tutti quanti tedeschi."*

Seriously, put in the professor's pretty daughter, this must mean that there were Germans actually in the village.

O'Hare got up from a chess game at the next table. "Haven't you heard?" he said. "They're at the Pensione La Perla. Have a whiskey."

The following morning, the Germans from La Perla were in the boat that came to fetch the group from the Buonsantis' landing. The "French" behaved politely, helping the Germans land their equipment as they helped everyone else, and the English lawyer, already sunning, was particularly assiduous in holding the boat's painter to steady it for the fat women's descent. But Laure, usually cooperative, refused to lend a hand.

"Mais qu'est-ce que tu as, ma petite?" chided her father. Laure would not reply and sat stubbornly at the water's edge, brooding and casting dark looks at the Englishman, who was chatting in German with the newcomers. Finally, when the others were in swimming, she explained.

In the boat she had seen the Germans staring pointedly at the number on Dr. Bernheim's arm. And to bear her out, that morning they all noticed still other Germans, from the Camping, eying the number too, passing and repassing the old man as he sat reading a volume of Stendhal, and actually stopping to get a better view. If Dr. Bernheim was aware of this, he gave no definite sign, but after his second dip he moved his place farther along the rocks, and before the boats came he asked François to row him back—he had taken too much sun.

"*Mais c'est inouï!*" burst out Hélène, when her father was gone. "*Que mon père ne puisse pas se montrer en public, à cause des allemands! C'est aux qui auraient dû se cacher!*"

No one could say she exaggerated; it was the Germans, not her father, who had something to be ashamed of, but it was the Germans who were making it impossible for him to appear in public. Because of the Germans ought he to wear a long-sleeved shirt? Or Covermark, as Mike sarcastically proposed?

This was the turning point. The next day, despite the children's protests, the "French" set out for Judgment Day Beach. The White Rock had been abandoned to the enemy.

Judgment Day Beach, like Raven Point, though pleasant for an excursion was not really a substitute for the White Rock. It was a pebbly beach, and the sharp stones hurt the tender feet of the younger children, who were not quite consoled by the stone collections made for them. Moreover, there was no shade— no protective cliffs, no cool caves. The small children sat in their straw hats in a row and demanded to know when Romeo was coming back for them. This was another difficulty. On calm days the boatmen did not like to go to Judgment Day; it was farther than the White Rock, but the price per head, fixed early in the summer, was the same. The advantage to the boatmen was that it was easier to land there, but when the sea was quiet this did not matter, and the boatmen, with the trade they now had, did not care to make the longer trip simply for the *"francesi."* Hence, every morning Pierino or Paolo or Romeo, pretending not to have understood the wishes of the "French," would try to take them to the Rocca Bianca, as if as a matter of course.

"No, Paolo, niente Rocca Bianca," some strong will among the passengers would have to interpose. *"C'è troppa gente. All'altra spiaggia."* Paolo, muttering, would yield, and they would sail past the marble rocks, as though past a siren, watching the British lawyer and his wife, who had declined to join in the exodus (they had met some lovely couples among the new folk at Rocca Bianca), wave to them cheerily from the marshmallowy cliffs. The boatmen showed their dissatisfaction by arriving late to pick up the *"francesi"* at lunchtime, with the excuse that they had first to pick up the various parties at the White Rock. Sometimes it was three o'clock before the boats returned to Porto Quaglia, and as they neared the landing, the Buonsantis would see tall Anna standing there, her hand shading her eyes, waiting to make sure they were aboard before putting on the spaghetti. Lunch, with a spoiled roast, would be served at three-fifteen. Those who were *in pensione* at the inn would find the day's specialty *"finito"* or sitting in tepid grease. Anna was cross; the waiters in the inn were cross; the lesser family cooks up and down the main street were cross. The "French" were being punished by the boatmen, and this punishment, like some Biblical malediction, spread over the whole village.

Only the old man with the rowboat and his grandson remained faithful to the "French," but it was a long row to Judgment Day, and the boat could not go back and forth many times in a morning. Soon another old man, with Garibaldi mustaches and an ancient dinghy, turned up at the pier; then a third, an octogenarian with a rakishly worn sailor's cap, a cheroot, and a leaky outboard motor. But this created further bad blood with the "regular" boatmen, who would sometimes decline to take a group they had seen patronizing the old men and the boy. In short, the balance of Nature at Porto Quaglia was upset. Some days it would happen that most of the "French" did not go to swim at all. After a family dispute, the sulking children would take their bathing suits and walk down to the *plage modeste* at the end of the village, while their parents sat at home fuming and declaring that they might as well be in Paris, Rome, or London. One morning the Brées and the Livios quietly crossed to Punta Sabbia—on the theory that the "Germans" encamped there had all gone to the Rocca Bianca. But this attempted "castling," as Arturo Buonsanti called it, did not work out either. The position was deadlocked: the "French," having surrendered Rocca Bianca, refused to be returned there under duress; the boatmen continued to outflank them by the device of marooning them at Judgment Day Beach. The Milanese publisher took to going late and bringing a cold lunch; Elisabeth, the American, brought steaks one day for twenty and cooked them on the beach. But the absence of shade at Judgment Day, as well as the absence of wood, discouraged these solutions.

By September, the "French" were talking of buying outboard motors for the children's rowboats; the engineer went to look at a sailboat that was for sale across the river. "Make yourselves independent of the boatmen," Mike counselled. But if every family had a boat, what then? Who was to promise them that next year the "Germans" would not push on to Judgment Day?

"You could sell them your boats," said Mike shrewdly, waggling his beard. But the "French" were cold to this idea and cold to the idea of acquiring shore property—another notion Mike broached. Though he was receiving cables telling him to get back to work from his editor nearly every day (with a two-hundred-lire delivery charge), he lingered, feeling it his duty as an American to exercise his ingenuity on a problem that the "French" by themselves could not solve.

"Why don't you get together and buy the Rocca Bianca?" he said to Hélène one morning as they were swimming. Far off to the right, they could see the white point jutting into the sea; from here it was evident that the marble there had once been quarried—slices had been taken off. This in fact was what had suddenly given him the idea.

"It is public property," said Hélène. "The shore belongs to the *comune*."

"Are you sure?" he said. "If the shore belongs to the *comune*, how come all the bathing establishments across the river?"

"They are concessions. Leased from the *comune* by business interests." But the Belle Arti, Hélène went on, would not permit anybody to lease a landmark like the White Rock. And they would be right.

She and Mike began to argue heatedly. He bet her that by bribery or influence the "French" could lease the White Rock and post it with "No Trespassing" signs. "Supposing you all got together"—he counted —"there must be at least twelve families of you, and some pretty important people, by Italian standards. You could fix the Belle Arti and the mayor—" "No," said Hélène.

"What do you mean 'no'? Assuming you could, for the sake of argument—" "No," said Hélène.

Mike took a few short exasperated strokes toward shore. Then he turned back. "I'll bet you," he said patiently, "that within ten years—no, five—somebody buys that whole cliff, leases the Rocca Bianca for ninety years, and builds a hotel. With a bar and a terrace."

"And dressing rooms cut into the rock," concurred Hélène. "And showers and toilets for *signore* and *signori*. And a night club over the water—why not? They would make a road and sell off plots of land for villas and *villini*. After that, a shopping center. It will happen. You are right. *Arturo a eu la même pensée*."

Mike's jaw dropped. He swallowed water. "Well, then," he said, spluttering, "if you see it coming so clearly, why don't you get in there first?" "Preventive war," commented. Hélène.

Mike ignored this. "Between you, you could raise the money for the necessary bribes."

"It would not be cheap."

Mike floated. "You'd buy the land above of course, too. You'd have to, to protect yourselves. And if you had the land, you'd build—the whole group of you. Why pay rent in Porto Quaglia? Say twelve houses." He narrowed his eyes, thinking. "You could build twelve houses in those trees if you kept them inconspicuous. In good taste. Blending with the landscape. Leaving green areas. You'd form a syndicate—incorporate. Get a good modern architect from Milan. Use native building materials."

"*C'est-à-dire le marbre*," said Hélène.

"Why, yes!" Mike ejaculated. "Yes. Come to think of it, you'd have a free marble supply. That'd be something to leave Laure and François. A marble house. How about it, Hélène?" If he could have nudged her in the water, he would have done so. "Don't laugh. I'm serious. They laughed at Columbus. How about it?"

"*Non, merci*," she answered, striking out for shore. "What do you mean, '*non, merci*'?" he called after her.

Hélène swung around in the water. Seeing the American's plaintive expression, she was angry. "*J'ai dit non*," she said. "*Mon père n'a pas été cinq ans à Auschwitz pour devenir propriétaire d'une villa en marbre sur la côte ligurienne*." "I can't understand you," yelled Mike. "You're talking too fast." "I said my father has not spent five years in Auschwitz to become the owner of a marble villa in Italy."

"I don't see the connection," called Mike.

"We are plain people," shouted Hélène. "What do you call it—wandering Jews."

Mike reflected for a minute. "I don't get it," he said. "Are you against owning property?"

"Yes," shouted Hélène, though this was not the truth—she was against being the kind of person who would preempt a natural marvel like some common piece of shore land, but she did not know how to express this in English, least of all to Mike, whose relentless American logic made it impossible, she said to herself, to have a reasonable conversation with him. Moreover, she had never known how to answer the insane argument that one ought to do something bad because if one did not someone else would do it instead. She struck out for shore again.

"You French have no vision!" Mike's voice roared after her indignantly. He backstroked a few moments, to cool off, not sure himself whether he had been joking about the marble villas and she had taken him seriously, in which case he would have a right to feel injured, or whether he had been serious and would have a right to feel injured at not having been taken seriously enough.

On the shingle they found another argument going on—one party asserting that the source of beauty was in Nature and the other claiming that Nature was simply a sentimental name for tradition, the way things had "always" been. A fishing boat, Elisabeth had said, belonged to Nature, while a smart motorboat did not. But Arturo begged to differ. A fishing boat on the horizon appeared to be a part of Nature because it had "always" been there, like the sun in the sky, or the mountains, or the stars. But the stars in fact had changed; the Pole Star of the ancients was no longer the Pole Star of today. A horse or a pair of oxen in a field were viewed as a part of Nature, but when there were no horses or oxen there would be another Nature, and a tractor, to Laure's children, would be an intrinsic part of it. For that, said the painter, you would need a new Millet; it was the artists who decided what was Nature and what was not. Why then, said Elisabeth, could you paint a good picture of a carriage, while an Alfa Romeo could "sit" only for advertisements? What about a plastic dish, said a woman's voice. The engineer said there was no inherent reason that plastics should be uglier than marble; it was a question of good design. No, said the editor; plastics offered no resistance to the manufacturer, which made them inferior to marble. "Inherently," he added tartly, skipping a stone across the water.

The discussion veered to the White Rock. It had not "always" been there, said Mike. *"Si!"* objected Hélène.

"No," said Mike. "Some acquisitive group around Dante's time must have formed a corporation to exploit the marble there. Originally, the whole point must have been green, covered with trees, like the rest of these slopes. Then somebody struck marble. The White Rock is the end result of man's tampering with Nature. If he'd left Nature alone, there'd be no White Rock."

"Il justifie le capitalisme," observed Laure in her still childish voice.

"Il justifie le progrès," said François sombrely, with a malign look at the American. *"Et tu es contre le progrès?"* asked his father, smiling. *"Mais naturellement,"* retorted François. *"Moi aussi,"* said Laure. *"Moi non,"* said Catherine.

"Regarde-moi ça, papa!" bitterly exclaimed Hélène. *"Mes enfants sont devenus conservateurs, grâce aux allemands."*

It was a fact, as already had been noticed, that the coming of the "Germans" was bringing out the worst in the community.

The doctor looked up from his Stendhal. She would not, he said tranquilly, want them to take all their views from books. They must learn from what they saw around them.

"From Nature's book, eh?" quoted Mike, with a loud laugh, clapping the old man on the shoulder.

And from what they heard, the doctor added in a lowered voice to his daughter: children, like old people, were afraid of any suggestion of change; one had to be careful how one spoke of it to them—let them see more and hear less. He looked at his watch. "*Viens, mon fils,*" he said to his grandson. "*C'est l'heure.*"

It was too early, objected the others, but the old man insisted that François should take him and the younger children home. Mike and Arturo pushed the rowboat off.

"*Regarde, mon fils,*" said the doctor, as the boat rounded into the harbor.

The boy at the oars briefly raised his eyes to the marble mountains in the distance.

"*Elles sont belles, les montagnes?*"

"*Oui,*" admitted François.

"*Pourquoi?*" said his grandfather.

All the children gazed at the white-capped peaks.

"*Parce que le marbre ressemble à la neige,*" the boy answered promptly. But it was a cheat, he added in his hoarse, angry voice. "*C'est truqué, quoi. C'est de la fausse neige. Et cela ne justifie pas le progrès.*"

Perhaps not, the old man replied serenely, but it justified snow. This afternoon, he continued, hopping out of the boat and holding the painter for his grandson, they would all go to see the quarries.

The youngest children looked doubtful. "*Elles sont loin, les carrières.*"

Not too far, said the doctor; they would start right after lunch.

It was the first time the "French" had visited the marble quarries, though for several years a sign, "*Visitate le cave di marmo,*" had been urging them to do so, on the road from Viareggio. This sign, in fact, which recently had begun reiterating its message in German, had killed their interest in the trip. But now several cars filled with "French" followed the doctor in his old Peugeot. The last car in the procession was the poet's battered Austin station wagon; having got wind of the expedition, he had brought his wife, a stroller, and four of his children—the baby had been left at home.

The first stop was at one of the quarries advertised on the road from Carrara. It was a "commercial" quarry: near the entrance was a stand selling Coco-Cola and beer and another selling marble souvenirs. Around the souvenir stand were German tourists in a group; a tourist bus stood waiting, and the cars parked along the highway were all marked with a big "D" for Deutschland. The quarry, which was not very deep, was no longer worked, and the principal attraction was a train track on which carts carrying blocks of marble shuttled back and forth. This was not the real thing, Mike protested.

"Bien sûr," said the doctor, but it would amuse the younger children. The real quarries lay beyond, high in the mountains; the doctor had telephoned the doctor from Carrara, who had suggested the itinerary. After the "play" quarry, they would leave the tourist area and visit the mills where the marble was cut.

The mills lay along a stream that had turned white with marble dust; they made an atrocious noise, cutting the marble into slices with big iron blades—the small children were frightened. They wanted to go back and see the little train again.

The adults glanced at each other. The poor mountain villages that straggled out from the mills were extremely dusty; everyone began to cough. The mills themselves were dismal; the water from the stream used in the cutting process splashed over the ground, creating a gray mud. The streets of the villages were caked with gray mud; there were no trees, and the air was cold and wintry, for the mountains cut off the afternoon sun.

"*Ça suffit, papa!*" exclaimed Hélène, but the doctor would not heed her, leading them from village to village, mill to mill, consulting from time to time a slip of paper. They ought to see everything, he said. In each mill, he asked questions, which Arturo translated, while the others paced restively about, the Irishman pushing the stroller; the doctor wanted to know the details of the cutting mechanism, the incidence of silicosis among the mill workers—were there many tuberculars?

"*Tu es en vacances, papa!*" irritably cried Hélène. "Yes, Doctor," said the poet. "Take it easy; you're on holiday."

Finally the cars left the melancholy mills and proceeded farther into the mountains along a narrow winding road, past chambers of smooth gray marble cut into the hillsides and heaps of marble gravel. Suddenly the doctor braked, and the "French" for the first time saw, right before their eyes, the "snow" fissures and gleaming "glaciers" they had known for so many years from across the river. These in fact were marble slides—avalanches of quite ordinary-looking stones that had tumbled down the mountainsides. Seen close up, they were not even white but a pale leaden gray in some places and a pale urinous yellow in others. Dr. Bernheim glanced at his slip of paper, and the cars continued upward till they arrived at a narrow bridge across a chasm; here a worker stopped them. They were at Fantiscritti, the last name on the doctor's list. It was the end of the road. Because of the dangerous marble slides, cars were not permitted to go any farther; if the *francesi* wanted to visit the quarries beyond, they would have to go on foot.

Arturo took the slip of paper from his father-in-law. "*Mais tu t'es trompé, Maurice,*" he said. "*Sûrement.*" This was the conviction of everyone— that the doctor had come to the wrong place.

Looking about them, they were conscious of a fearful disappointment. The spot on which they stood, surrounded by marble slides, looking into a chasm of rubble at the bottom of which ran a dirty *torrente*, was at the farthest extreme from what they had imagined. The scenery around them, far from being alpine, was a Cyclopean desert or monstrous manufactured wilderness that resembled, more than anything else, a set for some early super-colossal film, before the day of sound or color. The absence of sun in this pocket of the mountain combined with the bleaching light diffused by the monochrome stony gravel to suggest an interior, artificially lit and yet without shadow. There was no sign of a quarry or of a village—only a sort of frontier hut with a bus placard posted on it, around which some workers were loitering. Added to this, it was dusty; everyone was thirsty.

As they stood there, uncertain, a boy approached them and offered to accompany them to the nearest quarry, which he said was two kilometres off. They were in the right place, he assured Arturo and the editor. The quarries up there—he nodded toward the farthest mountain—were very old; Michelangelo had worked there before the birth of Christ, and slaves had carved pictures of Roman soldiers on the walls, which was why the place was called Fantiscritti.

The "French" smiled dubiously at each other and looked at their watches: to go or not to go and see for themselves? Looking up at the towering mountains, the younger children refused; they were afraid of the avalanches. Finally it was decided that the men should go ahead with the older children, while the women could stay behind with the younger ones. "I'll take Seanie in the stroller if you like," said the poet, speaking of his six-year-old, but the boy guide protested this arrangement and Sean was left behind with his mother.

The women walked across the bridge in the direction in which the others were vanishing up a mountain track; as they chatted, Sean slipped away from them and began to sidle down a sort of path that led to the half-dry *torrente*. Suddenly the women heard cries in a dialect they did not understand; a worker came running very fast across the bridge to warn them. What the boy was doing was dangerous. At any moment he might dislodge a stone and start a slide that would bury him.

But he seemed not to hear the workers' cries or his pregnant mother's pleas to come back, and Hélène started to run down after him.

"No, signora, no!" the workers shouted. A few stones began falling, like flour from a sifter, in her wake. She hesitated, saw the peril for the boy in her rashness, and turned back.

Then they simply waited, holding their breath, watching the child wave to them from the abyss; in the end, he returned coolly, unconscious of his danger, carrying with him a purple flower he had picked on the edge of the stream.

This nerve-racking episode confirmed the sinister impression made by the lonely spot. A bus came and collected the workers from the other side of the bridge, turned around, and started down the mountain. There was not another human being to be seen: they had not passed a single car on the way up; the women and children were alone.

"I don't like it here," "I want a drink of water," "I want to go home," the children whimpered, looking at the family cars, driverless, like a group of widows, on the other side of the chasm. Sean's older sister, Brigid, profited from the occasion by trying to imitate her brother's exploit; she was hauled back at once and spanked, with the approval of the child psychologist. Time passed; from the changing of the light, the women assumed that somewhere the sun had set. It grew colder, and the children were shivering in their summer clothes. The mothers fought down their hysteria, offering each other various explanations of why their husbands were so long in coming back. When the men and the older children at last returned from the quarry, they found their families huddled, terrified, in the automobiles, with the heaters turned on.

It had not been so different from the tourist quarry, they reported—another chamber cut into the wall of the mountain. The deep quarries, where they cut the white marble, were higher up; the workers walked an hour and a half every morning to get to them.

"Did you see the soldiers?" demanded the little children.

No, they had not seen the soldiers; the old Roman quarry had been closed a long time ago and the *fanti*, the foreman had said, were in the museum in Carrara.

"*On peut visiter, maman?*" said the children, coming to life.

But again they were told no; another day perhaps —at this hour the museum would be shut.

So instead, though it was dark and nearly their suppertime when they reached the bottom of the mountains, they all had ice-cream cones at the marble counter of a *gelateria* in Carrara, and the older children and the fathers heard about Sean's adventure.

"*Qu'est-ce que tu es venu chercher ici, papa?*" Hélène said thoughtfully to her father on the way home.

"*Rien,*" equably replied Dr. Bernheim. "*Une petite distraction.*"

Hélène shook her head. It was not just for amusement, she told her husband, that her father had brought them here. He wanted to tell them something. She knew her father, she said.

That night Arturo did not play chess. He and Hélène stood on the pier listening to the music coming from across the river. She was pensive, still thinking of the "scenery" they had visited, which on close view was an industrial landscape—a big gray outdoor mill. It was ugly, she said, turning to Arturo with a question in her voice. "*Très laid,*" her husband agreed.

She remembered the sallow marble slides and

shivered. *"François a eu raison. C'est de la fausse neige. Comme dans le théâtre. Nous l'aimons parce que nous aimons la vraie neige."* But everything here, she went on, was slightly false. The "French" were not French; the "Germans" were Italians; the "Jews" were a little of everything. The "Englishman" was maybe a German. Or a Jew, according to her father. "The "fishermen" were businessmen. Everything was in quotation marks. Even François' "birthday." His real birthday, which they had all forgotten, was today. She sighed heavily. *"C'est moi, tu le sais, qui l'a faussée."*

She was the one, alas, who had done it; she had moved his birthday ahead, two years ago, so that it would fall in the middle of the month, before the first departures. And now other families had followed suit, so that every child's birthday celebrated by the summer of Porto Quaglia was a false birthday. She gave a guilty, skittish little laugh. All was false, she repeated despondently—theatrical snow or the snow in a souvenir paperweight.

Arturo listened. *"Ce qui est vrai, Hélène, c'est le travail."* The work of the fishermen, the work of the miners in that fearful dust. It was work that joined man to Nature. Not vacations, despite what people thought.

"J'aime les vacances. Je déteste le travail," Hélène flung out. And it was true that she loved vacations and was already hating the day they would pack up and leave for the winter's work. After a pause, she asked in a different voice, diffident and stealthily curious, *"Et comment c'etait, dans la carrière?"*

Bad, Arturo answered; the work conditions were hard. Every other day, according to the workers, a miner lost a thumb, an arm, a leg. *"C'est pas joli,"* he added, grimacing. The work was unhealthy and badly paid; the less-skilled miners got a thousand lire a day.

"Mille lire!"

Arturo nodded. François, he said, had been very much struck by that; Laure too. There were many strikes, and many of the miners were Anarchists. *"C'est drôle que c'est la première fois que nous y sommes allés."*

Yes, agreed Hélène; it *was* funny that they had never gone there before, in all their years at Porto Quaglia. *"Les 'intellectuels de gauche'!"* she burst out after a minute. Another set of quotation marks, another cheat. Good, she went on bitterly, it was finished. They would not come back to Porto Quaglia another summer. She refused to live another summer with such trite illusions and echoes. *" 'Ah, comme elles sont belles, les montagnes de marbre!' 'Que j'adore la Nature!' "* Mimicking her own voice, she stamped her foot on the pier.

But it was the same everywhere, replied Arturo, smiling. All the desirable vacation spots were like that. All vacationers "adored" the poverty of the natives. *"Surtout les âmes sensibles."*

"C'est vrai," muttered Hélène.

Why not be honest, said Arturo. If they never came back to Porto Quaglia, what would be the reason? *"Je ne sais pas,"* said Hélène.

The true reason, declared her husband, was very simple: *"les vacances payées."* When they had first come to Porto Quaglia, only a few—professional people, artists, and salaried intellectuals like themselves—had a month off in the summer and a car or the price of railroad tickets to take them far from home. Now the many had it, especially the Germans. It was the "higher standard of living"—he quoted the words in English—of the European workers and small employees that had put Porto Quaglia on the map. The vacations of the masses were necessarily mass-produced. There was no escape from the "Germans" except for the very rich. Next summer the same problem would present itself. What would Hélène say when her *coiffeur* asked her where she was going for her holidays?

"Il faut avoir une réponse, Hélène. C'est une ques-

tion très importante. Tout le monde a le droit de sa-voir." The whole world had a right to an answer—the concierge, the grocer, the mailman, her editor at Gallimard. What was she going to tell them? An undiscovered Greek island? A wood-cutters' hamlet in the Alps? A hotel in Turkey? A cliff on the Dalmatian coast? *"Un château en Espagne?"*

Hélène did not respond to her husband's raillery. There were Germans everywhere, she agreed morosely. *"Bon, donc. Au travail."* She leaned her head against his chest. *"Mais comme j'aimais Porto Quaglia!"* Hearing the past tense of the verb that meant love, Arturo stared stiffly ahead of him into the dark.

"Oui, c'etait beau," he said.